FAITH ON THE ROCKS

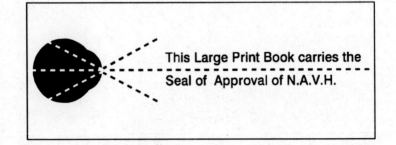

This Large Print Book carries the
Seal of Approval of N.A.V.H.

A DAISY ARTHUR MYSTERY

FAITH ON THE ROCKS

LIESA MALIK

WHEELER PUBLISHING
A part of Gale, Cengage Learning

GALE
CENGAGE Learning·

Detroit • New York • San Francisco • New Haven, Conn • Waterville, Maine • London

GALE
CENGAGE Learning·

LIBRARY OF CONGRESS CATALOGING-IN-PUBLICATION DATA

Malik, Liesa.
  Faith on the rocks : a Daisy Arthur mystery / by Liesa Malik. — Large print edition.
    pages ; cm. — (Wheeler Publishing large print cozy mystery)
    ISBN 978-1-4104-6382-1 (softcover) — ISBN 1-4104-6382-6 (softcover)
  1. Widows—Fiction. 2. Retired teachers—Fiction. 3. Love stories—Authorship—Fiction. 4. Murder—Investigation—Fiction. 5. Large type books. I. Title.
  PS3613.A43576F35 2013b
  813'.6—dc23   2013033678

Published in 2014 by arrangement with Liesa Malik

Printed in the United States of America
2 3 4 5 6   18 17 16 15 14

For Jay, Nicola, Sara, Chloe, and the pets. Life is made rich by the ones you love and share it with.
Thanks for believing in me.

For Jay, Nicola, Sara, Chloe, and the pets. Life is made rich by the ones you love and share it with.
Thanks for believing in me.

ACKNOWLEDGMENTS

Sometimes the best of luck happens because the people in your life push, prod, poke, harass, and otherwise encourage you to keep trying to do your best, even when your weekly ten pages lack conflict, grammar, or substance.

I am deeply indebted to all the people of the Southwest Plaza Thursday Night Critique group, led by Mary Ann Kersten, for gentle nudges in the right direction for writing. Couldn't have done this without you and the special friendships you've so generously shared with me.

Special thanks to Andrea Catalano, ZJ Czupor, Karen Goldsberry, Ed Hickok, Martha Husain, Kathryn House, Kathy Reynolds, John Turley, Bill Wall, and Kevin Wolf for enriching my writing experience with your wisdom and kind support. This critique group is also part of the Rocky Mountain Fiction Writers organization.

Thanks, too, to Sheila Seaver, my first reader and gentle critic.

I'm also deeply grateful to my editor, Deni Dietz, who has encouraged me through a number of submissions until the work presented met the standards for the original publisher, Five Star Publishing, and to the team there willing to take a risk on a new author. Hoping this is the first in a long line of successes together.

CHAPTER 1

I bit my lip, sucked in an overly long breath, and stared down at the manila folder sitting kitten-like in my lap. Inside lay seven neatly stapled packets of my work, ten pages each from my soon-to-be great novel, *Love Finds a Way.* I ignored the people coming and going through our public library doors, a swirl of happy sounds and thoughtful conversations as they passed by me sitting in the lobby, usurper of an alcove of comfortable chairs. I waited for my group and stared down at my work again.

Ten pages of fished-for thoughts, hard-captured words, and corrected fragment sentences sat on me with a comfy heft, still warm from the photocopy machine. I fingered the packets with hope and counted them again. These pages should force my writing group to respond with at least some small praise. After last week's calamity, I needed encouragement. Badly.

I'd always thought romance writing would be more fascinating than this.

"Hey, Daisy. Hear about the dead guy they found floating in the Platte?" Kitty Beaumont flitted lightly into our area, perched her pixie-sized frame into an upholstered lounge chair across from me, and dropped her oversized, overstuffed canvas sack on the tile floor.

Kitty was a delightful urchin fresh out of college, with a mind so sharp she put Ginsu knives to shame. Her energy wore me out quickly, but I couldn't help smiling when my tiny friend was around. We met when I joined the Hugs 'N' Kisses writing group about a month ago, and she'd kept me writing ever since.

Kitty hunched forward expectantly, as if I might add something to her dead guy news.

"Yes," I said. "Read about that in Saturday's *Post*. Paper said he was a bit wet behind the ears."

My young colleague shook her head and groaned. "Daisy. Your puns."

I knew Kitty liked my little jokes more than she admitted, but I turned more serious just the same. "Poor fellow. Drowned and dead for three days before they found him. Imagine."

"Oooh. Good and creepy. Imagine, here

10

in Littleton. Land of monotony and boredom." Kitty flung her arms wide as if to encompass the whole world around her.

I'd only seen her a few times but, whenever we met, Kitty created the impression of a woodland faerie on rainbow juice or something. Red, green, and gold colors all tumbled together in outfits I could never imagine, but on her they looked fabulous. Tonight's ensemble consisted of an array of violets and lavenders.

I smiled. "Careful what you wish for, my friend. Wouldn't want a dead person in the river daily. Besides, people die as often in Littleton as anywhere else."

"Yes, but not in the Platte. This town's too much the old, staid suburbia for someone to up and die in our only object of natural beauty."

Only natural beauty. Guess Kitty had forgotten the minor detail that Littleton's main backdrop, the Rockies, hover only a few miles away. They sleep a short one hour west of us and provide the backdrop to every human story found on the plains leading up to their solid, quiet, splendor. I'm most aware of them when I drive around town and they rumple the horizon, or when I sit near my Art's grave in the Littleton cemetery, wind chimes at the various graves

11

providing accompaniment to the peaceful rest my husband enjoys. The Platte is none too impressive by comparison.

I gazed toward the door. "Wonder who he was, the guy in the Platte. Maybe a handsome rancher or an oil man?"

"Probably some slimy homeless guy."

"Thanks, Kitty. Now there's a thought." I turned back to my manila folder. "Listen, I need to look over my ten pages for tonight's review."

Kitty reached over and patted my shoulder. "Too late for that, Daisy. Don't worry about it now. You'll be fine. Just take a deep breath and start reading."

"Easy for you to say. Especially after last week's disaster."

She laughed and leaned back. "It was a fairly rough first review, wasn't it? You sure know how to inspire your critics. Tell you what. Let's take your mind off things by playing the *what if* game."

"What if?"

"Yes. It's a brainstorming game from the Rocky Mountain Fiction Writers newsletter. Saw it a couple of months ago. Helps generate story ideas. You take something like a newspaper item and ask yourself 'what if?' questions until a story idea emerges." Kitty folded her arms and tapped her front teeth with a purple-polished index finger. "For example, *what if* the dead guy in the Platte was someone we knew?"

"Littleton's small, Kitty, but not that small. *What if* he's someone from Denver whose body swept downstream to Littleton?"

"Not possible. Platte flows north, and we're south of Denver. You know that."

I chewed my lip a moment. "But this *is* fiction, and not everyone knows the Platte flows north."

"Even in fiction, Daisy, there is a level of accuracy that has to be employed. Otherwise you get angry readers sending nasty emails to you and your publisher. Editors don't like that."

My heart sank. There was so much more to writing well than I'd imagined. How was I ever going to learn it all? I sighed.

Kitty relented a tad. "Okay. Say the guy was from Denver but fell in the Chatfield Reservoir south of here. Then *what if* he was murdered and didn't just fall into the river?"

"If he was murdered, we'd have to know a lot more about him and his situation. Look, *what if* I stop this game now and do a free-writing exercise on my next chapter?"

Kitty grinned. "Spoilsport." She reached down to pull a *Writing Magic* magazine from

13

her bag. "Who was he, our murdered friend? And imagine how he must've looked when they found him. Yuck!"

My thoughts drifted to the stranger in the news, the dead man in the Platte. Immediately, visions of bloated gray flesh and bulging eyes floated to mind. Being water-logged in a river for that long would do horrid things to a body. My stomach lurched at the thought.

Kitty slapped her magazine closed. "Honestly, I'd prefer being shot. Here one second, then *bang!* I'm an angel. Works for me."

For a supposedly innocent romance writer, she sure seemed comfortable with the harsher side of life. I giggled at the vision of a bang-angel. "Kind of makes last week's fracas seem bland in comparison," I said as I shook off my hideous images.

"You mean Rico and Todd?"

"Yes. All that noise over a manuscript. In a library no less. And when I found out Rico's a priest, I had to scoop my jaw off the floor with a shovel."

"I forgot you haven't been with us that long."

"*Rico* and *priest* in one thought? I didn't see it coming."

Kitty laughed. "You sure looked surprised over that 'Father Rico' Sandra pulls out

14

whenever she wants to remind us all to behave properly. What a load."

Sandra, our critique group leader, was a stickler for the rules. She seemed to be a perfectionist about everything, pushing here, prodding there. I guessed she was in those power years somewhere between mid-thirties to mid-forties and was used to being in control, but I had to admit, she intimidated the heck out of me. Where Kitty was a pint-sized powerhouse, Sandra was a veritable Amazon. When we met, my new group leader gave me a booklet, her "Little Guide for Being a Good Critic," and I felt like she would pop-quiz me on the contents soon. There were a ton of rules for such a small group, and I suspected that new ones sprouted in her Type-A mind each week. Only Rico seemed comfortable around Sandra.

"Are you sure he prefers *Rico* to the Father title?" I asked.

Kitty nodded and I shrugged.

She returned to her reading, and I grabbed a spiral notebook from my canvas writing bag on the floor beside me.

Now that I'm an aspiring writer, I need to do a lot of wordsmith exercises. When I taught special education, I dreamed of retiring and writing romances. Now that I'm retired, I miss my old job — I mean I need to focus on the writing I dreamed of.

I decided to do a quick free-writing project: write a question, set a time, then jot down whatever comes to mind, so I composed the first question that popped into my head: "What happened last week?"

Not a great inspiration for romance. I scratched it out and tried again.

"How can my hero . . ." Rico's face came to mind. "How can Rico . . ." Shoot! "What *did* happen last week?" I nibbled my pen, then began writing . . .

Each Tuesday evening our group of four to seven members meets in the Columbine library to read each other's work, critique it, and express hopes for that ever-elusive publication of our novels. I'm the newest member and had my first real reading last week. After agonizing for weeks to find precisely the right words, I offered up Chapter One of my book. I think it's good. Really. At least I hope it's good.

Why work so hard at a hobby? Hmm. Why not? It's not like I'm short of time. With early retirement, life stretches forever in front of me. Besides, who knows? Somebody wins the lottery. One day it could be me.

There's only one published author amongst us. Eleanor Rapp. She has an agent, four published books, and a real writer's office, although no one's been invited to see it. I think she's boring.

Kitty tapped my arm. "Look, Daisy. What luck. Here's an article on writing mystery plots. We can use this for our murdered guy in the Platte."

"You go for it, Kitty. I'm trying to write about love. Much nicer."

Kitty gave a quick, cynical "Ha!" and dove back into her article.

Now where was I? Oh, yes. Last week, after I completed my reading, Rico, the priest, the priest who writes romance novels, gave my critique.

I'm still jolted by a man of the cloth writing romance novels. I thought they were all married to God or something. But other romance writers are married, and I wouldn't think of them as cheating on their spouse. I wonder how that works. Oops! I digress.

Anyway, my cheeks still burn when I think about how I gazed into Rico's sinfully chocolate eyes and felt the wonderfully warm and intense electricity of his hand on my arm. The connection between us caused my chest to tighten. He stroked his thumb back and forth on my wrist as he talked, and acted as if we were alone. Breathing seemed superfluous.

Even though Rico used words like trite,

long-winded, *and* grandiloquent, *I could have listened to his trilling r's and soft Spanish accent for an hour. Everything else but the musky scent of his aftershave and the intense gaze of those eyes seemed to fade away. If only he were twenty years older or I were ten years younger. If only he were a Lutheran minister and available. Scrumptious.*

Kitty interrupted my writing again. "Says here that while the murderer has one main secret, the victim usually has several. That's how you get good suspects."

"That's interesting, dear," I said with as little enthusiasm as I could. Perhaps Kitty would get the hint. I started scribbling again . . .

Rico was scrumptious. I would love to hang on that thought for a while. But while Rico may have been kind, the rest of the group tore my reading apart. The others left both my work and my heart in shreds on the library lobby floor. What the heck does "tighten" mean anyway? Their comments and notes were absolutely brutal, if honest. Gee. Thanks. Not. I know I cried when I got home that night and had a nightmare with lots of red lines and sad faces drawn in it.

After my embarrassing review, Rico started his own reading. Like everything else about him, his ten-page submission seemed perfect.

I was more than halfway in love with Rico's hero, Reynaldo.

Kitty prodded me once more. "Says here, a murder victim might seem perfectly fine on the outside but usually has a really dark other life. Cool, huh?"

I bit my tongue. "Kitty. I don't need dark secrets. Hate to be rude, but I'm working here." I tried to show firmness and not annoyance, but was beginning to feel the latter.

Kitty threw her arms up. "Think how your hero would be so much more dimensional if he weren't all admirable and, well, *heroic.*"

"Another time." I waved Kitty back to her magazine, reread my own journal lines, then tried again . . .

I was more than halfway in love with Rico's hero, Reynaldo, when he and Tonya, the love interest, decided to run away.

At that point, the reading was cut short by an interruption from Todd Stevens. "Rico, stop, stop, stop!" said Todd, who is about as tall as Jiminy Cricket with strawberry-blond hair, ice-blue eyes, and an effeminate lisp. His face is quite handsome, I guess. But on top of being too young, he's not my type. Still, I like him. He's a fun-loving sort of guy most of the time. He sure wouldn't have dark secrets.

"This is the worst crap you've brought so

far," Todd had said, "and I won't have you humiliate yourself with more of it. Hand out the rest of your pages and we'll write our comments."

The shock I felt at such rudeness was reflected on the other group members' faces. Todd isn't like that. Wonder what was wrong with him.

And let's not forget about the rules. Rule Number One: The person reading is not to be interrupted, no matter how good or bad his writing. Though, to be honest, I rather wish the group had interrupted my reading last week. Even I was bored with it.

Rico glared at Todd and tried to resume his reading.

Todd pulled Rico's manuscript away. "I said, enough. Now, look, you b—"

Plus, can somebody talk that way to a priest? I mean, I didn't know he was a priest at the time, so maybe Todd didn't either, but still.

Kitty subtly cleared her throat.

"What is it?" I had a hard time keeping the edge out of my voice. Rico and Todd needed resolution.

"Did you know that murder often starts out as an accident or even a joke gone wrong?"

"Kitty, I'm sure all of this would be

interesting if I were writing a mystery, but I'm not. Please. Remember we're in a romance writers' group. I need to figure out how to inspire romantic feelings, not angry ones."

"I don't know, Daisy. They say there is a fine line between love and hate. I think I'll add a murder to my next book."

"You go for it, but I want to stay on the romantic side of things." Then it occurred to me that I'd spent the last ten minutes absorbed in writing about Todd and Rico's fight. I wasn't sure I understood what Todd had found to be so offensive in Rico's work. It was a sensitive story about Reynaldo, a man forbidden to express his love for Tonya because of outdated traditions in their community. I picked up my pen to start in again . . .

The rattling library door shook noisily, and with a blast of cool September evening air, our group leader, Sandra, swept in. Early season dead leaves swirled round her ankles like a tiny press corps following the general-in-charge.

"Good evening, fellow writers," said Sandra. Every strand of her blond hair was stuck precisely in place. No evening breeze would dare to disrupt the woman's hairdo.

Kitty and I exchanged glances before

21

responding. Such vigor from our leader meant only one thing: she would be reading tonight.

Sandra's story was about a perfect young woman who met her perfect young man. They were perfectly destined for each other. Even both sets of parents approved. Only one guy, nasty Garrick — the one character I tended to like — wanted to take the heroine for himself, and it looked like Garrick would fail. Blah. Blah. Blah.

I wished someone from our group had the courage to tell Sandra her story sucked. Instead, everyone politely critiqued the grammar, which was as perfectly controlled as her hair.

Soon the others came, and we began our work. I was the first to arrive with copy, so I read first. A barrage of politely phrased "this sucks" comments left me deflated, even if I got points for a tidy presentation. Why did I ever take up writing as an avocation?

Kitty read next. As she finished her story about a rancher's daughter and the local sheriff, I happened to glance up through the lobby glass into the library checkout area.

Our group was being watched by another, more somber-looking assembly standing with one of the librarians. Indeed, the librarian pointed at us while talking to them, and I felt a surge of discomfort. Had our group's incident last week caused the library staff to view us differently? I thought about how we had become louder as more people were pulled into Todd and Rico's argument. Were we no longer a welcome aspiring writers' club, but perhaps something noxious?

Suddenly, I recognized one of the mortician-faced people. It was Ginny's dad. Ginny was a special-needs student of mine a few years back. Then I also remembered her dad, Gabe, was a single and attractive police officer. I began to raise my hand for a wave and smiled.

"Yes, Daisy?" said Sandra.

I blushed like a kid caught passing notes in class. Rule Number Two: Focus only on the group while here. We do not have much time and certainly none to waste on socialization. Oops. My bad.

"Sorry, Sandra. I just saw a parent from my old teaching days."

Sandra sighed uncomfortably loud and long. The regal shake of her head completed the censure.

I fidgeted as Gabe and his group strode toward us.

"Sorry for the interruption, Kitty," I said. She winked at me to show no hard feelings, and I grinned back.

Gabe cleared his throat as he approached, standing behind Sandra's chair. I began to wave him away, but he ignored me to address the group at large. Perhaps he didn't recognize me after all.

"Pardon me. I'm Lieutenant Gabriel Caerphilly of the Littleton police. My team and I are here in search of something called the — er — hugs and kisses?"

"We are the 'Hugs 'N' Kisses Romance Writers' Critique Group,' " said Sandra. "A subgroup of the four-hundred-member Rocky Mountain Fiction Writers." The way she spoke made us sound a lot more important and professional than Gabe's reference.

"So you are," said Gabe, apparently unimpressed.

I felt a twinge of guilt thinking of him as merely Gabe, Ginny's dad, and not Gabriel, the forceful lieutenant standing before us. Handsome as ever.

He continued speaking. "We have some questions to ask you — each of you — regarding the death of one of your members last week."

"What?" said Sandra. "No one has notified *me* of any deaths. I think you must be mistaken." She looked around as if to accuse one of us of possibly dying without

24

proper notice. I'll bet she has a rule about that, too.

Kitty spoke up. "There are only two people missing tonight. Rico and Eleanor. But they're too healthy for a heart attack or anything. Unless . . . there was an accident?"

Lieutenant Caerphilly responded as if from a script. "The victim's name has been withheld from the papers, but Father Rico Sanchez drowned in the Platte River. This occurred behind the Aspen Grove shopping center sometime last week. We have reason to believe he was murdered. And, we believe the people of this group may have been the last to see him alive."

CHAPTER 2

Sandra was the first to break the shocked bubble of silence. She burst into tears and crossed herself, mumbling incoherencies like, "all my fault," and "my luckless Rico." For the first time since I met her, Sandra behaved as if there were a chink in her armor. And what a chink it was.

I stared in disbelief as the woman who controlled every piece of her life fell completely apart. Tears turned into wails loud enough to hear way down in Colorado Springs. She shook her head until her perfect hairdo flew apart in a riot of ratty blond waves, and stomped her high-heeled feet in a fruitless attempt to drill to China.

The spell broken, we all talked at once. The library staff must've thought we were the worst patrons ever, but we had good cause. One of our own had died. Correction. Was murdered!

I couldn't believe it. I remembered the

last time I saw Rico. So vibrant, so in love with life. Who would steal that vitality from someone? And why?

Toni, pale and serious, reached over to pat Sandra's back and hand our leader a tissue. Toni was a motherly sort of person who always had exactly what was needed in her big black purse. Tissues, aspirins, or extra pens magically appeared each week whenever someone was in need. Age had lightened Toni's bun at the back of her neck and given her a bit of a moustache, but everything seemed comfortable when she was around. She wore a black dress with tiny polka dots almost every week, and tonight was no exception. I was glad that she was sitting next to Sandra and not me. I wanted to be sympathetic, but Sandra seemed somehow too enthusiastic in her grief.

Toni looked up at Gabe. "What happened, sir? Can you give us any more information than that he was murdered? This is unbelievable."

Gabe shifted his weight from one foot to the other. "We can only tell you that Father Sanchez was killed sometime after your writing group last week. His body was found on Friday and showed signs of being in the water for a couple of days."

Kitty frowned. "That was in the news, Lieutenant. It doesn't tell us why you're here. Surely we can't really be the very last people to have seen him."

"We interviewed several people at his church. The pastor said Rico was a part of this writing group. He said his staff became concerned when Rico didn't appear for their weekly meeting Wednesday afternoon. Rico must have died between your get together Tuesday evening and Wednesday afternoon."

Kitty seemed to do some mental calculations, then spoke up again. "That's a lot of time, Lieutenant. Rico could have been killed by a lot more people than us. Why didn't the church staff call the police when Rico no-showed?"

"Look, Ms. —"

"Beaumont. Kitty Beaumont."

"Look, Ms. Beaumont. Like I said, we interviewed several people at the church. We're satisfied that our investigation needs to focus on this writing group for now." He looked at each of us in turn.

Todd, who until this point had silently let tears roll down his cheeks, shot out of his chair, grabbed his backpack, and headed toward the front door. "I need some air."

Gabe blocked Todd's exit. "Not so fast.

28

Like I said, we have some questions for you." He looked around the group. "All of you." Gabe turned back to Todd with more command than request in his attitude. "Please sit."

Todd complied, but his knee jerked up and down in a nervous staccato. Toni handed him one of her extra tissues. I looked around at the rest of the group. Sandra hunched into her hands, her moans loud and long as Toni, with more patience than I could imagine, kept an arm around her and seemed to be cooing soothing nothings to our group leader.

I thought I saw Toni roll her eyes once, but the look passed too quickly for me to be sure. Maybe I was the only one annoyed. Yes, it was shocking to have a colleague die so unexpectedly, but it wasn't like Rico was a close relative or anything. Plus, I've never been one to tolerate another's public displays of suffering.

Kitty, very serious, sat forward in her seat, all her attention on Gabe and his police companion, a striking woman who stood with clipboard in hand, looking at our group in a no-nonsense way. Like Gabe, the woman did not wear a uniform but projected authority with straight posture and a delicate but serious bent to her head. She watched intensly while each person spoke, as if memorizing everything they said or did. I'd bet she didn't miss a thing and was an excellent police officer.

I fidgeted with the blue-green threads on the upholstered arm of my chair, needing more information, knowing none was coming. Frustrating. If police and officials would only be more open in these kind of situations, I bet we could solve a heck of a lot more problems a lot faster. How could my group add any information to a story if the police weren't going to share what they already knew?

Gabe addressed the five of us with a nice-guy attitude. "The library staff have generously cleared their conference rooms tonight, so you won't have to make a trip to the station. Still, these interviews are likely to take a while, so if you need to phone home or use the bathrooms, now would be the time to do so."

Sandra jumped up. "Home! I have to be there for the babysitter. I have to get home for my son. How will I tell him? My poor Adam. Oh, what should I do?"

I thought I heard Todd whisper, "You should shut up," but I was looking at Kitty, who definitely rolled her eyes. How could our leader fall so completely apart during a crisis like this? I mean, I'd seen the old war movies where the officer crumbles under attack and some poor low-level guy with better leadership skills has to take over, but still. Was life really like that?

Toni stood and took Sandra in hand once more. She was a large, capable woman who seemed to have done this kind of soothing before. Sandra crumpled into Toni's arms and wailed some more.

Wish I could be as patient as Toni, who was talking in soothing tones. "It will be all right, dear. I'm sure your babysitter will understand, and you can call home to talk to your son."

"Oh, but Adam is a very particular friend of Rico's, and so sensitive. He lost another best friend a couple of years ago and has been having problems since. I need to tell my son in person. Rico's death will be a terrible setback for him. Oh, how can we cope?" She renewed her wailing efforts.

I never tolerated these dramatic shows of emotion from my students, so began to think Sandra was silly. What was with her theatrics?

Even Toni seemed to stiffen. "Please, Sandra. Let's calm down. For Adam's sake. I'm sure everything will work out."

Gabe turned to Kitty, Todd, and me.

"We'll let her have a chance to compose herself. Will you" — he pointed to Todd — "meet with me, and Ms. Beaumont, go with Sergeant Taylor." He indicated his companion, the woman with the clipboard.

"And me?" I asked.

Gabe looked at me for a long moment. "I know you, don't I?" He seemed to be searching his memory as he spoke. "Daisy?"

"Yes. Daisy Arthur. Your daughter's teacher at Independence High."

Gabe's face cleared, and he pushed a bright smile onto his features. The smile made me feel as if we'd been friends forever.

He nodded. "Yes. Daisy Arthur. So good to see you. We've missed — that is — if you'll wait here I'll come back for you when I'm done." He nodded toward Todd, who was following the trim Sergeant Taylor toward the conference rooms.

CHAPTER 3

A couple of hours, one *Writing Magic* magazine, and two pages of composing my romance later, Sergeant Taylor tapped me on
the shoulder.

"Ms. Arthur, would you come with me,
please?" The good sergeant had one of those
faces that arrests your attention with its
beauty. Even though she did not smile,
everything competent and wise shone from
her features.

I followed the sergeant to a conference
room. It was a small place without adorn-
ment, save a large-faced clock stuck next to
the requisite smoke detector high up against
the main wall. Pervasive beige swam under
fluorescent lights, and air conditioning running enthusiastically encouraged me to keep
on my sweater. An island table of chocolate
melamine ate up most of the floor space and
supported a stack of yellow pads.

"Wow. With all those notes, you must not

need anything I have to say." I forced a laugh to relax. Gabe looked up from the plastic chair he was using and nodded.

Sergeant Taylor still did not smile, but showed me to a seat opposite Gabe and walked to his side of the table. Her light perfume followed her like a drift of sweet wildflowers. She leaned over, pointed to places in the last pad, and whispered about the notes. Her right hand gently rested on Gabe's shoulder. "Sexual harassment" was probably the furthest thing from Gabe's mind. The two made a good pair.

Gabe looked up at the sergeant. "Thank you, Taylor." He seemed comfortable with the sergeant, as if they'd shared a lot of life together. "If you take these other notes to the station for transcribing, I'll finish up with Ms. Arthur and check in with you."

"No problem, Caerphilly. See you in, say . . . an hour or so?" Sergeant Taylor gave him a quick smile and was gone.

Like a revolving door, as soon as the sergeant left, a librarian popped her head in. "Will you be long, Lieutenant? I'm sorry, but the library's been closed for thirty minutes already."

Gabe looked at his watch. "My apologies, Ms. Goodwin. We'll leave shortly. Ms. Arthur, if you have a few minutes for some quick questions, I'll follow up with you tomorrow."

I bobbed my head. After waiting so long, I wanted to get this interview over and done.

The librarian left. Gabe blew a long breath out. I felt the breeze from my side of the table.

"Long day?" I asked.

"Very. But it's good to see you again, Ms. Arthur."

"Daisy. You, Ginny, and I have had too many conferences to be so formal."

"Daisy." He smiled. "You were always the rock we needed in those days. I had almost forgotten."

Those days. Gabe's wife left the family as Ginny began her hormonal urges of teenhood. The woman couldn't handle the new stresses Ginny's life brought, along with the difficulties of being a policeman's wife. In special needs families the divorce rate is as high as eighty-five percent, so it was no real surprise that the Caerphillys became one of those unfortunate statistics. As a result, Gabe, Ginny, and I worked hard as a team to get through the rough times. He was heroic, bouncing between his often stressful work life and teacher conferences, school basketball games, and teen woes with Ginny.

When Art, my husband, died, I thought

Gabe and I might make a good match, but I wasn't ready to pull out from under the difficulties of saying goodbye to my dearest man of over twenty-five years. As the months passed, Gabe's work drew him further off, and his little Ginny found her way into adulthood more or less independently.

"Thank you," I said. "How's Ginny?"

"Fine. And you?"

"Fine."

The clock on the wall hummed in the gap between us, but I didn't have any brilliant discourse, and Gabe, a tad grayer than when we last met, seemed comfortable only looking at me, keeping his thoughts to himself.

A knock on the door preceded the face of Ms. Goodwin. "I'm sorry, Lieutenant, but we really must lock up now."

Gabe glanced at the wall clock. "Yes, Ms. Goodwin." He turned back to me. "Daisy, I know it's a bit unconventional, but perhaps you could join me at Pete's Pub up the road? We can conduct a bit less formal interview there and perhaps clear up all our questions tonight."

"Sounds like a plan, Lieutenant." I stood, smiled, and gathered my things.

At the bar, Gabe proved to be the charming

man I had known in our Independence experience. He told me how Ginny had a job and her own "apartment" in his house. I told him I was still single and living the empty retirement life.

"But you're quite young for retirement," he said, leaning into the deep red leather booth back. I gazed down and fingered the hops plants embedded into the polyurethane tabletop.

"My husband was always good with things like insurance and wills. When he died, I was left financially comfortable, and, well, with the Colby Stanton incident, I guess the wind sort of left my sails."

"Colby Stanton?"

"I forgot. Ginny had graduated by then. One of my students had a bad accident. His folks blamed me, and the school administration wasn't up for a fight. Parents threatened to sue unless something was done about me. It was early retirement or public humiliation, censure, and firing. I chose to retire."

I pictured Colby. What a sweetheart.

A wave of anguish rolled over me. Rico. Colby. Art. I took to fingering the rolled-up napkin holding my silverware. Tears stung my eyes. Change subject, Daisy. No need to dump on Gabe. Change subject.

Gabe reached across our table but drew

back. Ever the proper policeman. "I'm sorry to hear that, Daisy. To me, you were one of the best teachers Ginny ever had."

"Let's answer your questions about Rico — Father Rico."

"Everyone stumbles over the guy's name. Why is that?"

"I didn't even know he was a priest until last week." Last week when Rico became Father Rico and then became the dead guy in the Platte. A knot formed in my stomach.

"And no one else knew?"

"Not exactly. Kitty said Sandra uses his title whenever she wants us all to behave better."

"Sandra's telling a group of adults to behave better?"

"Sandra's a bit of a control freak."

"Ah. Wouldn't have guessed so tonight." We both laughed, then Gabe said, "Now, tell me about Kitty."

"Kitty is as sharp as they come. I think she'd be happier having one of those controversial television talk shows, but, luckily, we have her in our writing group. I think she'll be the next one of us who gets published. Isn't she just the cutest thing?"

Gabe didn't comment on Kitty's cuteness. "How did she feel about Rico?"

"Not sure. She didn't ever smile at him,

and now that you mention it, she seemed to avoid him."

"Avoid him?"

"Yes. Don't know why that popped into my head, but I think she kind of worked to make sure she was never left alone with him."

"Good observation, Daisy."

"Thanks. Now, can you tell me how you knew that Rico was murdered and didn't drown accidentally?"

Gabe glanced around the bar. The bartender was wiping glasses and chatting with a pretty woman at the other end. The few other people there were engrossed in the televisions mounted above the assorted bottles of liquors.

"I really shouldn't tell you this," said Gabe, lowering his voice. "We try to hold things back, but there was a note and highlighted Bible passage at the scene."

"What did it —"

Gabe held up his hand. "No more. I've said too much already. Now, what about Todd Stevens and Toni Piccolo?"

I took a sip of the hot apple cider I'd ordered. "I like them both. Toni is the better writer, but Todd is a happy-go-lucky kind of man and a good friend, except for that fight between him and Rico last week."

"What happened?"

I briefly told Gabe about Todd's rudeness and how he and Rico fought over the manuscript, how Kitty remembered that *Tonya*, Rico's heroine, means "fairy queen," and she thought Todd and Rico were having a lover's quarrel.

"Did Stevens really say he wished Rico were dead? Ms. Beaumont mentioned that in her interview, too."

I thought again, picturing the fight. "Yes. Kitty's right. I forgot about that."

"That's okay. You sure don't miss much."

"It used to be my job. Observing, looking for strengths in people. Watching out for potential abuse situations for my kids. Generally I don't miss small but important details."

"Those are good skills to keep. Think you can keep 'observing,' as you say, and let me know if anything strikes you as odd or out of place?"

"Be a snitch for the police?" Although Gabe winced, I enjoyed the vision of Daisy, super sleuth, and wiggled my eyebrows. "I'd love to!"

CHAPTER 4

I dropped my car keys on the table beside the front door and my writing bag on the floor next to it. Magically, my cat, Georgette Heyer, appeared and sidled up to the bag. She performed her ritual sniff for goodies, then began purring.

"Hello, Georgie Porgie. You'll never guess what's happened." I lifted my sixteen-pound friend. Her multi-shaded fur danced in the air around my nose, and I enjoyed a good sneeze.

Georgette blinked her gold eyes as if to say, "I'm not impressed with any 'what's-happened.' Just scratch me, yes, right there, behind my ears. *Now* you may assault my peace with your trivial noise."

"We had a real to-do at writing group tonight," I said. "Rico, that priest from my group? He's been murdered!" I tried to picture every detail of the man I would never see again. He had a classic, square

41

jaw line, and round, brown eyes. Those eyes could bore into one's soul. He still had a nice head of hair that I'd thought about running fingers through in the last week. I wondered if he had on the silly royal blue vest he liked to wear when they found his body. What would I be wearing when I died?

As I stroked Georgette's back, I thought about why I found Rico magnetic. He seemed sort of dangerous, albeit in an attractive way. The kind of man my mother would have warned me against. Too good to be true. Odd, that. Rico was, after all, a priest. But why did he flirt in our writing group, and why didn't he make it obvious he was a priest? Most people love to talk about their work.

"Oh! And you'll never guess who I saw tonight. Gabriel Caerphilly, of all people. You remember me talking to you about Ginny, Gabe's daughter, don't you? She was always one of my favorite students."

Georgette began to knead my arms, a sliver of claw working its way into my skin. I gasped. "Now, don't look at me like that. I know, as a good teacher, I'm not supposed to have favorites, but I can trust my secrets with you."

We waddled back toward my bedroom, Georgette in my arms. I opened the door so that she could visit her own pet, Errol Fin. Errol is a Plecostomus fish Georgette fell in love with while we were shopping at the pet store. Must've been that permanent twinkle painted in his eyes that captured her heart.

I dropped an algae wafer into Errol's tank and closed the lid quickly so Georgette couldn't love him to death. We've had three Errols so far.

I sat down in my rocker to catch my breath. Its soft cushions in the pleasing rose pattern welcomed me with a marshmallow hug. Georgette leapt to my lap with a hard-earned oomph. I would like to say Georgette's a Maine Coon, but the vet has insisted her large size is due more to diet than genetics. Might need a new vet.

"Gabe Caerphilly. Can you imagine!" I mused.

Georgette began purring, so I kept talking and stroking her fur.

"He's as handsome as I remember and still not wearing a wedding ring." After enjoying a picture of Gabe across from me at the bar, I heaved a sigh. "Then again, there was a Sergeant Taylor with him and she seemed to have more than cops and robbers on her mind. I wonder how far their partnership goes. Yes, she's beautiful, seems competent, and I hate her already. What do

43

you think, Georgie?"

Georgette blinked and licked my wrist with her sandpaper tongue.

"I felt let down when Gabe didn't recognize me at first. At one time, under different circumstances, I might have been his significant other. Oh, Georgie, wouldn't it have been cozy? We wouldn't be so alone now, and you wouldn't have to be my therapist so often. Doggone that Sergeant Taylor."

Georgette's eyes closed. She likes to fall asleep to my chatter. Her purrs told me she was still listening.

As I talked, Georgette's purring turned to snores. I remembered that I was late getting home, so it was no wonder everything faded for me into a blurry wave of colors and faces, then black. I felt my head drop but didn't care.

I woke in my chair with a start. Strange, angry noises invaded my brain. I glanced toward my television. It wasn't on. The noises grew louder.

I tried to shake myself awake, and was rewarded with a leg cramp. Who was angry? More important, had I locked my door when I got home? Being a single person living alone was hard and scary sometimes.

I stood to relieve the cramp and felt sixteen pounds lighter as Georgette thumped to the floor. She wandered off.

I would have to go check that front lock. Don't turn on the light, Daisy. Makes you an easy target. What was that noise?

I tried to think. I lived in a safe neighborhood in the suburbs, for heaven's sake. Who would really want to hurt me? Had I ticked off that nerdy checkout man at the grocery store again? Had he followed me home somehow and decided to check me out?

The sounds came again and I jumped.

CHAPTER 5

A bit more awake and armed with one of my fuzzy pink slippers for protection, I crept toward my front door, but stopped when I realized the strange, angry noises invaded my bedroom through its open window. Two voices muffled by distance and walls wafted in. I grasped that it was a man and a woman. Shouting. Irate shouting.

I heard breaking glass, the deep barking of a big dog, and a slammed door. Soon, a car door opened and slammed shut.

I stepped back to my bedroom window in time to see the driver's royal finger gesture directed toward my neighbor, who was coming out his back gate. The finger-touting woman, now in her little red two-seater, backed out the driveway. Chip, my not-quite-thirty neighbor, ran toward her, wearing nothing but his dark striped boxers and white T-shirt.

"Ella, I didn't mean it," he called after the

car. "Ella, come back. Ellaaaaa!"

It was a bad remake of the movie that shot Marlon Brando to stardom.

What was the count? Four lovers lost in the past six months? Chip really had to work on his style.

He threw a last lure to recall the now-disappearing car. "I'll write a story about you. You'll see."

I sighed. That line would sure bring me running back into those scrawny arms.

Another neighbor called, "Shut up, Chip!"

"You shut up, lard mouth," Chip replied.

Georgette was scratching at my back door, so I let her escape and slipped out myself.

Chip sat on his back step, head in arms, shoulders heaving. He'd never been blessed with a normal growth spurt and looked tiny sitting there. Although taller than my own five-two, I could still look Chip straight in the eye when I wanted to, which wasn't often. His ferret-like activities and proclivity for prying ensured that Chip and I would never be great friends.

But last winter during a big snowstorm he bought a new supercharged snow blower and cleared my driveway. In return, I baked him the occasional batch of oatmeal-raisin cookies.

"Chip, are you all right?" I called. He

47

lifted his head. Even from across our driveways I could see his face was glistening; he was crying. This was more serious than I first thought. Still, he rubbed away tears and waved toward me.

"Lovely evening, eh, Ms. D.? What's the scoop?"

Something resembling fingernails on chalkboard crept up my spine. *Ms. D.? Scoop?* I forced a smile and said, "The weather this time of year is so lovely. I thought I'd enjoy some fresh air before retiring."

"I'm sorry if we woke you, Ella and me." A pained look crossed his face. "Ella and me," he said again.

Inwardly, I cringed. I didn't need a long night with an aspiring reporter. Even so, he was a neighbor, and Arthur, my wonderful husband, always said people in our country needed to reconnect to the responsibilities of being good neighbors.

"You want to come over for a cup of tea?" I called.

"Thanks! I'll throw something on." Chip's face brightened, and he disappeared into his house.

He was across in an instant, a ratty terry robe drooped over his Napoleon frame.

Time for the you'll-be-okay, you're-still-a-good-man chat. I only hoped it wouldn't take all night. We sat at my old Formica kitchen table, Georgette keeping watch from her perch on my windowsill over the sink.

"It's sad," said Chip. "I really thought Ella and I would make it. She's everything I always wanted in a woman." He stirred at least four spoonfuls of sugar into the teacup I offered.

"And what is that?" I said.

"Well, she's beautiful. Rich. Smart. She's, you know, compatible — in bed I mean." He blushed. I felt the teacher-slash-mother coming out in me.

"So far, I don't sense any real connection with Ella. What's her favorite color?"

"Blue, I guess. I mean she wears a lot of blue jeans. Oh, I don't know."

"How 'bout her favorite book?"

"Book? You mean to read?"

"Yes, Chip. It shows what's on her mind, the type and volume of reading she does. I mean, you're a writer, right? Don't you want to know that your partner might have an interest in reading?"

"Gosh, I don't know, Ms. D."

"It sounds to me, Chip, that you are thoroughly infatuated with Ms. Ella, but you're not in love. So what about you? How do you feel about yourself when you're in her company?"

"Ms. D., you could be a reporter. You ask great questions."

I wasn't going to let him off the hook. "Well?" I said. "Who *is* Chip McPherson when he has Ella with him?"

"I'm the Ken to her Barbie," he said. Then he sighed. "I'm an also-ran. I am the luckiest guy in town."

"Is she lucky, too?"

Chip hung his head and took a sip of tea before answering. "No, she's not. She's with some loser who can only advance her desire to be famous."

I laid a hand over Chip's. "Son, maybe you need a break. You need to spend quality time with yourself deciding who you are. Learn what's important to you, really important, and how you want to feel when that special woman of your life is around."

"You know me so well, Ms. D.," he replied. "Can't you find someone for me?"

Kitty flashed to mind — young, petite, bright, and funny. Nope. I love matchmaking in my head but know better than to express my thoughts. Trouble with a capital *T.*

"My quiet life doesn't give me much chance to meet many young people any more, Chip. You better handle this adventure yourself."

Chip looked as if I'd really disappointed him. The fool in me loosened my tongue. "Well . . ." I drawled, stalling.

"Yes?" Chip's face perked up.

"I do know one young woman, but she's part of my writers' group, and we're all under suspicion or something at the moment."

"Suspicion?" Chip's head sprang up, his beady eyes alert. The scoop dog was awake and could smell blood.

"It's nothing really," I said. "*Witness* would be a better word. The body they found in the river behind Aspen Grove, the one in the papers, was someone we all know and were possibly the last to see alive."

"Go on," said Chip, feeling around his robe for — and goodness, he found it — a notebook and pen. He smiled at my look. "Always need to be prepared, Ms. D. That's how you get to be the investigative reporter. Now, spill your guts. You can trust me to be accurate."

"I don't think so, Chip. The police are all over this. I'm sure they can give you the appropriate details."

"Oh, come on, lady. There are no secrets between neighbors." When I kept silent,

Chip rolled his eyes. "Okay, so I made that up. Still, I could give you a good profile with the story."

"No thanks, Chip. This is one article I'll be only too glad to stay out of. Besides, I don't believe anyone from my group —"

I paused. Why was Sandra's face coming to mind? Why did I see her as something more than a colleague of Rico? Father Rico.

I had to admit, my ferret-like neighbor has great instincts for the unsaid.

"You *do* believe someone you know is involved!"

"No. That is, I haven't any reason to believe otherwise."

"Tell you what, ol' girl. Give me the name you're thinking, and I'll check out the person for you. I'll even keep you in the loop if I find something."

"No thanks, Chip. You have enough on your plate. And please, don't refer to me as *old girl* or *lady,* as if you hardly know me." I grabbed our cups and moved to my sink.

Georgette stretched up on her haunches and glared at Chip.

"Sorry, Ms. D. I like to keep my informants on edge so I can get to the bottom of the story faster."

"I'm *not* an informant, and I have no story for you. Only a willing ear to hear about this Ella." I flipped on the tap and began rinsing our cups. Behind me, Chip's chair legs scraped my clean tiled floor.

"Ella! I forgot. I'm supposed to go to Fort Collins in the morning, and she was going to come by to take Thunder out for a walk for me. I guess that won't happen now."

I turned in time to see his dejected look. I shook my head.

"So you think you could do it for me? Please?" Back to weasel behavior for this intrepid reporter.

"But I don't know the first thing about dogs" — I shut off the water and turned to face him — "and yours sounds vicious."

"Thunder? Why he's simply an exuberant puppy. I'll put his leash in your mailbox when I leave in the morning, and thanks!"

Chip bolted.

As the door slammed behind him, I cringed. What was I getting myself into?

CHAPTER 6

Morning fought with my eyelids' desire to stay closed, and was reinforced by an obnoxious ringing in the direction of my telephone. I squinted at the clock, got up, and managed to pick up the phone on its third ring.

"Daisy? Hello, Daisy? This is Toni Piccolo."

I cleared my throat. "Hi, Toni. How are you? What an early surprise." I emphasized the "early" word, and looked longingly toward my bathroom.

"Sorry, but I had to talk with you." Toni sounded stressed.

"Are you all right, my friend?" Why did I answer the phone? I could've called back. Now it looked like I might end up in a long conversation that I didn't need. Bladder pressure.

"I'm fine. That is, I was fine." I heard her sigh before she charged into business.

"Look, Daisy, I took care of Sandra last night. All that crying and fussing. I even took her home when she said she was too upset to drive."

"What a good person you are." I couldn't imagine putting up with Sandra's agitation for so long.

"Thanks. But I'm not *that* good. I'm calling to dump her on you today. I've had enough."

"Dump Sandra on me? How?"

"She called two hours ago. Two hours! At five o'clock in the morning, that idiot was on the phone looking for a chauffeur for today. It woke my husband up. Now he's mad, I haven't had enough sleep, and the queen bee is expecting me to run errands with her this morning."

"No, Toni. That's too much." Then I spoke without thinking. "Can I help at all?"

"Oh, Daisy, I was hoping you'd volunteer." The relief in Toni's voice was genuine. "I like Sandra, really I do. Still, she's getting to me."

"I understand." I understood that babysitting Sandra was what Toni wanted from me. What I did not understand was why I complied. "What was with all the waterworks last night?"

"I'm not really sure, but she kept mumbling about things being her fault. I think I even heard her say she needed a drink when we drove past the bar."

A drink? Goodness! Gabe and I could have run into them last night. Our cozy chat would have taken on a whole new dimension. And it wouldn't have helped the objectivity of his investigation at all.

I looked over at Georgette, who was playfully tapping at Errol's aquarium. I put my hand over the mouthpiece and made a hissing sound.

Georgette put on that empty look teenagers have turned into an art form. I could almost hear her saying, "What? I wasn't doing anything."

I scowled. "Honestly, Toni, I thought Sandra was a lot tougher than that. Most of the time she intimidates the heck out of me."

"I call it insecure arrogance. The woman needs to be in charge more than we need her to be our leader."

"Then what do you think last night was all about?"

"I don't know. She's one of those screwed-up Catholics, always taken by surprise when there aren't miracles everywhere. When they find out life is merely life and no more."

I stared into my receiver then put it back to my ear. "That's a rather harsh commentary."

"Sorry, Daisy. Sometimes these religious zealots rattle my nerves."

"I take it you're not religious?"

"No. I follow that guy on television who's always poking fun at religious people. Calls 'em 'religerous' or some such thing."

"I see."

Georgette managed to get her paw into Errol's tank. I cradled the phone in my shoulder, shooed my cat away from the fish, and stuck a book on top of Errol's aquarium to keep it closed. Then I turned my attention back to what Toni was asking.

"And you, Daisy? Do you go to church?"

"No. I would like to find a way to express my faith, but I kind of agree with your TV guy."

"I know what you mean. I believe in God all right, but not church, and certainly not the Catholic Church."

"Why's that?"

"I don't like to talk about it."

"Okay." I tried to switch subjects. "How about Rico's murder? I can't believe someone from our group was killed. I've never been so close to this kind of violence before."

"Incredible. We're supposed to be all about writing romance, and now the police think we're scum of the earth who go around killing each other."

"Amazing. Do you really think someone from our group killed Rico?"

"No. I mean who, besides Kitty, is passionate enough for such a move? And can you see her subduing Rico, a guy at least seventy-five pounds heavier and a good foot taller than she is? Come on. The police are only whistling in the wind with our group."

I felt relieved. "You're right, of course. But if not us, who would kill a priest?"

"Rico had a slimy personality. All that touching and ogling. I think he probably got what he deserved and we're well rid of him."

"Toni!"

"It's true. Those guys throw on their stupid collars and the world is supposed to revere and protect them as if they're saints. Then everyone is astonished when their repressed sexual tendencies come out in inappropriate ways. Fuck them all."

"I've never heard you talk like this. You're always so quiet and gentle."

"Daisy, I'm sixty-three years old. I'm quiet because I don't have anything new to say. Old people like me are supposed to be gentle and quiet. Bah. When you're my age, you'll understand."

I'd been feeling quite old myself, what with menopause being such an intrusive part of my life and all. Toni was making me feel like a kid in comparison. "So you think Rico was involved with a lot of the wrong kind of people? That he asked to get murdered?"

"Not a lot of the wrong kind of people. He probably messed with one wrong someone. I know if my Fred had seen the way Rico was always hugging me and staring at my chest, he wouldn't have put up with it for a second."

Toni was voluptuously built, and for a woman almost ten years my senior, she looked very good. I hoped I could be so sharp and healthy looking a few years from now.

I returned to our conversation. "Maybe it's a cultural thing. I mean, Rico wasn't from around here."

"That's how you get to stereotyping people, Daisy. Best not go there. Let's leave the police work to the police. Now, will you take Sandra off my hands?"

"Shouldn't be a problem."

We said our goodbyes and hung up.

My heart sank. Sandra. How could I

handle being with someone who scared me at the same time she seemed so needy? At least I'd get to know my group leader somewhat better, and maybe she wouldn't be as difficult as I expected. I remembered all the crying from last night and my heart nose-dived again. Would she still be weeping and annoyingly dramatic? I would simply have to be strong and look at the bright side of things — if there was a bright side.

I turned to Georgette. The book on top of Errol's tank had mysteriously fallen off. "No, no, Georgie! Mustn't pull Errol from the tank. He doesn't like to play cat-and-mouse with you. Now be good. I have to go to the bathroom."

CHAPTER 7

I blew out my breath in frustration as Sandra Martin stepped out of my car and closed the door behind her. What is it they say? No good deed goes unpunished?

I'd called Sandra after talking with Toni. Yes, she said, I could help. She needed a quick lift to fetch her car at the library. Toni's kindness in giving her a ride home last night had left her with a bunch of errands and no way to complete them.

"Though, to be honest, Daisy, that Toni isn't a very good driver. She didn't listen to me at all when I gave her perfectly good directions. Then she even kept telling me to hush when I started crying. Oh, Rico! What a shock!" Sandra didn't exactly burst into tears again, but the quiver in her voice gave me warning to change subjects.

So, over an hour and several stops later, here I was, not at the library to retrieve Sandra's car, but at yet another "one last stop." If I'd been in Toni's shoes last night, Sandra might have heard more than "hush" from me. As for Toni, I was happily thinking of ways to get revenge on her when Sandra broke into my thoughts again.

"You coming?" She leaned back into my passenger side window to check on me. Her black outfit was definitely not her best color. Worse, she wasn't wearing any makeup. No denying this woman was in grief.

I smiled weakly.

Why didn't I just say no? Why didn't I say, you've about driven me nuts with your "did you see that stop sign?" and "you *must* have a tissue and trash container in your car," and "ooh, watch out, you almost hit that bicyclist." I wouldn't go another inch with you, Sandra, much less into that cavernous structure you call a church.

Instead, I managed a weak, "I'll be right along."

I loosened clenched fingers from around my steering wheel and followed General Sandra into her "last quick stop."

Most Holy Saints was built with the modern Catholic in mind. Lots of light walls and bright-colored signs. Other Catholic friends said that the actual messages were still the same guilt-ridden stuff they'd grown up with, although I saw lots of smiling faces and joy of giving sentiments that I'd seen in my own church often enough when Art and I used to go.

Sandra seemed quite at home as she marched past the sanctuary and into the business office. None of that "I don't know how to make it through the day" rubbish she'd been showing me all morning.

"Hello, Diane," she said to a secretary at the front desk.

A woman I'd guess was in her mid-forties looked up from a pile of work. Was that a grimace she covered with her quick smile?

The place had the air of a school office. Cluttered efficiency draped from overfull file cabinets and across flyer-topped counters right down to the requisite pothos plant trying to start its own jungle on one of the desks. Oh, and, of course, a cross hung on the wall.

Sandra tapped her foot. "I need to speak with Father Wright. Is he in this morning?"

"He is, but he's with someone." The secretary put on a grave expression. "Sandra, did you hear?"

"That Father Rico is dead?" My companion's bottom lip quivered, but the rest of her stood starched and tidy. "Yes, I heard. Who's helping with the funeral arrangements? Is the bishop going to give the homily? We really should start ordering flowers as quickly as possible."

Diane's face seemed to pinch a tad. "Everything's under control. We do have *some* experience with funerals here." There was a dryness to her reply that made me smile. I wondered if she'd ever been victim to any of Sandra's quick-stop adventures.

A new voice made us turn. "Sandra?" The voice was accompanied by a middle-aged woman whose gray outfit did nothing to reduce the years showing in her face. "Did you hear?" The woman sniffed.

"Yes, Agnes." Sandra allowed an accompanying sniffle. The two women hugged and whispered some sort of peace wish on each other.

A young woman with shoulder-length, dark hair entered the office. "So, we have an official mourning committee started?" She spoke with a soft Spanish accent and winked at Diane before continuing toward the office coffee machine.

I coughed to cover a chuckle and Diane shook her head, but smiled.

"Hello, Carla," said Sandra. The temperature in the room seemed to drop considerably. "So you know too."

"Who doesn't? The police came yesterday afternoon. There were hundreds here last

64

night for an impromptu Mass in Rico's honor. I must say I was surprised you weren't around to lead the choir."

"Father Rico," said Sandra with unnecessary emphasis on the *father* title.

Carla rolled her eyes. "Whatever," she said in an excellent California-girl imitation.

Agnes stepped nervously into the breach. "Come back to my office," she whispered to Sandra. "We can have a good chat there, dear, and perhaps some tea."

"All right. I have that financial report for the stewardship committee, too." Sandra started off with Agnes and then seemed to remember my presence. Turning my way, she said, "You can wait here. I won't be too long."

Diane's eyebrows shot up as she stared at the women's retreating figures. Then she gave me a feigned shocked look. Guess she sensed my annoyance at being dismissed so cavalierly.

I shrugged and rubbed my temple.

"Would you like a cup of coffee?" said Diane. "I'll apologize for them. We're a bit out of order this morning." To Carla she threw in, "God'll getcha for that one. Impromptu. Without Sandra. Hundreds there. You're a wicked thing."

Carla smiled like the Cheshire Cat.

"Yes, I see," I said. "I mean, no thanks on the coffee, but I was aware of your situation here."

"Oh? Sandra told you?" Diane looked as if Sandra sharing such news with me, the mere chauffeur and tag-along, was monumental.

"We heard it from the police during our writing group last night."

Carla had been on her way to an office marked *Youth Director* but turned at my comment. "Writing group? What writing group?"

Was I telling secrets? Surely not. "Sandra and I are in a writers' critique group together. Somehow the police figured that we were the last to see Rico alive."

"Now this sounds very interesting." Carla grabbed my arm. "You must come into my office and tell me all about it. I'm Carla, by the way."

"Daisy. Daisy Arthur. I can't really stay long."

"With Sandra in Agnes' office?" Carla laughed. "You must not know our oh-so-dear friend very well then. Did you know that one time she kept a monsignor waiting for over an hour only because — oh, but I shouldn't carry on so. I've been told I tell a few too many stories."

I felt my heart sink. So much for getting anything done today. I began a mental shopping list of items I needed to do, and ways I would be inconvenienced by Sandra's rudeness.

Suddenly I remembered Thunder and hoped he was okay at Chip's house. Though, if he made a mess, I hadn't *really* agreed to take care of the cur. In fact, my unwanted obligation with Thunder encouraged patience here. I allowed the young woman to drag me off to her workspace.

Carla's office emanated peace, decked out in figurines of saints and crosses. She had a small bookshelf filled with religious tomes and her walls were adorned with posters of happy children. A long, ornate walking stick rested in the corner like a shepherd's staff.

"How beautiful," I said, indicating the wooden stick.

Carla smiled. "Thank you. When I read about Moses and his staff, I think he must have had just such a one. It is my good friend."

"And Jesus, too. He was a shepherd, right?"

"Quite right." She gazed toward a painting of a man in Biblical clothing, a shepherd standing by a body of water, his staff in hand, his lone sheep enjoying a drink.

What a serene place.

Carla gave me a conspiratorial look. "Now, Ms. Daisy. Do tell about this writing group of yours."

"I'm not sure there's anything to tell. Sandra, Father Rico, and I are in a group of creative writers, working on romance novels." I wanted to change the subject. Who was I to talk about my writing colleagues?

"Yes? I wonder how a priest would write romance?" Carla seemed to look beyond the room we shared. "What experience might he draw from? Have you ever asked yourself this?"

"I only found out recently about Father Rico's job here. The romance writing is all about fiction, so I think maybe, for him, it's merely a hobby," I offered lamely. This subject was not in my comfort zone. "Carla, I'm as surprised about Father Rico being a priest as you are about him being a writer. Let's not dwell on it." I looked around again. "You've done a super job of making this space look homey. I used to be a special education teacher but was never able to keep the clutter under control. How do you do it?"

"Thank you," said Carla. "I try." She graciously let me lead the conversation to safer waters. She looked around her office, her gaze resting for an extended moment on a picture of a little boy. There was something familiar about his intense eyes staring out at us.

"Your son?" I asked.

"Yes."

"He's very handsome." The boy's smile was even and bright. Quite charismatic. Somehow familiar.

Carla's smile dropped. *"Mi Tobias."* She sighed. "He's dead."

"Oh!" A stabbing pain pierced my chest. I felt horrible for that young mother and half reached for her instinctively. "I'm so sorry."

"Thank you." Carla picked up the photo and gently fingered its frame.

I stepped closer to look at the boy more carefully. "I lost a child once too. Wouldn't wish that on my worst enemy. You have my heart."

Carla smiled at me through watery eyes. "It was God's will, I suppose. At least that was what Rico said before he suggested I needed more prayer time."

I sighed. "Parents shouldn't have to outlive their children. I hope he didn't have to suffer long." Memories of brave young cancer patients pushed themselves into my consciousness. I'd met them when my own

Rose was taken to the hospital with meningitis.

"No, he didn't suffer. It was an accident. He fell off a cliff two years ago, while on a camping trip. He was only eight."

"My daughter died in an influenza epidemic more than twenty years ago. She was three. It's been a long time, but I still miss her." For surviving mothers, I think pain is always close.

Carla came around her desk and we hugged, wrapped in a mourning that never ends. In my mind's eye, I saw my own Rose smiling at me and felt comfort in an indulgence of grief I didn't often allow any more.

I stood back. "It makes days like this, with Rico, er, Father —"

"You may call him Rico to me," said Carla, steeliness replacing her grief. "I know he was engaged in the secular world. I even wonder, sometimes, how such a man became a priest."

"Is that so? I didn't know him very well. I was only familiar with him for four or five weeks."

"Familiar?" Carla's tone of voice sounded accusatory. Did she think I behaved inappropriately with the priest? Did she think I took Rico's flirting too far?

"Oh! I would never!" Yes, Rico was handsome, but I don't think I would've put up with such a young man's amorous attentions. Who would fall for that? Why would Rico engage in such inappropriate behavior?

"My apologies, *Senora* Daisy," said Carla. "I knew Rico quite well. I thought you might have been one of his *special* friends?"

"Special friends?" I dropped my voice to a whisper. "You mean Rico had a lover?"

Carla shook her head sadly. "I know I shouldn't gossip, but so it is rumored. Rico's attachment to worldly activities was an illness for him. Forgive my assumption."

"But did Rico have a lover? This is important." Gabe would want to hear about it if what Carla hinted at was true. Maybe the right suspect wasn't within our writing group after all.

"Well, I shouldn't say, but I believe he consorted with several people." She nodded her head at my shocked face. "I understand he had a particular male friend . . . someone who's name is Thomas, or Timothy, or . . . ?"

Was she looking for information from me? How would I know? Wait. Did she mean Todd?

There came a knock on Carla's door. We turned to see a priest standing in the entry. Blood rushed up my neck to my cheeks.

Luckily for my middle age and ensuing hot flashes, there was a logical, if incorrect, conclusion to be made.

"I'm sorry to interrupt," said the priest. He turned as if to leave, but Carla stepped toward him.

"It's all right, Father John," she said hugging him. "Come in. Such a sad day." Carla didn't look sad at all.

Father John's face was a nice balance of gentle smile and serious grief. "All part of God's plan, I'm afraid. But I don't think we've met," he said, turning to me. "Are you here to grieve with us?"

"This is a friend of Sandra Martin's, Father," said Carla. Did she emphasize Sandra's name on purpose?

The priest's face remained warm, but I sensed hesitancy in his handshake.

Father John Wright was an average-looking man, except for a set of keen eyes that seemed to look into my soul. Quite different from Rico's more predatory gaze. The elder priest had thinning white hair and the hint of a stoop, as if he'd spent too much time bending low to give a discreet ear to even the smallest of his parishioners. I thought he must have been quite good-looking in his youth. Even now, there was a pleasant humbleness to his demeanor.

"It's nice to meet you, my dear," he said.

The man generated warmth even with his penetrating gaze. I felt somehow cleaner for being around him, though disappointed that he seemed not to trust me back.

Carla looked as if a new thought had only now struck her. "Father, I was entertaining Daisy until Sandra becomes free, but I do need to get some items put into the youth center."

"Say no more, Carla. Daisy, may I show you around our little parish?"

CHAPTER 8

I watched Father John as we walked in the garden. His garden. The priest stopped several times to pluck a weed or gaze at a flower, some memory bringing the wisp of a smile to his lips. I could envision him with trowel in hand, finding peace in working the soil, pulled weeds stacked like unwanted thoughts next to him as he meditated on his next homily.

Delicate and profuse red Cosmos bloomed in a circle around a statue of Saint Mary, and a cement bench was guarded by yellow straw flowers. We stopped to sit there. Beyond Father John and me, the place was bereft of people, yet it was not lonely. I felt honored to share this very private, public place with him.

When we had toured the classrooms, offices, fellowship hall, and even sanctuary, there was an air of bustling. I hadn't felt as though I ought to be quiet, as I did during services at my own church, but this casualness was awkward for me. I always thought of church grounds as a place of reverence.

Several times people interrupted us to share condolences about Father Rico, but mostly they seemed more intrigued with the news than being particularly saddened by the loss. It was as though Father Rico was very well known, but not particularly popular. What did I sense? Relief? This made Sandra's reaction seem that much more unusual.

Father John gave calming and appropriate answers to everyone, phrases that lacked any passion or true feeling. I guess, as a priest, he was used to dealing with death. That final passage shocks most of us, but priests live with it all the time as they tend their flocks.

Here, in the garden, Father John sank into a thoughtful silence. His shoulders drooped a bit lower, as if the weight of the world, or at least of his parish, were upon him.

"Father." I whispered the word, concerned not to break into his private world.

He looked at me as if startled he had a companion. "Oh, my dear. You must think me a terrible host."

"Not at all, Father. You've had quite a full morning. Perhaps you'd like some alone time?"

At that, the kind priest smiled. I felt like all the world glowed in its warmth.

"Daisy. How kind to think of my feelings. You are like the stranger at one's door." He patted my shoulder when I didn't catch his meaning. "From the book of Hebrews. *Be not forgetful to entertain strangers: for thereby some have entertained angels unawares.*"

"Me? Angel?" I laughed. Pictures of my Rose, Colby Stanton, and Father Rico popped into my head. "I'm sure no angel, father."

"Aren't you?" He looked at me thoughtfully, then stood, turned, and seemed to talk to a branch of his ornamental Maple. "What is your definition of an angel?"

"It's a messenger from God."

"Yes, but what does that mean to you?" He turned back to look at me directly. I felt like the kid who'd studied her homework but missed the point of the lesson. Angel. What is an angel? Memories of movies and television shows all showed people with wings and glowing auras around them.

As nothing came from me, Father John carried on. "Sometimes, when I need God's help most, I'm blessed with a gift that holds precisely the message I don't even know I yearn for. Sometimes a friend will give me a book or a news clipping. Sometimes our

76

music director selects a particularly poi-
gnant song. Sometimes I meet someone
briefly. These last encounters with God's
messengers are what I call angel moments,
and the people I meet, whether they remain
acquaintances afterward or disappear from
my life, are true angels, if only for a brief
time."

"You mean people are angels?"

"Who better to bring God's messages to
us?"

I thought about that a moment. "Was Rico
an angel?"

Father John blew a breath. "Definitely not
— or if he was, he was the wrong kind of
angel amongst us."

"What do you mean, Father?"

"Satan has angels too. I don't want to
jump to any conclusions, but I believe the
secular proclivities of my colleague were
possibly not good in nature at all."

"So it is wrong to be secular?"

"For most people, no. Most people find a
healthy balance between those things we do
as imperfect humans and a higher calling to
the Lord."

"But Rico didn't?"

"That man and his affairs! Now, even in
death, he plays with scandal." Father John's
nostrils flared as if he'd recently smelled

vinegar, but he quickly remembered himself and sighed again. "Rico was a good man, Daisy. But I fear his earthly needs tended to obstruct his higher calling."

"Earthly needs?"

Father John shook his head. "I've spoken too much already. Let's just say that you are more sweetly angelic than Rico. You have given me the message I needed to hear today."

"But I didn't hear any special message to give to you. I'm no angel."

"Daisy, you show a reverence in church that many in our parish seem to have lost. Your behavior on our grounds was the message I needed to receive. Words are easy, but it's how we act that, to me, God is most concerned with."

"So, you're saying people can be temporary angels, and not even know it?"

"It's not a common thought, but it has worked for my life. I even keep a log of angel moments, for comfort in difficult times."

"Wow. I want to think about that. People. Temporary angels. No glowing. No wings."

Father John laughed. The sound rumbled and broke on my ears with a joy that connected directly to my heart.

"Daisy," Father John said, almost to

himself. "Not only fresh, but —"

Sandra marched up to us as if I had somehow run away from where I was supposed to be. "There you are!" Her heels stomped and scrunched as they trampled on dried leaves and the last blades of green grass. "Daisy, I need to get to my gardening club meeting and now we're running late." She paused to glare at me, then remembered we weren't alone. "Oh. Hello, Father John."

"Sandra." His good priest mask slipped over his face almost imperceptibly.

"My condolences on" — her red-rimmed eyes glazed with fresh tears — "on the death of Father Rico."

"Thank you, my dear." They hugged with no warmth, said their peace-be-with-yous, and we all parted ways.

As Sandra and I left, I wondered more about that angel idea. What kind of angel might Rico have been? Why did Father John hint that he could have been inspired by a negative insight? Was, perhaps, Rico a bad angel?

If only I'd known him longer. I might have some answers.

CHAPTER 9

Sandra checked her watch. I bit my tongue. After more than an hour of her "just a few minutes" at church and with her friend, we were finally in my car headed to the library.

"Will you look at the time!" She tapped her foot on the floorboards. "Well, I didn't mean to be so long, Daisy, but I feel much better." Indeed, something about Sandra seemed more confident, like her old in-charge persona I'd seen in the first weeks of our writers' meetings. She sat tall and stiff, her dark clothes had found a colored scarf, and I think she may have put on some makeup. She even smelled like a mixture of breath wash and something more pungent. I looked hard at her and she tapped her toe again.

I tried unsuccessfully to keep the sarcasm from my voice. "Glad to hear it."

"Diane told me you got stuck with that Carla. What a blabbermouth. Hope she didn't chatter your ear off. Do watch out for that squirrel up ahead."

The squirrel was at least a hundred yards up the road, and Carla hadn't seemed like a blabbermouth to me. "I found her quite educational."

"Carla? Well, don't count on her *facts* too much. You know gossips can't be trusted with them. She's such an odd creature, always on hikes and walks with the church youth group. Now, keep an eye out for the police hiding around that next drive. They can be such pesky things. Once you're past them, we can speed it up. Remember, I have that luncheon with my gardening club."

"You have —" If I'd said more, I would've regretted it. Change subject, Daisy. "I didn't spend the whole time with Carla. Father Wright was kind enough to show me around the church."

"He's all right, for an older priest. I only wish Father Rico could've been there. Now there's a man who could have given you a tour."

"Don't talk to me about Father Rico. From what I heard today, I'm not sure you would've wanted him in our writing group if you had known."

"Known what? Oh, you mean the rumor that he was gay. I'm surprised at you. Even if Father Rico was gay, which I can assure you he wasn't, there's nothing wrong with that. Now, if you turn right on Jay Street, I know a shortcut to the library."

"But I thought priests didn't have any lovers, gay or straight." A memory flashed into mind. Rico was constantly throwing his arm around people. Toni, Sandra, Todd, even me. I hadn't seen it as an overture, but after talking with Carla and Father John, Rico's actions seemed more questionable. Could Rico have been asking for trouble, or did trouble come seeking an easy target like him?

"Priests are men before they are priests. The church doesn't sanction affairs, but you'd have to be a total innocent to think that all people completely abstain once becoming priests. I couldn't see Rico doing that. But still, Carla talks too much." Sandra crossed her arms as if I were the youth director and needed a lesson in discretion.

I thought perhaps it was Sandra who talked too much. At least her visit with her church friend, Agnes, left my group leader strong enough to discuss Rico without bursting into tears.

The memory of his handsome face floated above the road in front of me. His arm reached out to me. Then Rico's brown eyes, chiseled jaw, and thick head of chestnut-colored hair metamorphosed into gooey flesh falling from its skull.

I swerved at the thought. "Sorry. Pothole," I lied. "You have to admit, Sandra, this gay thing puts a different twist on Todd's outburst the last time we saw the two of them together."

"Todd! That wart! I'll bet he did it — killed Rico, I mean. You know, I always thought he wished Rico was gay. Now I'm more certain and hope he rots in hell for his sins."

"Hold on, Sandra. Todd's a member of our writing group too. I don't think you want to bash his reputation."

"Oh, yes, I do." She said his name on a snarl. "Todd. Don't you think it's pathetic, his being oh-so-in-love with our Rico? Why else be a part of our group? He's certainly not a talented writer. Rico probably rejected the disgusting gnat, and Todd couldn't handle it. Now Rico is dead and that queer wanders about with nothing greater on his mind than finding another potential mate. Horrid, horrid little man!"

I decided to put a lock on my mouth. Used to do that a lot with parents in denial about their children. Sandra seemed in denial about Rico, and I wouldn't be the one to change her mind. Why was she so certain about his love life? "Are we going to hold writing group on Tuesday?" I tried changing the subject again.

"Why wouldn't we?"

"With Rico . . . the investigation . . . suspects . . ."

"Nonsense. We should honor a great man who was taken from us too soon. Tuesday could be an opportunity to pray together and begin the process for his becoming a saint."

Saint Rico? I couldn't picture it, nor could I see some of our group members going for the public praying thing. Not comfortable with the direction of Sandra's and my discussion, I was glad we neared the parking lot of the library.

Sandra snapped her fingers. "Oh, darn! I forgot to stop for a herbicide on the way. Daisy, would you mind?"

"No!" I hoped the shout in my answer wasn't too obvious. But I wouldn't go a minute more than I had to with Sandra. "I mean, sorry, Sandra. I have an appointment myself." An appointment with my writing. My heroine, Gwendolyn, needed to fall in love. "Besides, here's your car."

"Oh. I didn't realize you had plans. You should tell me these things, so we can allow

for them in the future. Give us a hug, then."
Sandra leaned over. "Peace be with you."
She gave me some sort of gesture that
might've been a hug. No real chance to
wrinkle her black blouse, though.

"Okay, thanks," I fumbled. "Hope you feel
better soon."

I blew out some pent-up tension as Sandra
got in her car and drove off. My head was
filled with more stuff than I could sort
through. I turned off my ignition and
grabbed my writing bag from the back of
my car. No need to fixate on those things
now, even if I was Gabe's snitch. Creative
writing, here I come.

CHAPTER 10

I walked into the library foyer and felt rather ill. Twenty-four hours ago, this was merely my local library. Today, even though the tile was still beige, the walls still brick, and the atmosphere consistently nondescript, the library had changed.

As I walked through the lobby, ghostly memories jumped for a ride on my shoulders. I could see everyone so clearly. Todd, anxious to leave after Sergeant Taylor's interview, didn't even acknowledge the rest of us, but ran from the building. Sandra was too upset to do much of anything but give everyone else headaches. Kitty's subdued state was one for the calendar. Toni, the rock.

Now I needed to come to terms with the idea that one of those good people might have killed another person from our group. I felt a chill creep down my spine. Would one of my new colleagues really do such a

86

thing? Today, they were all back to their regular lives. Would I see them next Tuesday as usual, or would the group fall apart after the murder?

I grabbed a table in the back, a quiet spot where I thought I could work. The bookshelves provided a cave of safety for my restless spirit, a place where I could see out but remain unnoticed by most. All around, people went about their business, unaware that a patron had recently died. The librarians were chirping together more than I normally saw, but that might have been my imagination. Someone should care that Rico died and we found out about it in this very library, yet everything remained depressingly normal.

Why is it that the world keeps moving when someone dies? It should stop and take note. I kept quiet, but I wanted to shout out that the world had changed. Rico Sanchez, well-known Catholic priest, library patron, and aspiring romance writer, had died. Where was the mourning for the man?

I turned to my notebook. Gwendolyn. Perhaps if I wrote a short profile of my heroine, I'd feel better. Let's see. Ash — no, golden blond hair, cornflower blue eyes. What the heck is *cornflower blue*? I'd read that in a Georgette Heyer novel once and loved the description but had no idea what it meant. Maybe Gwendolyn should have Bronco-blue eyes, dark as midnight, but rich and warm as . . . as Rico's eyes were rich and warm.

Rico's eyes were brown but held such passion they compelled me to stare into them. *Father Rico,* Daisy. Rico's dead. Need to accept that.

I sighed and stood to wander around the library. I love scouting the shelves. Something about the solidness of books enveloping my sphere helps me relax. The worries of the world go away with the scent of pressed and printed papers, the intrigue of new titles, and the muffled atmosphere they create. Their words are as fresh and vigorous as when they were first published, and they wait patiently for any who choose a life of adventure and knowledge. Books are such good friends.

I wandered an aisle I hadn't been down much before and started fingering the spines. My whole body started to relax. Great! I took a deep, satisfying breath and began reading titles at random:

Bloodroot, by Susan Wittig Albert
The Potted Gardener, by M.C. Beaton

Throw Darts at a Cheesecake, by Denise
  Dietz
Foul Play, by Janet Evanovich
A Calculated Demise, by Robert Spiller.

My goodness! I was trying to write about romance and had been looking for inspiration in the murder mystery section. Brilliant. That's exactly what I was living through, a murder mystery. Could I possibly solve our murder? No, I was no amateur sleuth.

I went back to my table. Someone had left a book there. Another mystery.

Sometimes a friend will give me a book or a news clipping.

Could it be? Could I be having an angel moment? No way. I pushed the book aside and sat down.

I stared at my notebook, willing amorous thoughts to jump from my hopes to my paper. Nothing happened. Maybe I could kick-start my writing with a list. A nice, happy list of perhaps grocery shopping, or home tasks, or . . . murder suspects.

I gave in to the thing uppermost on my mind and wrote across the top of my page *Who Killed Father Rico Sanchez?* That should give the angels something to toy over.

I drew a line down the center of the page and titled column one *Hugs 'N' Kisses People* and column two, *Notes*. Column one was easy to fill in, except when it came to adding my name. As part of the writing group, I had to be on the Littleton Police suspect list. That gave me pause. Could Gabe really believe I'd kill someone? Had last night's chat been less friendly and more investigative than I'd thought?

If some people can be angels without knowing it, maybe some people are subconsciously, well, deviled eggs.

Murder starts out as an accident.

Where had I heard that before? I pushed the thought aside and wrote down everyone's name: Sandra, Toni, Kitty, Todd, Daisy, and Eleanor. Was Eleanor a suspect when she hadn't even been to our group in the past two weeks? I jotted down a note to call her, in case Sandra was still too upset over Rico's death to keep up with Eleanor. Then I added to my list after Sandra's name, "Why was she so upset over the news?"

I spent the next twenty minutes jotting notes about my friends. Sandra is controlling and forceful. She intimidates me easily. What made her crumble and cry so over the news?

Kitty, smart and close to hyperactive, didn't seem to like Rico. Need to ask her about that. I couldn't see how she would be strong enough to drown someone much larger than she, given her petite frame. Even Toni had noticed that.

Toni. She didn't seem to care for Rico and was in good physical condition. She also didn't like his religion. What had she said? *They throw on their collars and expect that the world will revere and protect them.* Interesting. Toni had sounded more bitter than I would have expected and seemed more upset over having to deal with Sandra than having to accept that Rico Sanchez had been murdered.

And now that I thought of it, why were the police focusing solely on our writing group? The people at the church hadn't seemed particularly upset either. Only Sandra and that Agnes woman were crying. Everyone else made appropriate motions, but without feelings to match. As Gabe's official snitch, I should ask him about that.

Maybe I could wheedle a bit more out of him about that note at the murder scene as well. My eyebrows started wiggling up and down involuntarily. This amateur sleuth thing had pretty cool possibilities. Problem was, I had a lot of questions, but no answers.

CHAPTER 11

After unsuccessfully trying to get some writing done at the library, I drove home, cranky and tired. What a wasted half day. A tasty tuna sandwich would be just the thing. I parked my car in the drive and headed to my mailbox. There, amongst my usual ads, catalogs, and bills, was a chewed-up leather string with a loop on one end and a large clasp on the other. Thunder!

I glanced up the neighboring driveway. Running back and forth along his chain-link fence was my charge. He barked and I shivered. Puppy, my eye. The black-and-tan German shepherd looked colossal to me. Slowly, I crept up the drive. His bark became more agitated. What was I supposed to do? What if he was a biter? The dog barked viciously as I approached the fence. I jumped.

The brute appeared seriously somber from head to tail. I gazed at him, looking for some sign of friendliness. He had no hanging jaw other dogs exhibit to smile. No cute little pink tongue. Instead, a big silver "pinch collar" hung around his neck. Not very warm or puppy-like. *Ferocious* was the word that came to my mind.

I glanced around Chip's yard. His puppy had already worn a deep path across the front near the fence, and evidence of chewed-up bones, dog toys, and even bits of lawn furniture were strewn helter-skelter around an otherwise tidy grass yard. I returned my attention to my charge.

Thunder stared at me, and I stared back. Suddenly, Thunder barked again. I wasn't sure I could do the dog walk Chip had asked for. Thunder's voice matched his name. Pit bulls would have had second thoughts about bothering my charge's house and yard.

I grabbed up all my courage and slowly opened the gate separating us. It squeaked, and I winced as the beast met me in my personal space. It hit me that this dog, this big dog, didn't really know me at all, and I was invading his yard. I stood still, a rabbit in the sights of a wolf.

He stared at me. Standoff. Suddenly, for no apparent reason, Thunder jumped up on me.

Seventy pounds of "puppy" were in my face. I screamed and fell back. I hadn't properly latched the gate, so when I fell, it swung open under my weight. Up flew the leash, down went my butt, and the puppy got tangled somehow around me. We rolled on the ground, and struggled to disengage ourselves. Big, white dogteeth were in my vision the whole time. I'm sure he saw a lot of my molars too, as I couldn't stop yelling.

Finally, I managed to sit up. This ridiculous situation reminded me of my first day of student teaching. The kids nearly ate me alive. And now here I was being defeated by one, albeit massive, puppy.

"Bad dog. Down!" I growled. To my surprise, Thunder licked my face, then dropped to a sphinx position. He let me hook up his leather leash before trying to make the tether his lunch. I reached for the now slobbery thing, only to see Thunder snatch it up in his large jaws and jump away.

"Good doggie," I said, feeling much the opposite. "Give me your leash now."

Thunder glanced through the open gate, then back at me, the tether hanging from his black muzzle.

"Don't you even think —" I struggled to my feet.

Too late. Although I made a grab for the

beast, he flew past me and down the street. For the first time, the dog looked truly happy.

I had to laugh. "You monster!" I called to my truant. I brushed dead grass from my skirt and prepared to go after him when a voice behind made me jump.

"That your dog?" Gabe Caerphilly had parked in front of my house and walked toward me. He strode with the natural grace of an athlete, a sardonic grin playing at his mouth.

"Go ahead and laugh. I'm trying to help a neighbor by taking his puppy for a walk."

Gabe chuckled. "Looks more like he's taking you for one. Just starting out or coming back?"

"Both." I shook my head. "I don't think I can do this."

Gabe crossed his arms. "What's his name?"

"Thunder, and it suits him. I'm going to catch that mutt and lock him back up."

"German shepherds need to have long walks or they get bored and tear everything apart." Gabe pulled a police whistle from his pocket and blew. A deafening sound exploded and my hands flew to my ears, but Thunder stopped his flight and looked back at us. "Here! Now!" Gabe growled.

The dog came running back and did a perfect sit right in front of Gabe. My jaw went slack.

"How old is he?" Gabe was leaning over by this time, making circular motions on Thunder's head.

The silly dog was responding as if petting had only been invented today. His eyes half-closed, solidly in a sit position, Thunder made guttural, happy sounds. If he could talk, I think the word he'd choose would be *heaven*.

"He's eight or nine months now," I said. "Imagine what he'll be full grown." I shivered.

Gabe chuckled. "So, you're an experienced dog-sitter?" His voice was as deep as Thunder's and fifty times more pleasant. I gazed into Gabe's smiling face and felt at home.

"I have tons of experience sitting. Just not dog-sitting."

Gabe leaned down and gathered Thunder's soggy leash as if it were not the most disgusting thing he had ever had to touch. "We'll finish the walk together. You need to stay on my right. The dog goes on the left."

"What? The dog goes somewhere other than all over the place?"

Gabe gave a quick jerk on the leash, said

"Heel," and started walking. Thunder fell into step immediately. What magic potion had Gabe used to get such cooperation? I fell into step on Gabe's other side. Novel idea, this discipline.

"So, Gabe, what brings you to my neighborhood?"

"Officially? To do a follow-up interview with you. Unofficially, to let you know what Ginny said when I told her I'd seen you."

"Oh?" I missed Ginny a lot.

"She said, 'Bout time, Dad. My Daisy makes good cheeser sand-itches. Will you tell her to come an' make me some?' "

We laughed. Ginny could sure get right to the heart of the matter. You make good sandwiches, she loves you. You talk too much or push too hard, she shuts down. Simple. Straight. Honest. I liked that.

"I'd like to bring Ginny a sandwich or two." It was a broad hint, but sometimes you have to help fate for good things to happen.

"Maybe. Sometime," said Gabe. I sensed he was not excited about the thought.

"But there's a problem?" Pride be damned. I was a shameless, pushy old woman who wanted back in Gabe and Ginny Caerphilly's lives.

"The investigation. Might be awkward.

97

You know."

"You mean I'm a suspect? That's kind of thrilling." I couldn't pass up an invitation to be a real person of interest.

"Not a suspect. Witness." Gabe looked down at me and the world seemed to still. His periwinkle-sky colored eyes captured my attention as much as the stillness of his voice.

"It wouldn't be too smart to get involved right now." Was Gabe talking to me or himself?

I nodded but couldn't look away. Gabriel Caerphilly's gaze was mesmerizing.

Suddenly his head jerked away. "Damn! Heel!"

Thunder had decided to run after a squirrel, apparently forgetting he had a policeman attached. Gabe's arm jerked forward, pulling the rest of him along. He tripped and fell. The dog yelped at the pinch from his collar and taut leash. The squirrel ran up a tree. It was good to know that Thunder could be an equal opportunity offender.

"Go ahead, laugh." Gabe glared at me.

"You took your mind off him," I replied. "That's the quickest way to get in trouble." I reached a hand down to help, and he almost pulled me down with him. Gabe was a big guy.

We laughed and chatted our way around two more blocks. In the time since we had last seen a lot of each other, Gabe had been promoted from sergeant to lieutenant, taken up cooking as a hobby, and had become even more protective of his precious daughter.

"I worry so much about some creep taking advantage of my Ginny-Bear," he said.

"That's not likely, Gabe. Ginny has always had good instincts about people. You need to trust her. She'll be okay."

He shook his head. "I know so many bad guys."

"Isn't that part of the work you do?"

"I suppose. Ginny is all I have, Daisy. If anyone hurt her, I don't know what I'd do."

"You'd help her pick up the pieces and move on. You two make a great family. Ginny knows she can count on you." I laid my hand on his arm and he squeezed it with his free hand.

Gabe seemed to give himself a mental shake, then returned to safer topics of discussion. He asked more questions about my writing group, and I told him about the various members. I didn't know any of them well, being so new to the group, but I tried to be open and fair in sketching their personalities. I was a bit harsh about Sandra. Thinking about the morning I'd spent with her still made me prickle.

"I don't know why I think this, Gabe, and I'm not sure why I'm even mentioning it, but every nerve in my body says Sandra is hiding something."

"Go on." He stopped. Then Thunder stopped, and they both turned full attention on me.

"That's just it. There's nothing specific to go on. Right now, it's only a feeling. Her constant edginess, her need to control, and then her falling apart last night. It doesn't add up. Also, only she and one friend at the church seemed to be genuinely upset about Rico's death. Everyone else went through the motions and words, but didn't really seem to care."

Gabe started walking again. "Thanks, Daisy. I'll check into it."

"Gabe, it's so nebulous right now. I'd hate to have you waste your time on my gut feelings."

He looked over and patted me on the back. "We're talking murder here. No investigation is a waste. Now, what do you think about Todd Stevens?"

"Todd? He's a really nice man. He's a graphic artist by day, and writes in his spare time."

"Is he honest? Do you trust him?"

"Yes. No doubt about it." I pictured Todd. "He would be the kind of son any mother would want. Open, friendly, happy-go-lucky in life."

"What makes you so emphatic?" Gabe was looking ahead, but I sensed he was listening very carefully.

I thought about it. How could I phrase my feelings clearly? "You probably know he's gay. That alone takes courage to admit. Colorado is still fairly conservative."

Gabe seemed to relax. "Okay, so he's open about his lifestyle —"

"And his life. He told the group about how frequently he was beaten up as a kid for being different. Goodness, Gabe. It was awful."

"And?"

"And he writes stories and tells us up-front that many women in them are really men he's known."

Gabe raised his eyebrows. "So his stories are autobiographical?"

"No. It's a writer's tool. Take two or three people you know, put them into a totally different body, and you have an interesting character. Todd uses it a lot and teases us when we try to guess if he's written about anyone from our group. He's lots of fun."

"Do you think he was serious when he said he wished Rico were dead?"

"Naw, it's only the kind of thing you say when you're really ticked with somebody. Hmm."

"What is it?"

"Now that I think of it, I don't know why he was so mad at Rico."

"Precisely," said Gabe. "Well, he's at the station being interviewed right now, so I hope Taylor and Hawkins will find that out."

"Taylor and Hawkins?"

"My investigative team. Young, bright, competent."

"Oh, yes. I saw Sergeant Taylor last night." Competent, bright, and a tad too friendly with Gabe for my liking.

Gabe grinned. "She's terrific. But Daisy, I wanted to ask you —"

I didn't want for a second to be talking about Sergeant Taylor. I decided interruptions were a good strategy. "For a cheeser for Ginny? Of course. You put Thunder into his yard right over there and I'll have one ready for her in a snap. My back door's open."

"In fact, I was hoping —"

"For a sandwich too? I'm making myself tuna."

"Tuna would be great, but I wanted to

ask you over for dinner Friday. To heck with discretion. Ginny misses you. I'd like to catch up on the last five years too. Will you come?"

I looked at Gabe. My stomach dropped as I stared into his face. One of my hot flashes chose that moment to attack. I felt the heat rise right up through my neck, my heart pounded, and my knees nearly collapsed under me. I swallowed.

"Daisy, are you okay?" asked Gabe, his face full of concern.

I felt my face tighten with a bigger smile than I'd produced in a long time. "I'm fine. And Friday sounds perfect."

Just then Gabe's cell went off. He looked down. "It's Taylor texting." Whatever he saw in the message inspired a gentle grin to bloom. "Have to go. Rain check on the tuna?"

I swallowed again, hot flash over. "Of course. I understand."

I understood that I was beginning to dislike this Sergeant Taylor. A lot.

CHAPTER 12

"Gwendolyn," said Grant, his periwinkle-blue eyes gazing deeply into her own misty brown orbs, "I cannot think how we will ever win over your parents' objections. But I love you with all of my heart."

Gwendolyn's own heart skipped a beat. "Love finds a way," she said with a sigh.

I stared into my computer screen, willing something clever to appear. Gwendolyn loved Grant, and now the reader knew their feelings were mutual. All should be well, but how the heck was I going to move the story beyond chapter three?

I tried harder to focus on Grant, the hero of my novel. I closed my eyes to picture him, but only Gabe's warm face came to mind. Those smokey blue eyes, the need for someone to show him the softer side of life, that devastatingly delectable smile. I gave myself a mental shake and tried again.

Another face came into focus. Deep-brown eyes looked at me imploringly. "I need justice," said the vision. "I need closure." Then the eyes bulged and the luminescent olive skin that encased them faded to gray and melted. Not exactly a starry-eyed vision for my work. Father Rico, what happened to you?

Memories of Rico danced around my consciousness. I saw him stare intently at whoever was reading their submission. He wore a bright blue vest most weeks. Not particularly attractive, but on him, it worked. He obviously exercised in a gym, but complained of a bad knee. Used to play soccer or something. No hint of a troubled life. If he were still alive, I might cast him in the role of my hero, Grant. But perhaps he was too good to be true. I know the hair at the back of my neck stood on end whenever Rico approached. What was under all that physical attraction? What kind of angel was Rico Sanchez, Catholic priest?

A new face replaced Rico's. I recognized Todd Stevens with his open look and smile that reached from his heart-shaped jaw line to his twinkling blue eyes. He was sitting in jail. "Don't look at me. I'm no help," the vision said. My mind replayed his and Rico's fight. The explosive anger over Rico's work.

The childish, angry exit. Then, last night, how Todd wanted so much to get away from the police questioning. How he didn't make eye contact with anyone when he left the interviews. Kitty's remembrance that Todd had threatened Rico. Could Todd kill someone? His were the actions of an impetuous young man, but not a villain. Yet, Rico was dead.

Apparently, so was my creative writing.

I felt restless. Dishes from my simple lunch called seductively from the kitchen sink. Laundry in the dryer whined silently. It *reeeeeeally* needed folding. Hadn't my car's fuel gauge shown I was low when I drove home? This cacophony of obligations plagued my creative soul. Which to address — my need to write or my house's need for order?

Georgette sauntered into my writing room. She played carelessly with a wadded-up first effort of my next chapter. Cats are so entertaining in their independent ability to enjoy themselves.

I watched my friend drop to the ground and paw at the carpet in anticipation of her kill. Her massive brown-and-gold stomach spread like margarine across the floor. Her tail, a feathery boa flag, waved and signaled to let me know she was on the hunt.

Georgette bolted and pounced before I could blink. The poor wad of paper had no chance. Georgette ravaged her prey.

Had Rico enjoyed any more of a chance with his killer?

I heaved a sigh at my computer and got up. No successful writing spurt going on today. My head was lost in the violence and mystery surrounding Rico's death.

On the corner of my desk sat a small booklet: "Welcome to Hugs 'N' Kisses Romance Writing." I picked up the folded and stapled pages.

Inside were a few "uplifting" words of wisdom from Sandra, some manuscript submission guidelines, critique rules, and a couple of writing exercises submitted by various group members.

Tucked at the back was a loose paper containing our member list, which Sandra updated quarterly. I had the latest list. My name wasn't on it, being so new to the group, but Rico was there and so were the others I knew. Sandra had thoughtfully added phone numbers, email, and even physical addresses.

I started to put the list back in place, but stopped. I withdrew it again and found Todd Stevens' information.

Todd might need a good friend after his

interview with the police. He might need to talk to a nonjudgmental listener. As an unofficial representative of the force, perhaps I ought to see if they forgot to ask him some small but significant question. Wasn't that my privilege — er — responsibility? I picked up the phone to call, then rethought the action. A visit would be better. Plus, the drive to his house would give my muse time to drum up a specific excuse for intruding. Every instinct said Todd was no killer, but if the police were zeroing in on him, a personal visit would be best to help prove my instincts right.

"Georgette, be good. I'll be home before long." I picked up my keys and headed to the door. How would I get Todd to talk? Why was I assuming there was more to Todd's story than whatever he would tell the police? Wouldn't it be great to ask the precise question that solved the mystery of Rico's death? I would love to be a hero!

Georgette yawned, exhausted from her recent battle with my manuscript. She leapt as gracefully as her massive girth would allow into my recently vacated seat and curled into a ball as if to say, "Yeah, I'll really miss you." Did she know something I didn't?

CHAPTER 13

The apartment door opened on my second knock. Todd stood behind it, ready to close his metal portal in my face. His eyes were red, and a stubble had grown on his normally smooth chin. He wore a wrinkled button-down shirt, also a step away from his usual neat appearance, and heaved a sigh when he recognized me.

"Oh, it's you. I was expecting — well, never mind."

"Todd, I wanted to see if you were all right. You seemed very upset over the police interviews last night, and Rico's passing. May I come in?"

"Now is not a good time." Todd began to close his door.

"Wait! Todd. I don't mean to be a bother. I wanted to see if I could help at all."

"What makes you think I need help?"

Fair question. Now for an answer that didn't include letting Todd know I knew the police had interviewed him.

"Well . . ." I lingered over the word. "When bad things happen, friends need to stick together."

Todd sighed and walked back into his apartment. The door being ajar, I guessed this was the only invitation I was going to receive. I followed him in.

Todd slumped onto a gray couch in his living area. Around him, scattered on the coffee table, were used tissues.

"I didn't realize you were catching a cold. Didn't mean to intrude."

"Yes, you did. You wouldn't be here otherwise. There's no cold. Just allergies. Police woke me up this morning to take me to their office for an interview." He said *interview* with contemptuous emphasis.

"No! Really?" I hoped the surprise act I practiced was believable. Hurdle one, about unexpected knowledge, was over. This police snitch role could be pretty intriguing.

"Really." Todd reached for another tissue. His wrinkled sleeve and display of refuse posed in stark contrast to his otherwise fastidiously tidy abode. The apartment living area blended with an eating nook and open kitchen, all of which were orderly and bare of clutter.

Todd wiped his face, then stared at me.

110

"Look, Daisy. I know you mean well, but can't this wait?"

"Of course. I only wanted . . . that is . . . Todd, I don't know why the police are focusing on our group. No one among us impresses me as the murdering type, and I don't believe for a second you killed Rico. I'm trying to figure out how to prove it."

"Prove it?" Todd rolled his eyes. "You? Are you a lawyer maybe?"

"No."

"How 'bout a detective or off-duty police officer?"

"No."

"Daisy, you're kind to offer, but I don't think I need your help. Please go home." Todd turned to another tissue and blew his nose.

"It's true I'm not a lawyer, spy, or anything special. But I hope I am a good friend, and friends don't need power resumes to support friends."

Todd smiled for the first time since I had arrived. "Okay. You win. What do you want to know?"

I returned his smile. "People usually say 'start at the beginning,' but you tell me what's most important to you. We can take it from there."

"Fair enough. The police station was filthy

111

and probably a breeding ground for every imaginable pollen spore. I have to bet that's how they get us bad guys to 'fess up' so quickly." Todd sniffed into his next tissue.

I murmured some indeterminate sound of sympathy.

"They were at my door around six-thirty, right as my alarm was going off. The creatures barely let me have time to dress and send a sick day email into work before hauling me off. Pigs! Sergeant Taylor seemed to understand, but she wouldn't bend on the escort to the station requirement either."

"I'm so sorry." I sat down in Todd's wing chair. "I guess Sergeant Taylor is a pain."

"No, she's all right. Under different circumstances I think I would like her very much. Don't worry. I'm only griping because, as you can see, I'm a bit sensitive." He swept a gesture around his coffee table top. There were prescription bottles and boxes of over-the-counter allergy relief along with the wads of goopy tissues.

"For your allergies?"

Todd nodded. "Indoors, outdoors, seafood, bug bites. You name it. I'm exaggerating, of course, but that's what it feels like. I use the excuse to be able to work from home as much as possible."

"I wonder how you make it to the library

each week."

Todd shook his head. "Have you ever seen me go past the lobby?"

"Good point." I took a moment to think. Visions of the library wafted up along with our group as we heard the news about Rico. Everyone seemed shocked and appalled. "What do you think of our group?"

"Why do you ask?"

"If you didn't kill Rico, somebody did. The way the police talked, one of us had the best opportunity. Maybe motive too."

"I'd put my money on Sandra." Todd gazed toward the opposite wall, banked with a stereo system of some kind, and nodded.

"Sandra? Why her?"

"She has a control thing going on big time, and she had the hots for Rico. Think the police will interview her?"

"I think they're talking to everybody. Though Sandra's showing affection doesn't necessarily make her suspicious."

"I know. Only wishful thinking on my part. She's just such a cow."

"Todd! I'm surprised at you." I said the words right, but spoiled the effect by giggling. He was right.

Todd smiled again. "Once, shortly before you joined the group, Madam Moo-Moo was quite cruel to Kitty."

"Really? How?" I leaned in to hear clearly.

"Kitty had recently broken up with someone, and Sandra told her that the way she dressed made it Kitty's own fault. Kitty started crying, so I let Sandra have it."

"She didn't! You didn't!"

"Oh, yeah, she did. And I told that heifer she dressed like a frump, then, for good measure, told her that her writing sucks."

"Todd!"

He grinned.

I laughed. "I knew there was a reason I liked you!"

Todd laughed too and offered me a cup of tea. We shared a few minutes of Sandra stories before he said, "And when Sandra came in with that 'bit of a bug' a few weeks ago, I was ready to strangle her. Why can't people stay home when they're sick?"

"You wouldn't really strangle anyone, Todd." I gazed at him. His choice of words was unfortunate at best, sometimes.

"Sorry, Daisy. I didn't mean it like that. It's only an expression, like when I said I could kill Rico. The police didn't appreciate that either."

"Not a great phrase, considering."

To my surprise, Todd began to tear up. At first I thought he was having an allergy attack and waited for the sneeze.

Only Todd slumped further in the couch and remained there, hand over eyes, silent. After a moment he began talking, much lower voiced this time. "I loved him once. He was so beautiful." Todd dropped his hand and stared at me with a face contorted in grief.

"Rico? You loved Rico?" I let my jaw drop.

"Of course. Isn't that what you really wanted to know? What you came to pry out of me? You're too slow, Daisy. The police have all my deep, dark secrets. I was the lover of a priest. Makes me a prime suspect. You happy now?"

"Todd, you poor thing! I didn't know. Even when you and Rico had that fight, I didn't conclude your argument might've been a lovers' quarrel." I reached forward in my chair toward this aching young man. "Is there anything I can do?"

He took my hand. After a moment, Todd said, "I guess you're right about needing friends at a time like this."

I changed seats to be nearer him. Todd rolled into me. He cried. His shoulders shook, and the sobs wrenched from his heart and bled with grief. I held him until his wave of sorrow passed. How different from Sandra's public wallowing. The cries from Todd were harsher, more difficult to listen to, yet somehow more real. I found it easy to rub his back as if he were my own child, to whisper words of comfort that I hoped helped. In a few minutes his sobs melted to small hiccups, then quit altogether.

When he finally spoke, Todd's head still rested on my shoulder. "What I didn't tell the police is that our affair was over — at least on my part."

"Over?"

"Rico and I didn't see the world the same way." Todd let go of me and reached for another tissue. "I'm proud to be gay. It's a lifestyle I have come to accept and enjoy. It took me years of knowing, of being beaten, before I came out. Now, I don't want to hide who I am from anyone."

"Good for you."

"But not for Rico. His precious collar was more important to him than any love he and I could share. Chained to it like a dog." Todd threw down his tissue and got up to pace his living room.

"I know there were others before me. He was sex-addicted. There may have been someone after me, but Rico said I was the love he had looked for all his life. Unfortunately, I wasn't enough for him."

"But if you were all he had been looking for —"

"All he wanted in an *emotional* relationship. He wanted much more than love. Was married to his job more than to his heart. Had thoughts of becoming a bishop, or going even higher in the Church. Selfish shit."

"Why didn't you tell this to the police?"

"Are you kidding?" Todd gazed down on me, eyebrows toward the top of his forehead. "Have you *never* watched TV, Daisy? Who *always* becomes the prime suspect? Who *always* seems to do the nasty deed?"

Years of watching *Law & Order* tumbled in on my miniscule brain. "The ex," I mumbled.

"Ex marks the spot," said Todd. He fingered his chest and sagged once more onto his couch. "The police figured I was his lover, so I was the most likely candidate for murder suspect. Add to that the notion we fought the night he disappeared and we have a solid case. If I had admitted we'd broken up, then what?"

"Right." I saw the logic from both Todd's and Gabe's perspective. Todd wouldn't trust the police any more than Gabe would believe Todd had nothing to do with Rico's murder. It would have been a difficult interview for both of them.

The young man spoke again. "Only they're wrong."

"I see." I didn't really see at all, but I wanted to encourage Todd to go on.

"Rico had so many secrets," said Todd. "He was incredibly afraid of not being the perfect priest, and worried that others would find out about his habits. As much as he loved everybody and wanted them to love him back, he was paranoid."

"Everybody?"

"Yeah. The stewardship committee, Sandra Moo Martin particularly, the church's youth director, even that kindhearted priest who's his boss. What a bunch of baggage Rico carried."

"And what was his baggage with you?"

"With me? None." Todd's face puckered in thought. "Only . . ."

I stayed quiet.

He bit his lower lip. "You know I do graphic art for work, but did you know I'm aspiring to make a name for myself in the fine arts?"

"No, are you?"

"Yes. I even have a painting I'm ready to enter into the Pink Arts Guild Show in November. Rico didn't want me to do it. He begged for it when we broke up. Said it would make complications for him. I still

118

wouldn't give the work to him."

"How come?"

"He'd only have hidden it away or destroyed it. Coward. It's a very powerful picture and I think it may make my reputation in the arts. Perhaps if I show you, you'll understand."

Todd led me back to the second bedroom of his apartment, which he had set up as an art studio. There was a corner desk holding his graphic work and computer and a large studio area with lights and a canvas for painting.

Todd stepped into the room's closet as I gazed around the studio walls. Sketches, mostly human studies, hung neatly on bulletin boards. What I guessed were artists' tools hung on a white metal pegboard. Triangles, pallet knives, brushes, color wheels. Cool setup.

"Here it is." Todd hauled a large rectangle covered in brown wrapping paper from the closet. He tore open the paper and revealed a beautiful painting. The main subject, in repose, was unmistakably Father Rico Sanchez.

I wasn't sure how the Catholic Church might have felt about the picture, as priestly garments lay strewn about the floor in well-rendered but disrespectful folds. And there amongst the garments, a playful grin upon his face, Rico Sanchez lay naked for the world.

CHAPTER 14

I was lost in thought as I descended Todd's apartment stairs. Rico's grin from Todd's painting shone through my mind. Todd's genuine grief, Sandra's waterworks, even Toni's harsh pronouncement about Rico's inappropriate gazes all bumbled around into a knot of inconsistencies for me. This morning, who could have known that I'd have become so painfully familiar with the members of my writing group? I groped in my purse for car keys.

A voice jarred my thoughts. "Heads up!"

I nearly bumped into a large cardboard box with legs that was ascending the stairs. "Whoa!" I dropped my purse.

The box stopped. A scraggly bearded face peered around at me. "I said 'heads up.' Didn't you see me coming?" asked the young man.

"Sorry. Lost in thought. Have to pick up my things." I bent down and scooped up my purse. "Moving in?"

"Yeah. Now, do you mind? This thing is heavy." Box-boy seemed annoyed that my lipstick had rolled down a stair and I needed to retrieve it. Once I collected the errant tube, I stood and squished against the apartment wall. No good. The box pinned me where I stood.

"Yo, whale woman, will you move?"

"It's somewhat difficult at the moment. And you needn't be insulting about it." This kid was becoming an annoyance. Didn't he realize I had thinking to do?

The young man tried to push forward, but I squeaked my discomfort. The handrail was digging into my back. The kid heaved a sigh and stepped back down a step. I wriggled out of my entrapment and back up to the landing. Box-boy followed and turned into the apartment below Todd's.

"Have fun with your project," I said with as much sarcasm as I could muster. The guy set his box on his foyer floor, turned to glare at me, then slammed his door in my face. Much as I liked Todd, I really didn't care for his choice of neighbors.

I paid sharper attention the rest of the way to my car. Didn't need any more boxes attacking me. I sat in my driver's seat mulling over the day.

Rico, our romance-writing priest, had been murdered, even though he seemed like such a warmhearted person. I pictured Rico with our group, smiling and doing his best to make each person feel like they were the only one on his mind.

He was also incredibly handsome. Even passersby would stare at Rico as they entered the main room of the library where we met. He noticed their looks and stared right back, like I'd seen Georgette stare at the cat toys I rolled across the floor for her. Jarring thought. Was Rico toying with us all? I bit my lip, trying to understand him.

Sandra liked Rico. Interesting. She didn't find too many people or things okay as they were in her world. Always fixing stuff, Sandra. I could see her in my thoughts, straightening the chairs we sat in for group, adjusting other people's collars, or letting them know if there was food stuck in their teeth. She even adjusted the paperclips that held her writing together so that they all lined up straight. But starched and straight Sandra had found Rico . . . What did she say? . . . *A great man who was taken from us too soon.*

I put my car in reverse and glanced up toward Todd's apartment. Poor, allergic Todd. I'd had no idea of his physical ailments until only a few minutes ago. Even with those challenges he appeared like such a happy, friendly man, especially toward Rico. I remembered Todd gently teasing his friend in several of our meetings. They always seemed to be sharing a secret. Now I knew. They had a secret love. Todd said *I loved him once. He was so —*

Screech!

I slammed on my brakes. I hadn't been paying attention and, as I pulled out, almost crashed into a car driving behind me. The glare of the sun on the other windshield hid what I guessed would be an angry face, so I waved my apologies and pulled back into my slot.

I caught a glimpse of the other driver as she passed, but she didn't look my way, so I hoped I was forgiven.

Art would not have approved. He'd probably have said something like "Daisy, you know I think you're a wonderful woman, but your driving is air-headed at best. Let's win the lottery and I'll get you a chauffeur."

Oh, Art. I have good, quick reaction time, so stop worrying. And if I don't survive? I get to see you and Rose again.

CHAPTER 15

The soft bedroom light on my nightstand played against the facets of my diamond engagement ring and made it sparkle. I swiveled my hand to play with the light for a moment, then took off both my engagement and wedding rings. I stared at them for a moment, then put them in a small, heart-shaped jewelry box next to the locket I normally wore in remembrance of Art and Rose. Friday had come, and I was preparing for my date at Gabe and Ginny's house. My sweet Art would have to understand. After six years, it was time to move on. I gave myself a mental shake and strode to my mirror in the bathroom.

I spritzed with vanilla body spray lightly, so as to not bother any allergens in my hosts, but honeyed enough to be feminine. It went well with my cute little pumpkin embroidered vest. I was looking good, smelling right, unencumbered by my wedding ring.

I looked down at my now-bare left hand. A wave of longing for my husband swept over me. Art. I had been so lucky in marrying him. How could I ask for more?

Art had been an engineer with Lockheed Martin forever. He was logical, neat, and orderly, and had progressed up the corporate ladder in good time. I loved watching him go to work in his white shirt, tie, and pocket protector. For Art's sake, I'd made myself into the stereotypical good wife, hosted parties with him, and endured friendships with people more interested in their own credentials and salaries than special education kids or interests I might have.

Ironic. I was the one to like life on the exciting side, to take risks now and then. I always thought I'd have an accident and die before Art. I wanted to go rock climbing and skiing. Art simply wanted peace when he came home from work. Hand him his dinner along with the television remote, and the man was happy.

But he did get excited about his sports teams; so excited, in fact, he had a heart attack yelling at the TV golf game six years ago. Art was gone before the ambulance arrived at our home, and since then I'd been alone. I was ready to fall in love again, though Art's memory hung around to make sure I behaved myself.

So why was I nervous now? Was Art sending me a message? What was I hoping for?

A knock at my back door made me jump, then I smiled. Art had sent me flowers on the day of our first date. Maybe Gabe had similar inclinations.

I opened the back door. It was no delivery man. It was Chip McPherson. I tried not to show my disappointment.

"Hey there, Ms. D.," said Chip. "Aren't you looking hot tonight." I could tell he was up to something.

"What do you want, Chip?"

"Does a neighbor have to want something because they pop round to say hello?" Chip tried a look that would bring guilt to the heart of a lesser-prepared friend. I stared back at him. He relented. "Oh, all right. I'm planning to go to the football game Sunday and am looking for someone to pet-sit for me."

"You've got to be kidding," I replied. "That brute of yours is quite a handful. I'm not the right person for that job."

Chip stayed and wheedled for longer than I wanted. Finally I let him know I was running late. He said he'd talk to me the next

127

day, when I had more time.

I tried to think of a place I could be all day Saturday so I could brush him off, but unless my date with Gabe went better than expected, I couldn't escape my neighbor. A picture of Gabe, complete with grin and strong arms, popped into my head. The eyes whose gaze I could drown in, the deep voice that held a tinge of humor. I smiled. Maybe tonight's date would go better than expected. I could always hope.

As I drove over to the Caerphilly house I realized I hadn't been so fussy about dressing since college, when I dolled up for some handsome jerk who had made me feel . . . Well, college was yesteryear. Thank my lucky stars that Art was there to pick up the pieces. I wasn't a child anymore. I could handle the single life and start dating again. A shiver ran through me. Date. Goodness! How adolescent that sounded.

CHAPTER 16

Ginny answered her door almost the second I rang the Caerphilly's bell.

"My Daisy!" She flung herself at me and wrapped her arms around my waist. Her face shone with a delightful smile, and she gazed at me with the same purple-blue eyes as Gabe.

There was never a doubt about where you stood with Ginny. No matter what happened with her father, this date already registered as a success for me. I laughed and returned Ginny's hug.

"Hello, Sunshine. I've missed you." I touched her cheek.

"I missed you too. Come on. Let's go find my daad, Gabriel John Caerphilly."

"Okay, Ginny. Let's."

Ginny stopped her move toward taking my hand when I raised my eyebrows. She sighed and dropped it to her side.

"I know, I know. We use grown-up behaviors an' we don't hold hands any more, 'less it's our mom or our dad. Right?"

"Right, good woman." My heart rebelled against being so standoffish, because I wanted to hold her hand, too.

Ginny led me across the living room right as Gabe emerged from the kitchen. He wore an ironed plaid, short-sleeved shirt neatly tucked into twill pants. A towel around his trim waist played the role of apron. Lucky towel. His smile in Ginny's and my direction was infectious, and I stood grinning back without a care in the world or a thought in my head.

"Daad, my Daisy is here," said Ginny from somewhere beside me. "My Daisy, this is my daad, Gabriel John Caerphilly."

The introduction gave us a chance to move closer, and I gladly shook Gabe's hand.

"Welcome, Ms. Daisy," said Gabe. "We're glad you could visit." He squeezed my hand, and I felt like tumbling into his arms right there and then. Honestly, you'd think I was still in high school with raging hormones and all.

Within a few minutes the three of us were chatting like the old friends we were. We migrated to the cozy kitchen and fixed last-minute items for our feast. Gabe busied himself with the roast chicken, and Ginny made a salad. It smelled so homey that I could have stayed there forever.

Gabe glanced toward his daughter. "Ginny, did you thoroughly rinse the lettuce leaves?"

"Yes, Daad," said Ginny, rolling her eyes for me.

Gabe turned to me. "Ginny and I grew a vegetable garden this summer and our salad is a result."

"Daad, *I* was going to tell my Daisy that!" Ginny threw her hands on her hips. "You talk too much!"

Gabe blew out some frustration. "Sorry, Ginny Bear. I didn't know you planned on that." He grinned at me.

I turned to my young friend. "Ginny, how great is that! You helped grow a garden. Will you show it to me after dinner?"

"I didn't *help* grow it. I was the boss. Daddy helped *me.* Let's go see it now."

"What about dinner?" I asked, looking toward my date.

Gabe seemed relieved. "It's okay. You two slip out to the garden, and I'll put things on the table."

I figured it might be easier on Gabe to have Ginny out of the kitchen while he finished dinner so I asked where the garden was. Ginny took my hand and we headed out back. I didn't stop the gesture this time. "Pick your battles" is my motto.

"My daaad is so stupid sometimes," said Ginny when we were alone.

"Ginny! You don't mean that."

"Yes, he is. He don't let me do anything I can do. I am a grown up now, an' he pertends I'm a baby. I want to have my own house and my own garden that he can't mess up."

"Ah, yes, I see."

And I did. How do you give enough emotional room for someone to be an adult at the same time making sure that their lack of cognitive capabilities aren't preyed upon by the nefarious among us? That question had plagued me throughout my career.

Ginny smiled. "I miss you, my Daisy. Here is my tomatoes, an' my lettuce an' my carrots." Ginny pointed to each of her somewhat gracefully laid-out rows and tended plants.

We were engrossed in a circular discussion of mean parents and carrots and peas when Gabe called us in. We smiled at each other, and I felt like I was on one of those happy family TV shows where everything turns out fine in thirty minutes.

"Daad, I told my Daisy you are stupid,

an' I want my own house an' she said yes!"
Ginny didn't stick her tongue out at her
dad, did she? Okay, TV show, twenty-eight
minutes till turning out fine.

I mouthed the word "no" to Gabe and
said, "Let's wash our hands for dinner." He
winked his understanding and nodded.

We soon sat at the table in Gabe's dining
alcove. The table was spread with a plain
gold-colored cloth, which went well with
the cream-toned plates we were using. It
was a simple setting, yet somehow nicer for
the lack of fuss. Ginny said grace over our
meal, and we began eating. Everything was
delicious. Soon our conversation was filled
with amicable exchanges between Gabe and
his daughter, and I was able to join in
comfortably. My empty ring finger itched,
but I ignored any memory of Art.

The Caerphillys' phone rang.

"I'll get it! I'll get it! I'll get it!" Ginny
jumped from her seat and started a dash
toward the kitchen.

"Ginny," Gabe said with that parental
I'm-in-charge-and-you'd-better-listen voice.

"Daad," Ginny whined back.

"Not during dinner," said Gabe. Obviously, this conversation had taken place
more than once before. Gabe shook his

head and Ginny slumped back toward her chair.

"But, Daad, it might be 'portant!"

"No." Gabe was calm but firm. It took a few minutes, but Ginny had a naturally fun-loving personality, and we returned to having a good time.

Gabe's cell phone rang at his hip. "Excuse me," he said rising to walk away.

"Daad, not during dinner." Ginny's phrase sounded awfully familiar.

"This is important, Ginny," Gabe said and returned to his cell phone. He obviously missed his daughter's point. She made a disgruntled noise as Gabe then stepped into the kitchen.

"Your dad has police work," I said. "Sometimes he's needed even when he's not at the station."

"He *always* has police work. He works in the morning. He works when we have lunch. He works when I come home from my job. He works an' he works. An' I hate his work!"

"I'm sorry to hear that, Ginny. Are you lonesome?"

"Yes, I am. Well, not really. I get to go to work almost about every day. I like my friends at my work. I work at Gigantos Super Market. I get to help people with

134

their groceries. I am good at that."

"Oh, Ginny, I'm proud of you!"

A steady job. Gabe and Ginny were a success. It would have been hard to place Ginny in a job, but if she got into a great environment like Gigantos', she was probably recognized for the true asset she was.

"An' at work — don't tell my daad — I have a boyfriend!" Ginny's eyes shone with excitement.

Boyfriend. I felt my forehead pinch. Was Gabe truly in the dark about this?

"His name is Bri-an, an' he's gonna call me. On the phone! He's gonna call me. It's 'portant."

Boyfriend. If Gabe didn't know about him, was Brian a person of trust? A knot of protective questions flew to mind. Was Brian an appropriate match for Ginny? What were his motivations in making her his girlfriend? Was the relationship romantic or something Ginny imagined? Why was he a secret from Gabe?

"Oh?" I said, hoping to draw information out of Ginny. But Gabe returned from the kitchen and sat down.

"Sorry for the interruption, ladies," he said. There was a soft grin on his face. "That was Sergeant Taylor. She's uncovered some new information about the case."

I was immediately interested. "You mean about who murdered Father Rico?"

"I use the phrase 'the case' at home," he replied in a low voice, as if Ginny couldn't hear. I nodded.

"Daad likes Ms. Sergeant Taylor. Daad wants to kiss her." Ginny sing-songed her words and Gabe blushed.

"Stop it, Ginny," he growled, but Ginny was enjoying her tease. She made kissing sounds. "First comes love, then comes marriage, then comes Gayby in a bay-bee carriage."

I felt my own face blush. Why hadn't I thought that? Of course, Gabe would have other dates than simply a frumpy, retired, special ed teacher like me. How could I have expected him to have no interest in women besides me for the past several years?

Gabe frowned at his daughter. "I'm sorry, Daisy. I really don't know what's gotten into my girl this evening."

Ginny giggled. "Your girl is Ms. Sergeant Taylor." She bounced and laughed in her seat, almost overcome by her own sense of humor.

"Ginny, now stop." Gabe rose from his seat. He had a big scowl on his face, as if they were used to this game of pretend fighting. "I'm warning you —"

Ginny screamed, but her face was full of real terror.

Gabe stepped quickly to her. "What is it? You know I wouldn't really hurt you." He blushed again, and his eyes registered a deep wound at Ginny's behavior. He gave Ginny a hug. She screamed again, eyes wide and hands flying toward her mouth.

I wanted to step in, to help, but it wasn't my place.

"A bug!" Ginny pointed at Gabe's plate. Sure enough, a tomato hornworm was creeping across the gravy. Its green body had left a wake through the brown sea. I felt my stomach churn a bit.

"I thought I asked if you'd rinsed the lettuce." Gabe frowned at Ginny. He scooped up his plate and headed toward the kitchen.

"I did," cried Ginny. "I rinsed an' I rinsed. Did you rinse the chicken? Did you rinse the 'tatoes? It wasn't a bug on *my* plate. It's not *my* fault."

Gabe turned back toward us, plates rattling in his grip. His frown deepened in his red face. "Go to your room, young lady. You don't talk to me like that."

Ginny burst into tears. She shoved back from the table and nearly tipped it over in the process. The gravy boat rocked and sloshed its contents. The roll basket overturned. Only the salad stayed placidly in its bowl. I imagined hundreds of worms using suction-cup feet to anchor the lettuce in place.

"You are a mean, mean . . . axhole!" Ginny shouted and ran from the room.

"Ginny!" Gabe's mouth hung agape. He turned to me, an I-am-so-shocked attitude sketched on his features. "She's never spoken to me like that before."

I thought about the garden conversation, the phone calls, and Gabe's attitude toward his daughter. I shrugged. "Seemed logical to me."

"What do you mean, 'logical'? She's behaving like —"

"Like a young woman whose father babies her?"

"I don't!" The plates landed with a thud back on the table. Silverware jangled, then fell off the china.

I shook my head. "It's the hardest part of parenting, Gabe. Give your child — your grown-up child — enough independence to satisfy her and enough rules or protection to satisfy you."

Gabe sat down hard in his chair. He stared at me over cupped hands that covered his mouth. Finally, he threw his hands out in a gesture of submission. "Nailed it. Any suggestions?"

I crossed my arms. "It's great that you say you've given Ginny her own apartment in this house. Where is it?"

"Downstairs, in the basement."

"Then why, when you sent her to her room, did she go that way?" I pointed toward the back of Gabe's house.

He shrugged. "Her apartment's really our rec room with some flowers and colors Ginny likes."

"No kitchen or bedroom of her own?"

"Can't risk her cooking on her own. And more often than not, she forgets to brush her teeth. Easier for us to cover the basics from up here."

"After the salad incident, I don't blame you, but Gabe, you still have to try. She has to learn by making and figuring out her own mistakes. And believe me, she will."

"World's too harsh on people like Ginny." The anguish in Gabe's face tore at my heart.

I stood and patted his back. "She'll learn. It'll be all right." We picked up the dishes and went to the kitchen. As we worked side by side with Ginny's crying in the background, I had to ask about what was on my mind. "Do you date with Ginny along often?"

I wanted the gory details of my situation.

Was Gabe dating me for myself, or me as a prospective babysitter for his daughter? Ever since I'd arrived, I'd felt like it was the latter. And, how close was he to this *Ms. Sergeant Taylor*? I remembered her touch on his shoulder when I first saw her, and the soft smiles that crossed his features whenever she contacted Gabe.

He slowly wiped dry one of the plates. "Well, no. Truth be told, I always take my dates out."

"I see." Babysitter. All my fussing over what to wear. All my hopes for a romantic encounter with my handsome police officer. Nothing. Nothing to this evening but a chance to get to know Ginny again, so I could be with her when Gabe went on dates with his Sergeant Taylor. I grabbed a plate and began wiping Indy 500 speed.

"I didn't mean it like that. I'm sorry, Daisy. Didn't think you'd mind." He turned and took the plate from me. He held my other hand in his. "When Piper — my ex — left, you were the stability both Ginny and I needed. I came to think of you as the person we could always count on if ever we had a problem we couldn't solve. You have a goodness about you that I only see in movies or read about in books. You helped us through one of the roughest years of my life, and I'll always be grateful for that. Then, when you were at the library the other night, it was like I was receiving a sign that I will be able to solve this murder. I brought you home to Ginny because you're so comfortable to be with, and I know she'll want you in her life always."

Comfortable but not kissable. Good and kind, but not exciting. I was getting a sharply focused picture. Gabe could trust me with Ginny, but didn't want me in his heart. I pulled away and tried to shift the focus of our discussion.

"Look, Gabe — Ginny seems to be at a particularly sensitive stage in her life right now. You and I talked about this while she was still my student. I know you want to guide and protect her, but she needs to be treated like the adult she's become. With or without cognitive strengths, your daughter is now a woman. Are you aware she has a boyfriend?"

"What!"

"That's what I thought. I think she wanted to answer the phone —"

"Because it was some rat-faced lout who wants to take advantage of her!"

"Gabe!"

"I won't have some wanna-be-stud going after my little girl."

"Your *young woman,* who has a mind of her own."

"Not if I can help it. Sorry, Daisy, but in my job I see the seedier side of humanity. Don't want Ginny to have any part of it."

"This may well be a good young man."

"Good? Who doesn't introduce himself to me?"

"It's your call, Gabe, but from a professional perspective, I think you'd be best working with Ginny on this instead of doing the dominant-dad thing." I put another dish in the clean stack and dropped my towel on the counter. "I think I should go —"

"Oh, no. Please, stay." Gabe's face contorted with the effort of trying to grasp this monumental new step in his daughter's life. "She has a boyfriend?"

"It seems to me, Gabe, you and Ginny need more time to talk than you and I do right now."

I made good my escape. As I left, I heard Gabe knocking softly on his daughter's door. So much for romantic designs. Kisses and hugs. What was I thinking? I ran to my car, shoved the keys to my ignition in place, and drove off.

I had to blink to clear the tears from my eyes. Gabe needed a babysitter and was happy I'd stumbled back into his and Ginny's life for that purpose. Alone. I hoped Georgette had had a restful day.

She would have a lot to listen to tonight.

CHAPTER 17

Gabe recommended taking Thunder to the park behind Aspen Grove shopping center when he'd helped walk my charge last week. I had no intention of pet-sitting the beast ever again. And, as being pulled around in the wilds by a rabid pup sounded as enticing as writing up curricular modifications for special students while overseeing detention, I promptly put the park out of mind.

So here I was on this picturesque October Sunday afternoon in Colorado, stuffing the damned dog into my Nissan Versa. How did this happen?

Chip might not have been an extraordinary news reporter, or a quiet, pleasant neighbor, but if all else failed, he'd do great in sales. The young man returned to my back door this morning with that lost-puppy look. I knew I shouldn't listen.

"I've checked with everyone else, Ms. D., but no one will help. And the Broncos are playing the Raiders. And I have tickets," Chip whined, as if that explained everything. When I looked unimpressed he added, "Tina likes football."

The new *amore*. That truly did make Chip's need clearer. I'd shaken my head and held out a hand for the leash.

"You're the best, Ms. D.," said Chip. He gave me a peck on the cheek. I felt sorry for Chip's mom, wherever she was. Her son was a real handful.

"You owe me!" I called to his retreating back.

Thunder's black-and-tan coloring did go well with my onyx blue car, and I thanked my lucky stars for having chosen a beige interior. Might hide some of the dog hair I was about to inflict on it.

"No drooling on my seats," I admonished, and we drove off.

We arrived at the park behind Aspen Grove without mishap. I opened my door and Thunder tried to leap over me to get out of the car. Eighty pounds of fur squeezed between me and my steering wheel. Thank goodness he wasn't full grown yet. I made a mad grab for the tether, hoping for something less than a disastrous tumble onto pavement. While not graceful, we managed to right ourselves and make our way toward the walking paths.

We saw a man leaving the park with a well-behaved golden retriever at his side. Why couldn't Thunder act so well?

Apparently, Thunder was curious about this too. He yanked me over toward the retriever to ask that question of the other dog's butt.

"Rocky, leave it!" The command, given with authority, came from the retriever's owner, a guy who looked as old as the mountains. Rocky obeyed immediately. I studied the man in admiration.

Although we were experiencing a warm spell, he had on a heavy vest with things clipped to and pinned over most of it, a floppy hat, and long rubber boots. The fishing rod at his side hinted that he and Rocky had been in the Platte. Rocky sat at the man's feet eagerly awaiting his next command.

"Wow." I allowed my jaw to drop. "How did you do that?"

"It's called training." The old geezer scowled. His gaze encompassed Thunder and me, and apparently we didn't measure up. "German shepherds are smart dogs. Yours would probably take to some good discipline."

I looked down. Thunder had *taken* to

chewing his leash and scratching his ear with his hind foot. Yeah, right. Smart dog.

"I'm only pet-sitting." I looked back up at the man. "Don't know too much about training or dogs."

"Then be sure to grab a bag." Mr. Geezer gazed significantly toward a fully supplied box on a post. A sign also attached to the post admonished visitors to pick up after their furry friends — it's the law.

I shook my head and cringed. "Oh, I don't think I could —"

"It's the responsible thing to do," said the ancient.

Just then, Rocky decided to help his owner demonstrate. Pee-Eew! To my horror, Thunder leapt up and pulled me over for an investigative sniff and lick.

"Oh, no, Thunder!" I yanked the leash. Thunder yelped, but stopped. The old guy shook his head and began muttering. I wondered how long before I would reach that muttering age.

Then Mr. Geezer calmly slipped a bag over his hand as if he'd been a surgeon in some former life, bent over, and picked up Rocky's residue. I couldn't help it. I made a face.

Mr. Geezer slipped the "cuff" of the bag back over his poop-holding hand and tied the top into a tidy knot. Pretty impressive. He made it look easy.

As the old guy deposited Rocky's bag into a nearby trash container, I called out to be helpful. "You missed some."

He glared at me and walked on. The muttering became louder. "Pet-sitter, bah!" and "Hope she steps in some" were the only distinguishable phrases I heard.

I tugged at the bag dispenser and took off. "This is just in case, but try to hold it until we get home," I said to Thunder.

I was going to walk on the cement path in the park, but Thunder had other plans. He pulled this way and that, up some trail I wasn't even sure we were allowed on. It had no pavement or other signs of civilization.

We struggled in a dance of dog investigating his earth while human authority figure loses all sense of control. I gave up and followed as best I could.

About fifteen minutes of wandering took us to a wooded area. Thunder and I came across yellow police tape. I heeded the "crime scene" warning, but Thunder hadn't learned to read yet, so he charged right in. Suddenly, I realized that this was the spot where Father Rico must have taken his last breath. A chill ran through me as we stepped forward.

I pictured Rico standing at the precipice, a peaceful smile on his face. This was a beautiful place of cool, restful greens and stillness. Traffic from the six lanes of Santa Fe hummed far away in another life. Standing here, you'd never know that a bustling shopping center was only a few minutes walk to the east. It didn't look like a murder spot either, though to be honest, I had no idea what a murder spot should look like.

How had Rico come to fall into that river? I glanced over the edge and saw the stream swirling viciously seven or eight feet below. Water tumbled over and around some very angry-looking rocks. I shivered at the thought of Rico falling . . . no . . . being pushed onto them.

If Rico fell here, it was possible for him to get a nasty bash on the head. If he'd been knocked unconscious he might have rolled over and drowned. But murder?

I guessed if Father Rico came with Todd, as the police seemed to think, my young friend could have pushed Rico over the side of the embankment. It would have taken quite an effort, as Rico was by far the larger of the two men. Todd would have had to run full force at Rico, and they both would probably have fallen into the river. I tried to picture the scene. It simply didn't feel right.

What a shame to be thinking such nasty thoughts. This was the kind of place I could've stayed in forever. I could've stayed, if not for the unpleasant thoughts of Rico's end. I could have stayed if I weren't so jumpy about potential run-ins with wildlife such as snakes, coyotes, and the like. And ouch! Those damned mosquitoes. What a plague. Still, I could have stayed if I had a friend with me and a can of bug repellant. I thought about Thunder and was glad to have him along, even though he was a difficult charge.

I returned to my reverie about the murder. Perhaps Todd had pointed to something interesting in the river. Then he could have caught Rico unaware and off-balance. A smaller shove would have had Rico fall just as hard. It could even have been done as a joke at first — the old think-fast shove.

Todd would have climbed down, perhaps intending to help his lover, but then somehow changed his mind. I could see there were fading lines in the muddy embankment sides where someone could have slid into the river. Todd might have helped Rico's journey to heaven by holding his friend underwater to drown.

My knees weakened at the thought. I tried to think of someone I was angry with, and

Chip popped into mind. Then I pictured holding Chip's limp body underwater. No. I wouldn't do it. Could Todd really have been angry enough for this?

I could have strangled Sandra. I heard Todd say that when I visited him.

I remembered Rico and Todd's fight and, yes, it was passionate, but neither man had made any physical move to dominate. No fists were clenched, at least none that I remembered.

Thunder, tired of standing still, wandered off as far as his leash would allow. He sniffed deeply into some weeds. Luckily for the rabbit he flushed out, the silly dog sneezed. The rabbit scooted away without my charge noticing. Smart dog, my eye.

Now, where was I? Todd and Rico fighting. Todd had said that Rico was the one upset over their breakup. Rico was more concerned about keeping their relationship secret than breaking it off. Of course Todd could have been lying . . .

Wait a minute. Hold on. Thunder sneezed!

I turned to gaze after my beast, who had resumed rooting around in the underbrush. In that instant, I knew without a doubt that Todd couldn't have killed Rico. I flipped open my cell to call Gabe. No answer at his house. I pulled his business card from my

151

purse and dialed the station.

"Lieutenant Caerphilly's office. This is Sergeant Taylor." Her voice sounded quite pretty in a no-nonsense kind of way.

"Lieutenant Caerphilly, please," I said, not wanting to identify myself, just in case my voice wasn't as inspiring.

"I'm sorry. The lieutenant has been called away from his desk. May I take a message?"

I hung up without responding. Sergeant Taylor could take that message wherever she wanted.

"Come on, Thunder," I said. "If Gabe and Sergeant Lover-Girl aren't interested, I'll bet Todd is."

Thunder gazed up at me. I guess I sounded like we were on a mission. The good, now smart, dog gave me no trouble, all the way back to my car.

CHAPTER 18

My eyes met an orderly sort of chaos as I pulled into the parking lot of the Gables Apartments. Police lights flashed red and blue atop several cars standing at odds with the yellow parking lines.

I pulled into a space, admonished Thunder to "stay put," and made my way through a gathering crowd toward Todd's apartment. Something big must have been going on, and mixed with my own anxiousness to speak to Todd, it leant a manic ambiance to the scene.

I approached a stern-looking police officer. "We need you to step back," he said, dark blue uniform crisp over muscle-bulging arms.

"But I've come to visit someone who lives here," I replied and tried to step around him.

"Not today. Crime scene. Residents are in the community building." He gestured with his thumb toward the building furthest away. He was all business, so I guessed arguing wasn't going to be my best tactic.

I started walking away, when a flash of orange caught my eye. It was Gabe Caerphilly. He wore a Broncos jersey over his jeans. He also wore a very grim expression on his face.

"Gabe!" I called out and waved. "Woo hoo, Gabe."

He looked up, handed a clipboard to the young woman he'd been talking to, and stalked over. She looked familiar. Was that Sergeant Taylor?

"What the hell are you doing here?" Gabe's face was sober and none-too-friendly looking.

"It's nice to see you too." I employed my coolest sarcasm. Maybe we didn't have the best time on Friday's date, but he could still show some civility.

"Sorry. This isn't a good place for you right now."

"I came to see Todd Stevens. I'll go over to the community center and find him there. By the way, what's going on?"

"You won't find him," said Gabe. He blew out a sigh. "Todd was murdered."

My stomach did a roller-coaster drop. "What? That can't be!" Shock left me without a thought. Suddenly the early autumn air was too thick to breathe.

"It's not a pretty scene, Daisy," Gabe continued. "You should go."

As if on cue, two men carrying a stretcher topped by a black bag emerged from the building. They wore surgical masks, and even from this distance I caught a whiff of something awful. It smelled like meat that had been left on the counter far too long.

My hand flew up to my mouth when I realized who the men were carrying. I gasped, turned, and ran. At a nearby hedge, lunch, breakfast, and remains of last night's dinner all made their quick exit from my stomach.

Tears stung my eyes. Todd! It couldn't be. Gabe must be wrong. I had only visited my writing colleague a few days ago. We'd shared hugs. I could still feel them. No, no. He was so young.

I felt a hand on my back and through my tears managed to see a blurry white tissue. I grabbed for it and wiped my face before turning back toward Gabe. "Thanks."

"I'm sorry you had to find out this way, Daisy." His voice held the compassion I was more used to sensing from him.

"Me too. More than you know. What happened? Was there a note like with Rico?"

"I can't tell you much, you know that . . .

How did you know about the note?"

"You told me about it. At Pete's. That first night."

"Where? I did? I don't talk about evidence to —"

"Pete's Pub. You told me. Right after I told you about Colby Stanton, how I retired so early."

"I'll let that go for now. Todd was killed sometime late last week. With this warm spell, you can imagine that it didn't take long for the neighbors to complain about the odors. The manager checked the apartment an hour or so ago and called us."

"Oh, Gabe, he was such a talented young man. Did you find his picture of Rico? I'd still like to see it entered in that art show he wanted."

"What picture?"

"It was a nude painting. Wasn't it there?" Sometimes crying helps, but I didn't feel any better with tears streaming down my face.

A young officer stepped up to us holding a clear plastic bag in his surgically gloved hand. "Rabbit," he said.

I could barely make out one elongated ear from the bag. The rest was a stew of reds, browns, fur, and indistinguishable guts.

"Note was with it." He handed Gabe

another plastic bag, this one with a single sheet of paper in it.

It was all too much. I wheeled around and retched again.

Gabe patted my back. "Will you be okay, Daisy? I can get a medic for you, but I really have to go back to work. We need to finish tagging and fingerprinting the scene."

"Fingerprints? When I was here last week, I might've touched things. Would that be important?"

"What the f— what in the hell were you doing at Todd's? Of course your fingerprints will be important. You know what this means, don't you?"

"No. What?" I sensed a growing frustration in my detective friend. He ran fingers through his hair and tapped his foot.

"Never mind. We'll have to get a sample of your fingerprints to compare with what we find." Gabe waved over the young woman he'd been speaking to when I arrived. "You go with Sergeant Taylor here, and she'll take care of it. Linda?"

I looked at the comely young woman. Sergeant Taylor was in a dark blue Broncos tee and jeans, so I guess that both she and Gabe must have been off duty when this situation arose.

I tried not to ask myself if they were together when the call came in.

CHAPTER 19

I looked around the crime scene parking lot, at all the police and emergency people. What a crummy way to spend your life, happily watching a favorite football team one second and investigating murder the next.

Murder. Todd. Tears welled in my eyes once more as I turned to Gabe. I wanted to ask a thousand questions about my friend's death, but knew there would be no answers. Instead I focused on immediate needs. "Will this take long? I have Thunder with me, and I don't trust him to behave well if I leave him in the car for long."

"You left that dog in a car on a hot day like this?" Gabe's eyes bugged out at me and I flinched.

"It was only for a couple of minutes. We came from our walk behind Aspen Grove. Oh, Gabe! That's how I knew Todd couldn't have killed Rico. You see, Todd has —"

"That your car over there — one with the

windows *rolled up?*" Gabe pointed as he spoke.

If I were a criminal, I'd confess to killing Santa Claus at Gabe's look. I stepped back and nodded.

"When did the dog last get a drink?"

"Well, he dove around in the river for a bit. I suppose he drank then."

"Give me your keys." Gabe held out his hand. His frown deepened, and his foot-tapping became louder and more insistent. I pulled my keys from my purse and held them out with shaking fingers.

"I don't have time for this," Gabe said through gritted teeth. "Linda, print her." He strode off toward my car.

"If you'll come with me, Ms. Arthur, we'll take care of the printing and you can be on your way."

"I'm afraid I must have touched some things in Todd's apartment," I said as an attempt at pleasant conversation. "Poor Todd! I can't believe it. I was just visiting him."

Sergeant Taylor eyed me full in the face, and I felt like steak on a plate when the dinner bell rings. "You were in his apartment? Why were you there? When? Are you quite good friends with Mr. Stevens?"

"I only wanted to commiserate with him on the loss of Father Sanchez," I said.

Sergeant Taylor whipped a notepad out of her pocket. "How did you know the deceased?"

"Who? Father Rico or Todd?"

"You knew them *both*?"

"Yes. They were in my writing group, remember? I saw you last week when you and Gabe told us about Rico."

Sergeant Taylor moved to put her notepad back in a pocket, disappointment scribbling itself across her features. "Sorry, ma'am. You were questioned last, after I left. I forgot you were part of the group." Sergeant Taylor moved her lips toward a conciliatory smile but continued to stare at me. "And you came over today to . . . ?"

A shout in our direction caused both Sergeant Taylor and me to swirl around. "That's her!" I recognized the scruffy-bearded boy from Todd's stairwell. He was pointing at me, talking with another officer. Why would he be so excited about recognizing me?

"She was the one coming up the stairs as I was going down!"

Sergeant Taylor turned from watching the boy back to me. "Excuse me, ma'am. When precisely were you here last?"

"On Thursday afternoon, I think. Or maybe it was Wednesday. I was leaving

161

Todd's apartment when I bumped into that young man." I nodded in box-boy's direction.

"Going up the stairs?"

"No, going down. He's confused. He was carrying a big box up, so we only had a glimpse of each other."

Box-boy heard me.

"Unh-unh," he said eloquently. "You had a box of stuff too and made me back up the stairs. I had a hard time seeing your face, but you were rude and in a hurry."

"Excuse me?" I couldn't believe what I heard. "That's not at all what hap—"

"Then there was some thumping around above me. That's the last time I heard anything outta the dead guy's apartment." Box-boy acted as if finishing his sentence made his memory accurate.

The officer that box-boy had been speaking with turned toward Sergeant Taylor and me.

Sergeant Taylor nodded in my direction as she spoke. "Friend of Caerphilly's. He can vouch for her." To me, she spoke lower.

"You're sure you met this guy coming down, not going up the stairs?"

I nodded.

"Were you carrying a box?"

"He must have me confused with someone

162

else. I was here, but I didn't have any box."
I raised my voice. "And that guy," I pointed
to the scruffy young man. Two could play at
his game. "That guy was coming up the
stairs, squished me against a wall, and called
me a whale!"

Sergeant Taylor pinched her lips together
and tapped her pen on her clipboard.
"Okay. We'll leave that for now. Why are you
here today?"

"I came over to tell Todd I knew without
a doubt that he couldn't have been Rico's
killer. You see, he said he was concerned
about becoming a prime suspect. It was
Thunder, as a matter of fact, that proved
the point."

"The thunder?"

"No, not the weather. The dog. I sometimes pet-sit for Thunder and take him on
walks. He's the one in my car. I don't know
much about dog-sitting, but my neighbor is
such a hopeless manipulator, I was talked
into it before I knew what was happening."

"Talked into what, Ms. Arthur?" Sergeant
Taylor leaned in toward me, pen at the
ready.

"Walking the dog. That's what I was doing when Thunder sneezed, and I knew
Todd couldn't have killed Rico. It's all so
clear. Don't you see?"

Sergeant Taylor rolled her eyes, her pen slipping from her fingers. I guessed she didn't see at all. She stared at my face, then stooped to pick up her pen. When she stood back up, her eyes bored into me with less-than-friendly interest.

"Look. Are you playing some sort of game with me? Try running that story by me again, this time in a straight line."

"It's quite clear. Poor Todd couldn't have killed Rico."

Taylor's voice took on a mocking edge. "Especially as he's dead now too. Very conveniently dead."

What Taylor hinted at was ridiculous. "You don't think I . . . ?"

She tapped her notes. "I see you here at the second crime scene. I see you flirting with the officer in charge of the case. Maybe throwing him off the trail? I see you're part of the group most likely responsible for the first vic's demise."

"This is silly. And I am not flirting with anyone." I hoped the last bit sounded honest. I felt a hot flash coming on. At that point I could have poked the oh-so-efficient Sergeant Taylor right through her clipboard.

Lucky for us both, Gabe came back right then, Thunder in a heel at his side.

"Got him some water, but you need to

take this guy right home and see if you can put him in a kiddie pool or cool bath," said Gabe toward me. "Dogs can overheat in half the time it takes humans. Have the prints under control, Linda?"

"We're headed that way, sir," said Sergeant Taylor, still glaring at me. "Ms. Arthur was illuminating some details of the crimes for me."

Gabe huffed. "I can see I have to do everything myself." He grabbed my arm. "Come on, Daisy. Thunder, heel."

We walked toward a police vehicle. I didn't want to upset Gabe any more so I tried to play the conciliator. "Don't be upset with her, Gabe. She was only asking me some questions." Uncomfortable questions, but I supposed it was her job after all.

"Shh," he hissed. He didn't look at me, but glared at the police truck in front of him. I readied a pithy remark about the offensiveness of shushing, but he handed me over to the fingerprint person. Silently the print expert took my patterns with black goopy stuff that required a lot of rubbing with paper towel to get off.

Gabe walked me out away from the police van. "You shouldn't have conversations at a crime scene. It could get you in deep trouble."

"Oh, I don't think —"

"That's the point. Police are hoping to come across people who talk without thinking. That's a great way to catch our perps. What did you tell Taylor anyway?"

"That Todd couldn't have killed Rico because his allergies wouldn't have let him go into Aspen Grove woods to do it."

"Well, say no more to her or anyone else, you hear? I know you, Daisy, and I'm confident that you wouldn't hurt anyone, but with your fingerprints at the crime scene and with your being in the Hugs 'N' Kisses writing group, you've elevated yourself to the prime suspect list."

"Oh." I formed the word slowly as my mind took in the enormity of what Gabe just said. "You mean the police could think I'm not a helpful witness, but I might murder someone?"

"That you killed both men? Yes."

"But that's silly. Why would I want to do that?"

Taylor was back in step with us. "Only you can tell us." Did the woman never go anywhere without her annoying clipboard? I pictured her in the shower with that thing, writing a hundred times, "Daisy is not to be trusted."

I looked from Sergeant Taylor to Gabe,

then stared into his eyes, looking for something between us that could give me reassurance.

Suddenly, Gabe smiled. "Oh, don't look like that. Of course we don't suspect you. You're a schoolteacher who walks her neighbor's dog. I'd be more inclined to believe you guilty of befriending all the fleas on Thunder than killing someone."

Sergeant Taylor gave a discreet grunt. Something told me she didn't feel the same way.

"Thanks. I think." I wasn't thrilled with Gabe's assessment of me. It sounded wimpy. Better that, however, than his harboring any thought about my ability to murder someone. Gabe smiled again. Then he turned to his right-hand woman.

"Taylor, how 'bout you go catalog evidence with Hawkins."

She looked like cataloging evidence was the last thing she wanted to do, but to her credit, she acknowledged her orders, turned on her heel, and walked away. Gabe watched her for only four or five steps. He turned back to me.

"Look. We had a rough time of it Friday with Ginny and that disastrous dinner. Then when something like this happens" — he gestured at the commotion around us — "I become short-tempered. How 'bout we start again. I'm Gabe Caerphilly." He placed a hand on his chest. "And I'd like to take you to dinner."

I smiled and made ready to reply when the officer who had been talking with Todd's box-carrying neighbor stepped up. The officer pulled Gabe aside and spoke softly to my lieutenant. I didn't hear much. Maybe a few words like "your friend," "seen entering," and "silence after." I shrank inside.

Gabe and the officer glanced my way. They both looked very serious. I had to do something, so I scrunched my shoulder and finger-waved.

"Thanks, Matt," said Gabe. He patted the officer's shoulder and stepped back over to me.

Thunder, who had been behaving very well, chose that moment to wind his way around Gabe and me, his leash pulling us together. My heart skipped a beat as I took the dog's strap from Gabe and disentangled myself. "Sorry," I mumbled.

"Daisy, prelims put Todd's death at three to five days ago, which is about the time you were seen going into his apartment. Can you explain that?"

"No. How could I? He'd been at the police station right before he let me in. You were the one who told me about that, remember? I came over to offer comfort as any friend would."

"You know how this looks, don't you?"

A vacuum of energy stole through my spirit and I dropped my head. "I suppose."

"I don't personally suspect you, Daisy, as I said." Gabe pulled my chin up. His hand had a strong sickly scent. Dead body smell. "Still, you have to admit, your visit appears rather suspicious to my team."

His team. Linda Taylor. I could imagine her thoughts.

I controlled another approaching retch, and nodded. "Maybe I could take a rain check on that dinner."

Gently, I pushed back on Gabe's chest. I wanted to do precisely the opposite. I wanted to grab on and snuggle into his comforting hug but knew things didn't bode well for me, and it wouldn't be fair to stick Gabe in the middle of more mess. Fresh tears pushed their way forward, so I turned and walked away before Gabe saw them.

"Daisy?" he called.

I pivoted and looked back. "Yes?" Everything was in motion except Gabe. He stood tall and static, his Broncos shirt gently rippling in the autumn breeze. I wanted nothing more than to run back toward him, but his next words stopped me.

"Stay out of this investigation." He stared at me with no hint of a smile. The lines around his eyes spoke of a weariness I would never come close to understanding. "I don't want you hurt."

Too late. Sergeant Taylor and Gabe's team suspected me, so I was already involved more than I'd ever wanted.

I gnawed on Gabe's words for a moment before answering. "I didn't kill either Rico or Todd. Maybe today you believe me, but others on your team don't. I can't sit around to let their suspicions take hold in your heart. It's important to know who did these horrid murders. Besides, if I'm so close to the situation, I could become a victim too."

I turned and walked away. Gabe didn't follow.

CHAPTER 20

The faces of my writing group members all appeared reluctant to critique the chapter I'd just read. Maybe their reticence came from the damper of losing another group member. Poor Todd!

Yesterday, everyone had apparently received the same police visit. Knock on the door. News of Todd's death, then the request to come to the Littleton police station. The searching looks at our homes. Notes. Always notes. Later the police exited, sucking our spirits along in their wake. All they left behind was the big question: *Who would do such a thing?*

I looked around at my group once more. Sandra slid reading glasses down her nose to edit my work while still sitting up straight. Interesting. No hysterics over Todd. She seemed calm and focused as she wrote her comments. If she had seen what I'd seen Sunday, smelled that awful smell . . . which

Sandra would have been here today?

Eleanor found something to study intently out the window. This was hard to do, as night had fallen and you couldn't really see outside. So much had happened since she last came to a meeting. Was she thinking about my work or about the missing group members?

Toni found the edges of my manuscript fascinating, judging by the way she picked at them. Was she uncomfortable because of Todd's murder or my work? Must be his murder. My pages had to be good. I'd labored too hard for them not to be.

Even Kitty decided to fidget in her over-sized handbag for who-knows-what.

No one looked at me. Not a good sign, no matter their thoughts in this situation.

"I know its not the best chapter," I ventured.

Sandra held up a finger while maintaining her gaze on my manuscript. "No speaking by the author until all critiques are complete." She scribbled something else across my words.

Oh yeah, Rule Number Four. Thank goodness for the rules. I blew breath into my cheek and glanced around the library lobby.

The glass wall that separated Hugs 'N'

Kisses from the main book room provided cozy privacy at the same time we enjoyed the buzz of community around us. A few library patrons walked past and went on. They reminded me of ants, set in fixed paths and on their own missions. Tonight it might have been my imagination, but I thought the patrons tended to stare at our group as they walked by us. I'd have to guess that the whole world knew us more as some seedy Poison Pen Club than the Hugs 'N' Kisses they'd been so comfortable with only a couple of weeks ago.

Sandra put down her pen. "Eleanor, you're to the immediate left of Daisy. Will you begin, please?" She nodded to Eleanor, who glared back.

Eleanor readjusted herself in her chair. She tossed her ash-blond hair over a shoulder, revealing an equally pale face, centered by a nose that looked as if it had been broken more than a few times.

When I'd first met Eleanor and she found I hadn't written any novels before, she gave me a glacial smile. Then she turned to Kitty, practically shouting "God save us from amateurs!"

I studied Eleanor's misshapen nose. Could it be our published author had led an interesting life as a boxer before joining our group? Maybe she'd had to defend herself against rude comments about that large mole protruding from her chin. Maybe she was tougher than she looked. Maybe she was strong enough to push someone down an embankment. Or bash someone on the head. It was fun to think that Eleanor could be the murderer, and I would soon see Gabe leading her away in handcuffs.

Eleanor spoke with a wispy voice that grated like Limburger cheese. "Ahem. Daisy, I think you need to cut this down. Your plot is weakened by a lack of direction and conflict."

Off to a great start. I sighed inwardly, pasted a fake smile in place, and meekly replied "thank you" to the person who could take her four published books and go start a library in Siberia as far as I was concerned.

"I agree with Eleanor," said Toni. The woman seldom says anything in our group other than "I agree with" whomever speaks right before her. It would be interesting to listen to Toni in a political debate. I wondered how she came up with any original story ideas under that dark brown-gray bun when she worked so hard to be unoriginal. "That, and you need a more compelling protagonist. Gwendolyn sounds too weak and indefinite for the role you have thrust on her."

"I see," I said. I didn't bother to say thank you for helping me feel like forgotten leftovers in the fridge.

"There are definite grammatical problem areas," said Sandra. "You need to remember how to place your commas, to stop splitting your infinitives, and to work harder on eliminating your passive voice."

"Hey, everyone." I'd had enough of this. "What happened to Rule Number Two?"

The group stared blankly at me.

"You know. 'Say something nice before ripping someone's work apart'?" I figured I'd been coming to the group long enough to be able to voice a forceful thought, even if apparently my heroine, Gwendolyn, couldn't.

Toni spoke in a stage whisper, "Boy, you can tell she was a teacher, can't you? All rules and numbers." Everyone laughed but me.

Then Kitty, sitting on my other side, chimed in. "Don't be discouraged, Daisy. You are getting better. But you won't improve if we don't point out weak areas."

Kitty was right, of course. But I needed positive comments. It felt like everything I wrote was subpar, and I was going to spend another night crying into Georgette's fur.

Sandra addressed the group. "However, Daisy does have a point. What we need is Father Rico here. Now there was someone who could be clear without being harsh."

"In your opinion," shot Eleanor. "In mine, he was a hack who didn't belong in our writing group. Imagine. A priest who thought he knew enough about the topic of love to write about it."

"He wrote beautifully!" said Sandra. Her face registered complete shock at Eleanor.

Eleanor examined her fingernails. "If he wrote so beautifully, how come he was never published? My editor wouldn't read past the first four lines of anything he submitted."

"But your editor has a weakness." Sandra's shocked look gave way to a venomous smile. "She *likes* your work!"

And they were off. Eleanor and Sandra entwined in a verbal battle, punctuated with nasty barbs and dagger looks. They made me think of cobras, bobbing, weaving, and spitting out aggressively toward one another. Best strategy in this situation was to try to look for conversation elsewhere.

Kitty whispered to me. "Daisy, we really like you in our group. You're fun to be with and kind, unlike some others" — significant glance to Sandra and Eleanor — "and over time your writing will improve. Keep trying."

I smiled at my friend. "Thanks, but maybe I'm not writer material."

Kitty grabbed my arm. "Nonsense. Heck, none of us was great to start with. We've all had our challenges. And we've invited in all sorts of people who didn't write well. Some didn't have the personality for writing either. The absolutely hopeless ones left after only two or three reads."

"This is my second read," I said.

"Well," Kitty said, dragging the word out to buy time, "you're different. You fit in. We had one guy, Loathsome Les, who was a creature from the scummy bog. You remember him, Toni?" Kitty turned and waved to encourage Toni to come sit nearer us.

"Les the pervert? Of course. Who could forget?" Toni dragged her chair into a cozy threesome.

"The pervert?" I asked.

Kitty nodded. "Yep. This guy wasn't really writing romance, but weird, violent sex acts. Left us all feeling that's what he wanted — to abuse and hurt us for real. Oooh. I still get creeped out just thinking of him!"

I was glad for having missed the man. "What happened to Les?"

Toni said, "Sandra invited him to her house for dinner. That way her hubby could be around when she refunded Les his group fees and told the slime to go away."

Seemed to me that Sandra was a good strategist, even if she wrote boring prose.

Kitty laughed. "Yeah. Now whenever Sandra invites someone over, we know that their hatchet time is coming. Hey! I wonder if the police know about Les? He seemed to relish spewing his crap in front of a priest."

"You're right," said Toni. "Maybe he's the murderer. I remember him having words with both Rico and Todd after one of our meetings. They were trying to get him to stop submitting that offensive garbage."

Eleanor's voice rose to a shrill siren. "Well, I'd rather have my four published books than your twelve high-school essays any day!" We all turned to look at her.

"Eleanor, if I weren't the leader here and so keenly aware of our situation, you'd be out on your ass."

The ex-teacher in me came out. I couldn't let this go any further, so I stood up. "Now, now everyone. The last time we became this passionate over our work, someone *died*. We need to settle down. Look. The librarian is glowering at us."

Sure enough, Ms. Goodwin was staring

and frowning. She raised a finger to her lips in a silent "shush" gesture. Everyone turned with guilty expressions back to each other.

I continued my authoritative stance. "Okay. We've all been through a terribly shocking time, what with the murders of Rico and Todd, but we need to maintain our composure here."

Sandra burst into tears. "Rico!" she moaned.

Toni rolled her eyes and dug into her purse. She hauled out a wad of tissue and thrust it at Sandra. Not quite the consoling friend she'd been last week.

I decided to ignore Sandra's outburst, and carried on. "I think we need to help each other come to terms with all that's happened."

Kitty spoke up. "You're right, Daisy, but what do you suggest we do? Find the murderer ourselves?" She gave a nervous chortle. "None of us is going to be all right until we figure who among us is a killer."

Kitty had to be wrong. I tried again. "We need to get over the idea that the police think one of us killed Rico and Todd. We need to look for suspects elsewhere. But" — and I held up my hand to stop Kitty from interrupting again — "I also think we need to consider disbanding for a few weeks until

179

this murder business is resolved."

"No!" Sandra shouted. She dropped her tissues long enough to glare at me.

"Our best ideas come from being here together," added Eleanor.

"I like our group." Toni picked up her notepad and started scribbling. "Even if you and Kitty want to stop coming, we have three people who will keep our commitment to Hugs 'N' Kisses."

"You can count me in," said Kitty toward the others.

I sighed. "Okay, we stay active, but we need to address the elephant in the living room."

Sandra's head snapped up as she glared at me. "What do you mean?"

"I'm not trying to push myself into your role as leader, Sandra, but the Littleton police, and" — another library patron stared in our direction — "and the community seem to think one of us is a murderer. How do we keep working together if we have to constantly look over our shoulders, worried about who's behind us?"

Toni looked up from her notes. "Fair question. How do we know we're all safe to be around?"

Kitty tapped her teeth with a finger. Tonight's polish was gold. "Keep your friends close and your enemies closer. Not sure how to do that."

Sandra chimed in. "We could do a phone tree. If anything unusual happens, we can call each other and spread the word."

Eleanor snarled, "And how does that help if one of us is the murderer? Daisy may have a point after all. I think I'm going to my cabin in Keystone for a while." She picked up a Kenneth Cole briefcase and strode toward the exit.

Gabe Caerphilly entered the library directly in Eleanor's path. "Not so fast." He guided her back to our group. Tonight he wore a mock turtleneck shirt over twill pants. How had this man stayed single since his wife left him?

"Good evening," said Gabe. "I see everyone's present tonight. Excellent. I won't have to repeat myself. Clear up any questions at one time. With two murders in as many weeks, we have the possibility of a serial killer on the loose."

Shocked exclamations met this pronouncement.

Gabe waited for the noise to subside. "Todd and Rico only had two things in common — their friendship with each other and this writing group. While we'll continue to investigate all possibilities, this group remains important to our investigation."

"You think one of us did it." Kitty jumped up. She looked tiny in the face of Gabe's height. Her bright red sweater matched the spark in her eye. "Well, that's plain stupid. Look around you, Lieutenant. Most murders are committed by men. Do you see any men here?"

"No, Ms. Beaumont, I don't. But even if rare, women have been known to kill. We can't rule you out solely because of your gender."

"Granted, but we're a group of romance writers. We focus more on love than hate."

"Okay." Gabe looked directly at me. "Let's say that sometimes the romance sours. Problems occur. Accidents happen."

I returned Gabe's look and bit my lip. Was he going to arrest me in front of my colleagues? Gabe turned and addressed the group at large.

"Therefore, I'm making it official. Consider yourselves 'persons of interest' with the Littleton police, in regard to the murders of Rico Sanchez and Todd Stevens. Don't plan any out-of-town trips in the upcoming weeks, including" — he looked at Eleanor — "Keystone or any mountain vacations."

CHAPTER 21

At the end of our meeting, we all agreed to "buddy up" for protection. We wouldn't go any place that might put us in danger without a friend along. And we would call each other daily to check up on one another. Then Kitty asked everyone over for a girls' night in on Friday.

"At least we'd have strength in numbers," said my diminutive friend, "just in case. And besides, a party is a good way to make the best of our disturbingly dangerous situation."

Everyone said they'd think about Kitty's offer. Then Eleanor and Sandra decided to share rides to any errands or other necessary events away from home. Kitty and I buddied up to help our growing friendship. Toni said her husband and his family were well equiped to protect her and strode off into the night by herself.

The next afternoon I went shopping with

Kitty. We drove to Southwest Plaza, a block or two from the library. The mall was quiet. Young couples held hands as they walked the floors while indeterminate music played over the sound system. The tunes mixed with echos of those few screaming toddlers who never seem to catch on that shopping is supposed to be fun.

"Hel-oooh, Daisy." Kitty waved a delicate hand in front of my face. Her apple-green nail polish gleamed to perfection. One day I was going to have to see her closet. Amazing.

"Sorry, Kitty. My mind's been taken over by dust bunnies." We were walking around the department store in search of gifts for her mom's birthday.

"You seem out of sorts, my friend," said Kitty.

"Guess I am." I made like a swimmer emptying her clogged ear. "Sorry. I'll try to focus more."

Kitty laughed. "No problem. Wanna talk about it?"

How could I talk about *it*? *It* was huge. Rico. Todd. Murder. My heart palpitated in response to the thought. Kitty didn't need me to bring that up. And Gabe Caerphilly, perfect candidate for the next Mr. in my Mrs. sort of life, had not been exactly lover-like. Since we'd re-met a smidgen over a week ago, Gabe had behaved as if I was interesting only because I was a suspect in *his* murder case. And who really was the bad guy in that? *Somebody* had killed two of my writing colleagues. Would there be others? Could Kitty or I become victims too?

"No," I said giving myself a mental shake. "We came here to shop for your mom's birthday present. What's noodling around in my brain has nothing to do with that."

Kitty grabbed my arm. "I hope you don't mind. I really don't know what a woman turning fifty would want. I mean, she has everything, and I have precisely fifty-eight dollars and some pocket change for a present."

"Remember it's the thought —"

"Yeah, yeah. But I don't want her interpreting my thought as 'Quick! Run to the store and get some gawd-awful doodad at the first place you see.' Mom deserves better."

"I'm sure we'll find something."

"I suppose you're right." Kitty sighed. "But I'm getting desperate. Imagine. Fifty whole years! How ancient."

Fifty whole years. I wished I could still be looking forward to that birthday.

Kitty brightened. "Maybe I could get her a gag gift. You're supposed to tease people on their decade birthdays, aren't you?"

I couldn't think of a worse thing to happen when a person reaches "that certain age." But Kitty knew her mom best. We headed for the Laugh Shack. I did my best to hide a cringe.

We found the store. Why is it that these "happy" places are always dark, with an overabundance of black lights bouncing off skull figures? How happy is that? We entered to some ghoulish prerecorded laughter that crept up my spine with anything but a fun spirit. I spied a stack of "Over the Hill" cards, walked over, and began reading: You know you're old when . . . you look into a bowl of prunes and think it's a mirror . . . Fifty is nifty . . . only if you're old enough to remember what "nifty" is . . . Talking blue bowling ball says, "Being a blue hair is better than . . . being a no-hair . . . Sad. Still, I giggled at the lines. They were so wickedly true." I put a few in my purse to share with Kitty.

Meanwhile, my friend armed herself with an "Over the Hills" shirt that showed baggy boobs crudely drawn on its front. She also grabbed a pair of "glasses" that displayed wrinkle-lined eyes to anyone walking up, but buff young men in tight swimsuits plastered on the inside of the lenses.

Note to self: good investment, those glasses.

"These are great!" said Kitty. "Mom will love 'em."

"She will?" I tried to keep my face calm. "No kindhearted side to the present?"

Kitty bit her lip. "I don't know what she would find 'kindhearted.' You have any ideas?"

I looked around. "Old Fart" stared at me from a cap stand. I shook my head. "I don't see anything here. Tell you what. Let's go have a snack and think about it."

"Sounds like a plan." Kitty paid for her stuff and we walked out.

We turned down the main hall toward the sound of clanking trays, humming voices, and lovely junk-food smells. At the food court, we stood in line for the sub shop, where I spotted someone who looked familiar. Where had I seen her before?

I couldn't see her face well, but the woman wore a black pantsuit with a white, scoop-necked shirt. Her raven hair was tied in a neat ponytail at the nape of her neck. It was her cross, though, that nudged my brain into gear.

Carla Brown, from Sandra's church, stood

in line before Kitty and me. I hadn't realized when I'd met her what great shape she was in. The jacket nipped in nicely at her waist and seemed even a smidge tight across her arms. Not an ounce of fat showed against her skintight pants. Oh, to be young again.

"I know that woman," I said to Kitty and reached out to tap Carla on the shoulder.

The line moved and she stepped toward the counter without noticing me. "Roast beef 'n' cheese," Carla said, tapping an impatient toe.

"No problem-oh, *Senorita,*" replied the server. "*Mi* sandwhich *es su* sandwhich." He wiggled his eyebrows and grinned at her playfully.

"Are you making fun of my accent?" demanded Carla. "I only order a sandwich and you are laughing at me?" The tapping toes metamorphosed into a stamped foot. Lightning fast, her hand snapped out and grabbed the server by his shirt. She pulled him into her scowling face. "You want trouble, you ferret? You want a complaint to your manager?"

"Sorry, lady," said the hapless server. "I didn't mean anything by it. I like your accent."

"Well, *Inglés* is my second language. What's your excuse?" Carla shoved the boy back. He nearly fell. She sniffed and flipped her dark pony tail off her shoulder. "Never mind. I don't have time for your crummy fast food anyway." Carla stomped off, leaving the young man open-jawed.

"Whoa," said Kitty. "You *know* her? What's her deal?"

I shook my head in disbelief and stared after Carla, who had disappeared into the mall.

Meanwhile, the boy spoke out to anyone who would listen. "I didn't intend anything by it. I mean I have lots of Hispanic friends. Dang, that doesn't sound right either." The poor kid blushed to the roots of his carrot-colored hair.

I stepped to the counter and patted his arm. "It's all right. She's probably having a bad day." I would never have guessed that the peaceful youth director I'd met a week back could be so venomous. Was she more upset than I realized over Rico's death? Had something happened at church to make her so angry?

"Sheesh," replied the sandwhich guy, then remembered his job. "Welcome to Sub-O-Mania." His blush and any hope of a smile vanished. "What would you like to order?"

CHAPTER 22

Kitty and I found seats in the parking-lot-sized hall of empty tables at the food court. Not exactly cozy, but when on a shopping mission, snack atmosphere is a low priority.

"So?" Kitty put down her food tray, sat, and leaned in.

"That was the youth director for the Catholic church off Platte Canyon and Bowles. Most Holy Saints." I mirrored Kitty's actions.

"You're kidding! Bet the kids *love* her."

"Actually, when I met Carla, she was quite friendly. I took an instant liking to her. Maybe Rico's death upset her more than I'd realized. They were colleagues, and I think they spent time together on youth missions. Carla also lost her eight-year-old son a couple of years ago in an accident. Perhaps Rico's death retriggered her grief. I'm having a hard time with all this myself, and I hardly knew the man."

"I see," said Kitty. "I'm having a hard time too. Rico's murder is awful news. I shiver every time I think of it. Do *you* believe someone from our group did it? Killed him? Killed Todd?"

I took a bite of my peanut butter cookie and spoke through the crumbs. "No," I swallowed, "not really."

Fact was, I'd been hashing over those very questions since Gabe first approached us at the library. While he might be unsure, I knew I didn't kill Rico or poor Todd, even if I had my fingerprints where they didn't belong. So the question was, who did? And why?

"Then you *do* suspect someone. Come on. Give," said Kitty. A smile played at the corner of her mouth. Minx!

"It's silly, but I keep thinking about Sandra."

"She's such a tool." My friend rolled her eyes.

"Kitty!"

"Oh, come on, Daisy. No one in the group likes her. She makes a great suspect. I think that even Sergeant Taylor has doubts about her."

"Sergeant Taylor?" The sergeant who put so many awkward questions to me at Todd's murder scene? The sergeant who accused

191

me of flirting with Gabe, while she was the one mauling him in the interview room? I scrunched my nose.

"Don't you like her, Daisy? The sergeant? I think she's great. You know, she's only a few years older than me and said I might make a good police officer, what with my interest in the law. She was even nice enough to suggest I could help her with info about our group."

"Really." I had found the good sergeant efficient and serious, but nice? Didn't quite sense that with her. And she was developing her own snitches. I hadn't considered that possibility.

Kitty nodded. "Yes. Sergeant Taylor said I have the right aptitude for police work. Cool, huh?"

"Yes, I suppose that is cool." I swallowed a sip of cola and fought the desire to say that Sergeant Taylor was not someone I trusted or wanted to know.

"But let's not focus on the police. What is it about ol' take-charge-and-pain-in-the-butt Sandra that has your attention?"

"She's unpopular at the church too." I pictured the office gossipers. "I was thinking about her reaction to the news about Rico compared to hearing about Todd. It was almost like she was two different people.

There is something uncomfortable about that woman. I have a hard time understanding her. But you can't make someone a suspect solely because you don't like them."

"I can." Kitty tapped her tooth with her small green nail. "Still, like the TV detectives say, means, motive, opportunity. Let's see. Means. Well, she's a giant and looks very strong. I bet she could've pushed Rico in the water. I don't know what happened with Todd."

I nibbled my cookie. "Bludgeoned, I'd guess."

Then there was some thumping around above me. That's the last time I heard anything outta the dead guy's apartment.

Kitty wriggled in her seat. "Ooh. That's gruesome, but I can see her doing it to Todd. She never liked him."

I swallowed another bite. "And Rico? Why him? She seemed very fond of him. What would be her motive to kill someone she so obviously admired?"

"Motive? Maybe he'd heard one too many confessions from her. Maybe she let him know that secretly she leaves her bed unmade when her husband is out of town." My young friend winked a smile at me and I burst out laughing.

"Kitty, you are incorrigible. I can't imagine Sandra leaving anything out of place, much less her bed." I laughed again.

"Yeah, but that's the fun of gossip," said Kitty. She sipped her soda. "Exaggerate the bits, and you've got a great story. Wanna be my next suspect? I need the practice for my new novel."

"Thanks, but no thanks."

"Aw, come on, Daisy. It'll be fun. Let's see . . . As a special ed teacher, you used to have to lift the wheelchair-assisted kids. That makes you strong enough."

"Assistants did that. No insurance coverage for me."

Kitty threw me a quieting glare. "And then the first time you read for our group, Rico was hugely insulting to your work. There's your motive."

"Everyone was insulting to my work." The memory still stung.

"Yeah. Your writing does kinda stink, but I think Rico was particularly cruel. I think he said you didn't belong in our group, your writing was so dreadful."

"He did not." I felt a hot flash coming on. Or was it simply heat rising up my neck? "My writing *stinks,* Kitty?"

"At the risk of understatement, let's say your room for improvement is about the size of Invesco Field." Kitty swept her gaze around the food court as if to verify the room size for my improvement plan. "Oh, don't look so sad! Everybody starts badly. You'll get there." She reached over and patted my arm.

"Thanks, I think." I felt a lump of cookie dive down my pipes unpleasantly.

Kitty didn't notice. "Where was I? Oh! You're familiar with the park behind Aspen Grove, where they found Rico's body?"

"Who on this side of town isn't?"

"There's your opportunity. *Voila.* You're the murderer."

"Let me be sure to remember you in my will, friend." I took another, more aggressive bite of my cookie.

Kitty laughed. "Come on, Daisy. It's all a tease. I'm definitely going to put a murder in my next book, especially since we're dealing with one now." Kitty grabbed her writing notebook and began scribbling. She rattled off a few ideas about killers and their motives.

I stared at my friend. "How do you do it?"

"Do what?"

"Come up with all those ideas? You're nonstop with your writing, and I struggle to get the next chapter out. Then, when I do, the group isn't very enthusiastic about my work. I'm beginning to think maybe I wasn't meant to be a writer." Maybe being alone one more night a week wouldn't be too lonely. I could watch some television shows with Georgette, after all.

Kitty worried her bottom lip, then said, "Let's face it, Daisy. You're not exactly a natural at this writing business. No one in the group likes your work." She grabbed for my arm again as I pulled away.

"No one? Perhaps I should call Sandra to resign this afternoon."

"Look, just because we don't like your work doesn't mean we don't like you. Who cares if you're not a natural? No one is. There isn't a Shakespeare born every day, you know."

"Great, I'm a likable writing flop. Let me engrave that on my headstone."

"You wouldn't want me to lie to you, would you?" Kitty splayed her palms in my direction.

I shrugged. "Actually, I would. People need affirmations to keep motivated."

Kitty straightened in her chair and gave me a measured look. "Truth? Your story doesn't seem to be going anywhere. I know you're working hard on it, but even Sandra finds it boring. And she's the queen of boring prose."

"Sandra finds *my* story boring? Sandra of the awfully perfect pair of lovers? Sandra, the uncontrolled controller?"

Kitty smiled and nodded. "But I think you make her feel good. At last there's someone in the group who's worse than she is."

I got up. "I'd better go."

Kitty reached for me again. "But I think I can help," she said. "I know the one thing your work lacks above all else."

I hesitated. "Okay. I believe in magic. One little thing and my stuff will be readable?" I sat back down.

Kitty sighed. "Conflict."

"What?"

"Conflict. You don't have any in your story. It's like eating steak without salt, curry without cumin. Your story has no spice. Your heroine, what's her name?"

"Gwendolyn."

"Ugh. I'd change that too. Too old fashioned. Anyway, Gwen needs to have goals and overcome conflict throughout. She has to have fights with people, with nature, within herself. Conflict is the set of cogs that drags the reader and the story along to the last page."

"But I don't like conflict."

Kitty blew out her breath and closed her eyes. "No one really likes conflict. But we all find it interesting. What would happen if newspapers simply said today was another great day in Littleton? Weather? Clear and bright. Stocks? Holding steady. No thefts or burlaries or —"

I couldn't resist. "Or murder?"

Kitty nodded. "Or murder."

"But I write romance."

"Even in romance, there is conflict." She shook her empty hands the way a basketball coach might at a particularly obtuse player. "The world's full of conflicting goals and motivations. They are the heart and soul of a good story. What happens when you want to follow a path one way and your friend walks another?"

I pictured my few outings with Thunder. "Crash," I said.

Kitty smiled. "Crash is right. You have conflict. Expand on that for a few more incidents and you're suddenly building a story. Look. I have an exercise for you."

I patted my pockets. "Wait. I don't have a notebook to write it down."

"Ah, conflict. You want the exercise, but you have no paper. What will you do?" Kitty at last looked satisfied with my lesson.

"I could try writing on my napkin, or do you have a sheet of paper I could use?"

"Here." She handed me a sheet from her

notebook. "Now write down these words. Ready?"

"All set. Ready for the magic." I leaned in to capture every last syllable of this sage advice.

"Conflict. Is. Good."

"That's it? Conflict is good? That's all you have to say? Where's the magic?" I felt hood-winked.

"Keep writing." Kitty was hitting her stride. She made a sweeping motion to keep me at my work. "Must. Should. Needs to. Wants."

"What in heaven's name are those?"

"Goal words. Write down as many of those as you can, then put Gwen's name at the top of a page and fill in goals for her. Doesn't matter how big or small, just give her some. Do the same for your other main characters."

"But what if Gwen wants to go shopping, and her mother's goal is to have Gwen go to a movie instead?"

"Bingo! You have conflict. By George, you've got it!" Kitty's fake English accent was pathetic, but her enthusiasm made me feel better.

I started scribbling "Okay, so conflict doesn't have to be live-or-die stuff."

"Right. We're writing romances, Daisy.

Nobody has to die."

Flashes of other group members' faces popped into my head. Lots of conflict there. I sobered. "Rico and Todd did, Kitty. Had to die. At least someone thought so."

"Daisy. That's a scary thought." Kitty stared hard at me. "Sometimes I wonder about you."

We chatted on for another twenty minutes. We talked through our notes, cookies, and drinks, but the subject always seemed to gravitate back to the murders. A subdued Kitty finally said, "I almost died once too."

"Really! What happened?"

"I was twelve and at camp." She looked into the distance to find her memory. "It was a really hot afternoon and everybody was in a cabin for quiet time. I sneaked out with one of the junior counselors and a couple of other girls. We swam out to the camp raft for sunbathing.

"After a while we got bored and started roughhousing. I lost my footing and fell in. As I fell, I choked on a mouthful of water. When I tried to swim to the surface, somebody jumped in on top of me. Then another girl jumped in, and I was pushed further down. That's almost all I remember until I woke up in the hospital a few hours later. That and the panic of searching for a way to breathe."

"Oh, my stars!" I clasped my throat. "How frightening for you."

"Oh, I was okay. I hardly knew what happened. Now my mom, *she* was frightened. And angry."

"What did she do?"

"Do? To me? Nothing but hug and kiss me until I called her gay. But, boy, I felt for Mrs. Patterson."

"Mrs. Patterson?"

"The head of our camp." Kitty twinkled at me in a most mischievous way. "I come across as a dynamo to most of my friends, but I'm nothing compared to Mom. I thought she was going to tear Mrs. P. limb from limb. Mom was a hurricane!"

I laughed. "I guess you'd call that conflict all right."

Kitty smiled. "You're catching on."

I thought of Colby Stanton, then of my Rose. "I'd guess a mother's protective love is very powerful stuff." Kitty nodded. I continued. "If this were my fiftieth, I think I'd want to share special memories with you. Here's an idea for your mom's present. Let's go to that engraving store and buy your mom a picture frame. You can put in a favorite photo of you two."

"That's perfect!" Kitty stood, gathering

her stuff.

I was about to retrieve my purse from the floor, when a man in a blue rent-a-cop uniform approached us. "Excuse me, madam," he said to me.

"Yes?" I glanced from him to a pimple-faced girl at his side, who scowled in my direction.

"It's her," said the girl pointing. "She's the thief!"

"Thief? I haven't stolen anything," I said.

"Look!" said Pizza Cheeks. She pointed to the floor. There stood my purse, and from the outside pocket jutted three or four white envelopes. Then I remembered Shabby was the kid behind the counter in the gag shop.

"Oh! I must've forgotten those. I was going to show them to my companion here." I looked toward Kitty, who stared at me incredulously. "I'm so sorry. I'd be happy to pay for them."

The security guard leaned down and retrieved my purse. He had on rubber gloves, for goodness sake.

"That's what you're supposed to do *before* you leave a store, madam. Follow me," he ordered.

"Daisy," called Kitty as I was being escorted away, "can I do anything?"

"Call Gabe Caerphilly!" I yelled back. "This is *not* good conflict!"

CHAPTER 23

The muscle at the back of Gabe's jaw danced an angry rhythm. I wondered if he practiced that tough-guy look in his mirror. Very effective. But as I was witnessing it from the passenger side of Gabe's car, it wasn't at all pleasant. I shivered.

He'd rescued me from the security team at the mall and had driven me home without a word. We sat parked outside of my house. I wanted to be anywhere else but here.

"Thanks for the ride," I ventured.

Silence.

"I truly am sorry for your inconvenience," I tried again.

His thumb tapped angrily on the steering wheel. He stared straight ahead.

"Will you say hi to Ginny for —"

"Zip it, Daisy!" Gabe turned and glared at me. "Leave my daughter out of this."

I felt as if I'd been slapped. My breath caught in my throat. "Gabe, don't be so angry. It was a small misunderstanding, that's all."

"I am not angry. I simply don't want my daughter associating with you for a while."

"Yes, you are angry, and you're being unfair. I feel awful —"

"As you should."

I could almost hear my Art speaking. He was quite as censorious as this sometimes. Art would listen to my woes and assume that somehow I blew the incident out of proportion or that it was my fault. Damn him! And damn Gabe too.

"I didn't do anything wrong." I could hear my voice taking on a whine.

"Didn't — wrong! — Since I met you last week, you've been doing nothing *but* wrong!"

Ouch. I rubbed my cheek. Tears welled up unbidden. I hate crying when I'm mad.

"That's an awful thing to say. How dare you!" I wasn't going to put up with this.

"How dare I? Me? Now you listen. First you're mixed up in some stupid group called, of all things, Hugs 'N' Kisses." He held up his hand as if to tick off my many shortcomings. "Romance writing, my eye. One of your group *murdered* Rico Sanchez. Real romantic, don't you think?"

I puffed up my courage. "I think you have

it wrong, Gabe. No one from the group committed that horrid murder. It will work out. You'll see."

Gabe shook his head and ran his fingers through his hair. "Daisy, can't you understand how serious this is?"

"I understand, but most murders, Lieutenant, are conducted by men. We have no men left in our group."

"You got that from Kitty. And don't be ridiculous. Plenty of murders are committed by women. Your group is full of strange women, none of whom I would trust."

Ooh! That wasn't fair.

Gabe's face was turning red, but he continued, on finger two. "Then, at Todd Stevens' place you left *your* fingerprints all over."

"Who else's fingerprints would I leave?"

"Don't get insolent with me, madam. Todd is dead too. Can you explain that? You know about the notes at the scenes of the crimes . . . and no, no. Don't tell me I forgot I told you about them. I never mentioned them."

"But you did tell me! At the —"

"I did not! And now" — he threw up both hands — "now you're caught shoplifting. All this may be a 'simple misunderstanding' to you, but you're going to land in jail for a long time if you're not careful."

Perry Mason couldn't have built a better case against me. Gabe was right, and it made me *really* mad.

"I hate you!" I started crying. Damn, damn, damn! I grabbed the door handle and shoved. It flung wide, and I fell out. I didn't care that my skirt flew up over my butt. I stood up and brushed it down again. "You're a despicable Cretin and I hate you, hate you, *hate you*!"

Gabe got out of his side of the car. His was a much more graceful effort, and I despised him the more for it.

"Hate all you want, but you're not rid of me, Daisy Arthur. Remember, *you're* the prime suspect in a murder case, and I won't let you off the hook just because you cry so well. I should have let them put you in jail for shoplifting. At least then the rest of your group would be safe from you!"

"Oh, go away, you awful man!" I reached into the still open passenger door for my purse and bumped my head on the door rim. Blood spurted immediately from my eyebrow. I cried harder and fell down again.

My head swam from the pain of the cut, the headache from crying, and the broken feeling in my heart. I heard the sounds of my neighborhood and felt embarrassed to

207

be providing such a scene. Some child down the street was wailing, cars rumbled out on the main road, a dog barked, and a drumming pounded in my noggin.

Gabe reached my side instantly. Wouldn't you know, he was the kind of man who carried cloth handkerchiefs in his pocket. He held the soft material to my eyebrow and gently tilted my head back. I cried on.

Gabe's face switched from rage to worry in an instant. "Daisy! Are you okay?"

"T-to th-think I was attracted to you," I moaned. "To think all I wan-wanted was to be your —"

"Wait! You're attracted — to *me*?" Shock registered in those periwinkle eyes so close to my face. His hand seemed almost to tremble as he turned his attention to my cut. I lay still in those wonderfully capable arms. If I were braver, I might even have snuggled into his warm chest. If this were in one of my novels, surely his kiss would be coming any moment. A kiss that would assuredly make everything all better. I waited and hoped.

Woof! Woof! Woof!

A deep bark preceded the feeling that both Gabe and I were flying totally off balance. Suddenly all I could see was sky. Then I heard Gabe yelling somewhere near me.

"Off! Off, you brute! Oww! Off, damn it!"

I rolled over to see Chip come running up. "Thunder!" He grabbed his fiercely growling dog away from Gabe. "Sit!" he commanded.

Thunder did as instructed but still growled at my policeman.

"Keep that dog under control. I could have him put down for that." Gabe stood up and rubbed the arm that Thunder had been mouthing a moment before.

"You were physically molesting my neighbor," replied Chip. He crossed his arms and stared coolly up at Gabe. "You're lucky I didn't give my dog the kill command."

Kill command? Thunder hardly knew how to sit and heel. *Kill?* Gabe backed off a step just the same. Wow.

"It's all right, Chip," I said. "Gabe is a police officer. Gabe, my neighbor and reporter for the *Post,* Chip McPherson"

The two men nodded. Thunder's tail began to wag. Kill. Not sure about that one.

Gabe brushed off his pants. "If that mutt really can kill, I don't think you should ask Daisy to walk him for you so much. She can't control him."

"I can too control him!" I allowed my chin to drop open. Gabe had managed to deeply entrench himself on my loathe-list. Both men turned to look at me. They might as well have shouted a sarcastic "yeah, right" in unison.

"Thunder, come!" I said, to prove my point. The silly mutt wagged his tail but made no other effort to respond to me.

Gabe turned to Chip. "And she leaves him in cars with windows rolled up."

Add *tattletale* to Gabe's infinite list of sins.

Chip looked at me in disbelief.

"Only once, and for just a couple of minutes," I said to Chip before throwing a glare at Gabe. The two of them shook their heads in some male-bonding ritual against all useless women.

I felt a deep rage against the obtuse feelings of the opposite sex well up within me.

"Oh, go home. Both of you." I didn't want to start accidentally crying again.

"We're not done, Daisy." Gabe shot me an earnest look before heading to his car.

I turned on my heel to ignore the law officer and started walking toward my house. Men! Maybe I should stop writing romances.

A scrawny arm wrapped itself around my shoulder. Chip had me on one side, and Thunder trotted next to me on the other. Not quite Gabe, but it still felt great.

"There, there, Ms. D. It'll be okay."

"Chip, I thought Gabe was the one for me. He really is terrific most of the time." I sniffed, tears threatening to tumble down again. "Can I have a hug?" I slumped against my reporter friend.

Chip let me stand there for a few seconds before he spoke. "What's his favorite color?" Chip pulled my chin up.

"Color? I don't know."

"What books does he read?"

"We haven't explored . . . that is, I'm not sure —"

"It sounds to me, Ms. D., that you're thoroughly infatuated with this Gabe guy but nothing more." Chip stared at me blandly. Then he winked.

"*Touché,* my friend." I gave him a watery smile and he squeezed my shoulder.

"Don't worry. There's lots of good guys out there. We'll find you one."

"I'm not desperate, Chip," I said, but grinned in the warmth of our emerging friendship. Chip and Thunder and me.

Internal memo: Introduce Chip to Kitty sometime. There may be gold there.

CHAPTER 24

Kitty called to re-invite me to her party as well as to prod for news of my shoplifting adventure.

"It'll be great fun, Stoolie," said Kitty, after I gave her all the details. "Girls' night in. We'll watch chick-flicks and eat ice cream sundaes. All nice, safe, and alibi-riddled for the weekend. I won't let anyone else die on my watch."

I couldn't help but get enthusiastic when Kitty was up to one of her plans. "Who else will be coming, my friend?"

"Toni and Eleanor both said they would be interested. Sandra was noncommittal. And my roommate will be there."

Friday didn't seem like the best night for a "girls' night in," but starting the weekend with friends was a lot better than a micro-wave meal with Georgette and television reruns by myself. Plus, with Rico and now Todd no longer a part of our group, we couldn't exactly have a First Friday Pot Luck. "Count me in," I said. "What do you want me to bring?"

Kitty said she'd handle the food, then added, "I'm hoping if this works out, we can have the party move from house to house and maybe meet once a month or so."

Socializing once a month actually sounded good to me, so here I was, knocking on Kitty's apartment door. She opened on my fourth rap.

"Hey, Daisy. Glad you could come."

Kitty swept an arm wide to welcome me in. "You're first to arrive. Make yourself at home while I check the stuffed mushrooms in the oven."

"You shouldn't have gone to such trouble. I thought we were going to order pizza or something simple like that."

"No biggie. I love to cook. Used to do it with my mom all the time." She waved me into her living room. "Sit. Sit. I'll be out in a jiffy."

The apartment smelled as I imagined home would in a Norman Rockwell painting. Savory scents emanated from the kitchen, and a lit, scented candle sat on the coffee table. There were small bowls of munchies set out. Looked like Kitty was planning a real party.

A couple of minutes later, a young woman came strolling out from one of the two bedrooms in her bathrobe, pulling a cell phone from her ear. "Kitty. Woman here says — oh! Sorry. You must be one of the Friday night women. I'm Carol, the room-mate."

I smiled. "Hi. She's in the kitchen."

"Thanks." Carol strolled that way, talking as she went. "Somebody named Toni's on the phone. Can't come." She pressed through the kitchen door and disappeared.

What a shame. I liked Toni. I wasn't really looking forward to either Sandra or Elea-nor. Still, Kitty was a vivacious hostess. She'd keep the party going.

An hour later, Sandra was a no-show and Eleanor was sitting with inordinate formal-ity on Kitty's lounge chair, a napkin placed delicately in her lap. Only one mushroom off her plate had a bite out of it. Kitty, Carol, and I stretched on the floor with throw pillows.

Kitty grabbed her tray of food and offered us all more.

Eleanor shook her head. "On a low-carb diet," she said. "Have to watch the weight, you know."

Killjoy.

Carol heaved a sigh. "Hate to leave such a

lively do, but there's a bar with my name on it and some cute guy sitting there waiting for me." She pulled herself up.

"Don't go." Kitty and I cried together. Carol gave us a feel-sorry-for-you smile.

"We have movies," enticed Kitty. "*Emma* and *Sleepless in Seattle.*"

Carol shook her head. "You can call this writing research, but I call it needing a life. *Ciao,* babes." She grabbed a coat off the hooks in the front hall, waved bye, and was gone.

Eleanor made as if to leave as well. "Research. That reminds me. I have to get some done before meeting with my agent on Monday."

Kitty looked disappointed. I felt desperate to help out. I poured a little wine in all our glasses. "Eleanor," I said, "before you go, Kitty mentioned that I might have a slight problem or two with my writing?"

Eleanor snorted. In fact, she produced the kind of scornful sound that normally drives people nuts. I grinned through gritted teeth as Eleanor formed her response.

"Daisy, *slight* and *problem* don't go together where your writing is concerned. I wouldn't know where to begin with you."

"Oh," I said. "Is it — am I that bad?"

Both Eleanor and Kitty burst out laughing. Perhaps it was only because this had been the first opportunity to laugh since Eleanor arrived at the party, but I still felt a bit taken aback as they overdid the enthusiasm bit.

Kitty turned to me. "Have you ever had an English course in your life?" Kitty might be smart, but she could still use a lesson or two in tact.

Eleanor joined in. "Have you any notion of the concepts *beginning, middle,* and *end?*"

I felt like Bambi in the hunter's scope. "I thought it would be fun to be a published author."

Kitty stared at me with large eyes and a gaping jaw. Eleanor put her hands on her hips and glared at me. "Fun?" she said. "*Fun?* Writing is fucking hard work! You pound out thousands of words only to throw half of them away. You struggle for plot and character ideas twenty-four-seven. You have something brilliant strike you at two in the morning and don't have a notepad handy, so it's lost."

Guess I'd been naive about being a writer. Eleanor shook her head and a finger at me.

"You hole up in some writing closet and pray for inspiration that never comes. Then, when you're published, with a royalty that pays all of half the month's electric bill, they want you to go and do the whole thing all over again."

"Gosh, I didn't know." I was truly abashed.

Eleanor was on a roll. "Then they parade you from bookstore to bookstore where you're supposed to say, 'It just came to me and I jotted down this sweet little ol' story. Gosh, I hope you like it.' Daisy, writing is not fun. It's a profession and a compulsion."

I had been in the audience for a few authors' signings, and Eleanor was right. Authors tended to make light of their creative processes as they pushed three-, four-, or five-hundred-page books. The books only took me a few days to read, so I never imagined how long they took to write.

Eleanor continued. "Do you really want to be an author or do you want to come to our writing group and pretend that someday your great American novel will be on everyone's bookshelf?"

I bit my lip and murmured a reply.

Eleanor hovered over me. "What?"

"I said, I want to be an author."

"Do you want to be published or do you want to write?" Eleanor was relentless.

"I want to write. I want to write well."

"Okay, then." She nodded as if coming to

a decision, then rolled up her sleeves. "Let's get to work."

Eleanor's leadership made Sandra's look weak and impotent. Gone was the wispy voice she used on Tuesday nights. She commanded another glass of wine and a notepad from Kitty, who happily complied. We blew out the candle and shoved any delicate nibbles aside.

Eleanor started pacing and pointed at me again. "Now you," she said, "you take notes. This is probably a hopeless cause, but I will try to start you in the rudiments of creative writing."

Kitty piped in. "What about me? Will you help me too?"

Eleanor smiled at her. "Honey, in a few years I'm going to be asking that question of you."

For another two hours and three bottles of Yellow Tail wine, I was plied with more thoughts on writing than aspens have leaves. Inciting incidents, ramping up tension, plot points, attributions, cutting fat all danced through my mind and got scribbled down as both Eleanor and Kitty took me in hand to make me a writer. Or at least, a tad more writing-literate.

Eleanor swigged the last of her fifth glass of wine. "Oh, yeah, and don't forget to keep files on each of your main characters."

She had a slight slur in her voice. Diet forgotten, Eleanor had scarfed up all her hors d'oeuvres and one of the bowls of Chex Mix Kitty put out at the beginning. "Man, writing makes me hungry. Who's up for pizza?"

Kitty chimed in. "It's Friday night, oh Lawdy, Mama, I'm feelin' right!" She had Elton John's spirit if not quite his words.

I chipped in. "I've got a cellulite phone. We could ask for a no-carb, no-fat, no-taste pizza or keep it simple. Ask for the works."

"Works!" said Eleanor, wine glass refilled again.

"Works for me!" said Kitty, who chortled over nothing particularly funny.

By the time our pizza arrived, I had enough sheets filled to submit a full book. *How To Write Stuff* by Daisy Arthur. Thoughts were scribbled in from all directions. Kitty reached over to jot things with her purple gel pen, and Eleanor dashed out words and diagrams in black from another side of the table. My notes turned the dot from any stray "i" into a flower.

I gave my new best friends a dizzy smile. "Gosh, Eleanor. I don't know how to thank you. You too, Kitty."

Eleanor frowned at me through whatever

fog rolled in on her brain. "Hey. Have to ask. Why do you talk like that?"

"Like wh-what?"

"Like you're some sort of kid. 'Golly gee' and all that crap."

"I don't like to swear."

"How come? I think it fucking well feels great." Eleanor rattled off enough profanity to make the devil blush.

"I jus' want to live a G-rated lifestyle. I don't like things scary and — conflicty — and all like that. Plus, I used to be a special needs teacher. We teachers never swear, don't you know?"

Eleanor snarled. "Oh, get a backbone. Are you a wimp or something?"

"Yep. I'm a wimp, and I like it that way."

Kitty chimed in. "How are you going to write r-real—istically with that attitude?"

I smiled at her. "I have a pretty Kitty — oops — a Kitty witty — memory. I jus' write down what other people do."

"Careful," said Eleanor. "Somebody will accuse you —"

"Of what?" I burped. " 'Scuse me."

"Yeah. Of what?" Kitty asked.

"Pagerism," said Eleanor. She nodded her with certainty.

I needed help with that. "Pagerism? Goofing around with a Senate page?"

Eleanor shook her head at us. "No. You know." She rubbed her forehead. "Rico? He was a slimy shit. 'Cused me of pagerizing."

"No!" Kitty and I gasped in unison.

"Yep." Eleanor put her finger to her lips and blew a long *shh.* "Shithead said I stole the story he gave me to edit. I only took a teensy-weensy bit."

"What did you take?" Kitty asked.

"First four lines of a suspense he was writing." Eleanor giggled. "Only decent writing he's ever done. He was so mad when *Dark Night in Houston* came out. I thought he was going to kill me." She giggled again.

"Whoa. What did he do?" I asked.

"Said I owed him. Started fingering where he shouldn't. 'Can't do that,' I said. 'You're a priest,' I said. He said I was fucking ugly anyway. Then he said he'd tell if I didn't make my agent look at his next book. Dickhead. Didn't you notice? He was no priest. He was a walking erection."

Kitty and I laughed.

"I don't know about his writing, but I agree that Rico was a creeper," said Kitty. She took a big bite of her pizza, so Eleanor and I had to prompt her for more information.

"Well, I'm embarrassed to say. See, I went to the Florida coast for spring break during my undergrad. Got drunk — kinda like tonight — drunk."

"Then what happened?" I nudged Eleanor, who nodded.

"Well, I sorta did the 'Girls-Gone-Wild' thing." She tittered. "Bad Kitty, kitty. Anyway, somebody posted my pictures on the Internet. Oops."

Eleanor leaned in. "Okay. Where does Rico fit into this?"

"Creeper Rico found 'em on some porn site. What's a priest doing on a porn site?"

I hugged my petite friend. "Oh, Kitty. That's awful."

"Nooo. What's awful is job hunting. Potential employers find those pics, and I get one of two things." She held up her fingers to count. "One: 'Don't-call-us.' Two: Best job description ever with all the benefits. *They* get the benefits."

"What a fucking lousy break." Eleanor sipped her wine.

"Oh, well," said Kitty, "saves me from being the overachiever I was in high school. Working bars instead of taking the bar is okay by me. And I took tonight off to be here."

"But Rico finding the pictures . . ." I said.

"Was like Employer Number Two. Told him I'd chop up his balls in my Vitamix if he ever came near me. I could do it too. Just to be safe, though, I stayed away from Shithead Rico as much as possible after that."

"No offense, Kitty," said Eleanor, "but you're practically a goddamn midget. How could you beat up Rico?"

Kitty smiled. "See all those martial arts awards?"

She pointed to a wall filled with trophies and ribbons. "They aren't my roommate's, don't you know."

CHAPTER 25

I spent the weekend nursing my hangover from Friday's soiree and putting out Halloween decorations. Pre-lit pumkins danced across my front porch, a witch found herself and her flying broomstick crashed into my ash tree, and candy corn tumbled happily into a glass bowl at my kitchen table. As I reached in for the first handful of the season, I knew I would have to buy another bag before Halloween. Sorry, teeth.

I stretched down into my Halloween storage box once more, then recoiled. At the bottom of the box a ghost stared up at me with a glass-eyed grin. I normally hung Casper on my front door. Somehow, this season, it didn't seem right. Funny, I hardly ever thought about what a ghost was until all this business with Rico and Todd. I closed the lid on the casket-shaped container with more enthusiasm than was necessary and shivered. Was that someone walking over my grave?

Luckily, Chip came over Sunday afternoon and brought a sumptuous piece of beef. I roasted it along with a few veggies while he raked away the leaves in my yard. We shared dinner, mostly because his latest lover, Tina, was busy at a friend's house.

Chip sighed in frustration. "Tina doesn't read anything much but the sports pages. I thought that was a good thing until I discovered she reads only to hunt down who's single among the Broncos players. Good tip on that interest thing, Ms. D. I'm not sure she's the one for me, but we can have fun for a while."

I shook my head in feigned concern. "So you think she's just 'horsing' around with you?"

"Ugh, Ms. D.! Broncos. Horsing. You have to stop those putrid puns." Still, he laughed.

We spent a quiet evening together playing Scrabble. Sometime between debates over suspect words and a bunch of laughter, I realized that I was beginning to like my young friend's company. How did that happen?

Now, a couple of days later, I revisited the writing notes I took at Kitty's. Unfortunately, between progressively illegible writing and the wine spills, I had a hard time deciphering much of anything. My Tuesday afternoon was eaten up by retyping and sorting through the thoughts I remembered as being brilliant at the time but which disappeared with the light of sobriety. What had Eleanor said about losing thoughts at two in the morning?

I looked up from my work. Five twenty-five, and I hadn't made dinner yet. I fought off the panic of being late. Critiques started right at six. Peanut butter and jelly would have to do for dinner, but if I hurried, I'd only be a couple of minutes late. I raced to find presentable clothes and make my sandwich.

Forty minutes later I walked into the library and over to my group. Something was different. I couldn't quite put my finger on what was odd, other than that no one smiled or chatted and a strange young man sat with us.

"Sorry I'm late," I said, hoping to sound as breezy as Eleanor when she did something outrageous. I grinned in hopes I'd be forgiven quickly.

Sandra looked up and nodded her acknowledgment. Normally, I focus on Kitty's various fashion statements, but tonight my eyes zeroed in on an excessively large wooden cross that hung around Sandra's neck more like a political statement than any piece of jewelry. "Glad you could make it, Daisy. We were just talking about you."

"Me? Why me?" I tore my eyes away from the party-store reject hanging on Sandra.

Kitty spoke up. "Well, I couldn't get hold of you today, buddy." She emphasized the word *buddy,* and I slapped my forehead.

"Goodness, Kitty, I'm sorry I forgot to call you. I was typing up notes on writing, and I guess the battery on my phone must have died." Bad choice of words. I flinched.

Toni spoke up. "Daisy, this is my grandson, Jamie. He's come home from college for a few days to be with me."

Home from college in the middle of a semester? Strange. Kept that thought to myself as Jamie and I shook hands.

"Shall we start our readings?" said Sandra. "Toni, you were here first. Ready?"

Toni pulled out her copies and began handing them around. Then I figured out what was different. "Hey," I said. "How come everyone's so spread out? We won't be able to hear each other. Let's scooch in."

No one made a move. People acted as if they hadn't heard me. I moved my chair toward Toni on one side, and Kitty on the other.

Toni pushed her chair back a few inches.

Odd. Kitty was busy fishing in her writing bag for something. I noticed she didn't have her ever-present copy of *Writing Magic* with her. Some magazine with a martial arts cover poked out instead.

Toni read her night's submission. The story was about a good Italian girl who was thinking about marrying a Mafia boss. Made for a disturbing romance but a great story. I was hooked.

Sandra of the cross gave her review first. "Toni, splendid story, but I'm wondering why, especially with Maria and Gino so set to marry, you haven't brought in a good priest character. I think the Catholic church is a very important part of the culture."

Toni scowled and stared at Sandra's cross. "I don't want a goddamn priest in my story."

Sandra's mouth formed an "O". "I don't think you mean that, dear."

Toni stretched taller in her seat. "Sandra, I'm well past the age of not saying precisely what I mean. To me, priests are charlatans, and the church hides them from prosecution. I'd have to guess our precious Rico probably asked for the trouble he got. If I put a priest in my story, I'd have the Mafia be sure to bump him off."

Jamie laid a hand over his grandmother's

arm protectively. "My uncle Sal was molested by one of those creeps in robes when the family lived in Dallas. Even the diocese covered up the charges. We haven't been to church since."

I felt for Toni. Her son, Sal, had been hurt so badly that her faith, at least in her church, was stolen away too. I had to ask. "So nothing happened to the priest? And your son?"

"My son," said Toni, a tear rolling down her cheek. "My son shot himself."

There was a communal gasp, then silence. How horrid for Toni. No wonder she didn't like priests.

I fumbled for words. "Toni, I'm so sorry for your loss."

Jamie piped up. "Oh, he didn't die. Just lost a finger. Thank the fates for Uncle Sal's bad aim. Always was a bit clumsy."

"What happened to the priest?" I expected to hear that he at least apologized or was sent for counseling.

Jamie spoke up again. "Let's say my dad had friends, and that priest took a well-deserved, permanent vacation." Jamie's smirk held no humor as he stared at each one of us in turn.

I felt a chill run down my spine.

"Jamie, boy, don't you tell stories," said

Grandma Toni. "The priest was sent to a small parish outside the country, where most of the parishioners were of retirement age. It's simply that I've read enough pedophile stories since Sal's problems that I don't care to place my faith in the church anymore."

Eleanor shifted in her seat and her handbag fell to the floor. A heavy clunk sound followed. She jumped nervously, staring at the purse as if it were alive.

"Eleanor, you okay?" I asked.

"Fine, Daisy. Fine." She dove down and fiddled in her bag.

"What do you have there?" I said.

"Nothing," said Eleanor, reemerging. Her rosy face said otherwise, and the something was something big. I continued to look at my new friend. She hung her head.

Everyone's attention switched to Eleanor.

She looked back up and jutted out her chin. "Okay, okay. So I have a license. I'm not doing anything wrong. I only want to protect myself." She pulled out a black, shiny item, and we all gasped again.

Jamie jumped up. "Down, Grannie. Gun!" He made a human shield in front of Toni, who had let out a small squeal. Kitty's chair scraped noisily as she pushed back. She jumped into a made-for-movie martial arts pose.

Sandra screamed and crossed herself, mumbling frenetic Hail Marys.

I clasped a hand over my heart. Ms. Goodwin, the librarian, came running. "Is everything — Oh, my, no!"

I reached for Ms. Goodwin. "It's all right, Ms. Goodwin. Eleanor has a license for that. Eleanor, dear" — I put on my best school-teacher-with-hysterical-student voice — "Eleanor, let's put that thing away."

As Eleanor complied, Ms. Goodwin leveled a glare at all of us. "For the past three weeks I have had to deal with nervous patrons, police interruptions, and this group's loud and obnoxious behavior. Now, a gun in my library? A *gun*? You're no longer welcome here. Get out. Get out now or I'm calling the police!"

Sandra spoke up. "Ms. Goodwin, now, now. We're all a bit upset at present. Our group will most certainly go home for the evening, but let's you and I go talk about this."

Ms. Goodwin looked skeptical, but allowed Sandra to lead her back to the library offices for a chat.

The rest of us packed up our things and left, no one looking at each other. As Sandra was occupied with Ms. Goodwin, Eleanor teamed up with Kitty for the walk to the parking lot. Toni held on to Jamie's arm, and for the first time, I really saw the age in my writing associate. What a harrowing night for us all.

Kitty turned toward me. "You coming, Daisy? I think Sandra will be all right with Ms. Goodwin."

"Thanks Kitty. I'm heading straight home in a minute. You and Eleanor go ahead. I'll be all right. There's still a little light left."

I looked around at the remains of our meeting and sighed. For the first time, our group hadn't reset the furniture or picked up after ourselves. Remembering the angst of our librarian, I straightened up a bit, then headed out the door.

Outside, a light rain fell. I heaved another sigh and dropped my writing bag to the ground, bending to search it for my collapsible umbrella.

A man's voice made me jump as I snatched up my things.

The voice was low and soft. "You all right?"

I swirled around to see Gabe standing no more than three feet from me.

"Gabe! What are you doing here?" Was

the relief I felt obvious? Even though we didn't part on the best of terms last time we met, I suddenly felt completely safe.

"I came to make sure you got home all right. You're out of your meeting early, aren't you?"

I glanced at my watch. Our meeting, normally three hours long, hadn't lasted more than forty-five minutes tonight. I suddenly felt defeated and worn. I dropped my writing bag again, and looked up to Gabe.

"Can I have a hug?" I said.

He opened his arms, and I stepped into a more secure world.

After a few seconds Gabe spoke. "Daisy. What's wrong? Can I help?"

"Yes, you can help. You can stop making all my writing friends your murder suspects. Everybody is completely on edge. Eleanor even brought a gun with her for protection tonight. Toni brought her Mafia-infatuated grandson, and Sandra brought a cross big enough to send vampires running across the world."

Gabe chuckled. "You do have some colorful friends. What about you and Kitty?"

"Kitty is apparently polishing up her martial arts skills."

"And you?"

"Me? I guess I'm stupid. I still don't

believe anyone from our group is a killer. Plus, I trust that you're going to find out who's to blame soon. You *are* looking into other suspects, aren't you, Gabe? Did you find that Loathsome Les guy?"

The police lieutenant peered down into my eyes. His arms around me felt so strong and warm. I could trust this man forever.

"Loathsome Les moved to Minneapolis three months ago. I'm always open to whatever possibilities exist, Daisy, but your friends, as you call them, are legitimate suspects. Anyone who brought a weapon tonight could've easily planned to use it for something other than defense. Father Sanchez and Todd Stevens weren't suicides, my girl. I want you to be very careful with these writers of yours."

Did Gabe realize he'd called me *his* girl? Inside my spirit smiled.

"Be careful? Me? *I* could be the killer, for all you know. 'You're the prime suspect in a murder case, and I'm not going to let you off the hook' is what you said. You know what a despicable creature I am."

A slight breeze caught me by surprise. I shivered with the creepy feeling that someone was walking over my grave.

"I'm sorry," said Gabe. "I don't know what came over me last week. I didn't know that you, well, that you . . ."

"That I liked you? That I was attracted to your stupid blue eyes and trim figure? That I thought being invited to dinner was a date? How boneheaded of me. Well, there's more to relationship-making than that, isn't there?"

Gabe looked at me with such sweet sadness, I wanted to melt. He took my hand. "Yes, Daisy. There is." He picked up my writing bag with his other hand, and we walked toward my car in silence.

As we neared my sweet Versa, Gabe said, "Suspect or no, my friend, try to keep away from that group." He looked around the parking lot as if in search of group members. Patrons of the library formed ghostly shapes heading back and forth amongst the cars and trees that bordered the place.

"I do see what you mean, Gabe. But still —"

"No *buts* about it, Daisy. I want you to be careful." He put down my sack and reached into his pocket for a small canister. "Here."

"What's that?"

"Pepper spray. It won't hurt anyone permanently, but you could use it to get away in case of emergency."

"No thanks, Gabe. It's very thoughtful of you, but I can't carry this around." I pushed the canister back toward him.

He looked exasperated. "Do you *want* to become a victim, Daisy?"

"No, but if I carry something like this, that's exactly what I will be."

"I don't get it. Why not use this? It could save your life."

"Gabe, my age makes paranoia attack me constantly. Who's at the door? Am I going to get ripped off by phone solicitors? What if my identity's been stolen? If I give in to it, I'll soon find myself agoraphobic. I don't want that. I want to believe in the goodness of people. We may have our problems and bad behaviors as a species, but over all, people are good." Even angels occasionally, according to Father John.

"My work would argue differently." He put on a stern face. "I have to assume everyone is bad, only disciplined enough to follow the absolute rules laid out for them by the law."

"How sad for you." I reached up and touched his cheek.

He looked at me for a long moment, then smiled. "Daisy, you are one special woman."

Gabe took the keys from my hand and unlocked the car door for me. If nothing else, I would always love his gentlemanly ways.

But, I was a doggone suspect, and he, a police officer. Fate can be such a cruel jester sometimes. I stepped into my car, started the engine, and flipped on the wipers.

"Maybe, when this murder thing is over," I said through my open window. Then I flipped back off the wipers. Someone had put a stupid flyer there. "Gabe, could you? —" I pointed to my windshield.

"Yeah, when this is over." He reached for the paper. It fairly crumbled apart from the rain. One advertising dollar wasted. Gabe's brow furrowed.

"I think it was a personal note," he said. "Newsprint. Teacher paper? The writing's bled from the rain. I can barely make out a few words. 'Stop' — something — somebody's 'work'? — 'Else' —" He shook his head. "Can't read any more."

"What the heck does that mean?" I asked, annoyed. "Here, let me see."

"I don't think you want to. There's a squished spider all over it. Black widow, I think."

"Eew!"

"And I think this means your life has probably just been threatened." A frown knitted Gabe's brow as he gazed at me, and I felt another walking-over-your-grave chill go down my spine.

Right then, Sandra stepped over. "Daisy, I'm glad I caught you. Hello, Officer Caerphilly."

"Sandra," I said, "how'd it go with Ms. Goodwin?"

Sandra smiled like the kid who'd hoodwinked her teacher out of a hall pass on test day. "She was quite upset to begin with, but I have a certain persuasive ability. We can come back anytime."

Gabe made a disgruntled sound nearby. Guess that wasn't the best news for the police.

"That's great!" I said.

"I'm heading to Pete's Pub for a nightcap. Join me?" said Sandra. She smiled again. I didn't remember Sandra as being a particularly smiley kind of person, but she should've been. She looked so much better with that softened look. Not half so scary.

Gabe cleared his throat. "I'd better be going. Daisy, remember what I told you. Be careful." He turned to Sandra and nodded like a Wild West sheriff. "Ms. Martin." He moved away into the dark.

I turned back to Sandra. "Sure. Pete's sounds fun." I shrugged. I knew Gabe had warned me, but what could happen at a bar? Would Sandra attack me with that ridiculous cross of hers? "See you there." No way was I going to get caught in another "errand run" with Sandra. See, Gabe? I was being careful.

If Sandra was offended that I didn't invite her to ride with me, she didn't show it. I waited for her to get in her car, and we drove off. A small voice in my head whispered to be careful. Gabe's face floated into my imagination. I guessed only my heart was at risk.

CHAPTER 26

We walked into Pete's, and the hostess trotted straight up to us. "Hi, Sandra. Eating at the bar?" The young woman flashed a comfortable smile, almost as if we had been expected.

Sandra returned the gesture. "Hi, Shelly. Yes. We'll find our own way." We headed toward a booth in the back corner. As we passed, the bartender stopped wiping a glass he was working on long enough to wave. "Hi, Sandra. The usual?" She nodded and said a quick "Hello, Ted," then kept walking.

Gosh, how did these folks know my group leader so well? As we sat, Sandra said, "I come here after our library meetings occasionally. Philip works late a lot, so I stop on my way home. Quick unwind. You know, good for sleeping."

Sounded logical to me. I settled into our booth.

Almost instantly two glasses of water arrived, courtesy of the bartender, Ted. I took a big gulp and realized too late that my glass didn't precisely contain water.

Sandra laughed at the choking fit I was thrown into. She downed her drink and waved back toward the bar. Ted stepped over again.

Sandra smiled. She'd sure done a lot of smiling this evening. "I don't think my friend is up for vodka tonight. I'll have another, but she'll have . . ." She paused and looked at me.

"Water," I choked out.

"Water," repeated Ted. He and Sandra shared a conspiratorial roll of eyes before he disappeared toward the bar.

Suddenly, our casual stop-in after group didn't feel quite right. I decided immediately that I wanted to go home. I hardly drank a lot anyway, and Sandra's multiple personalities were becoming harder and harder to keep straight. "I think I should go, Sandra."

"No, you're okay. Stay for one quick drink." She reached across with a look that implied there was more to her invitation than I was aware of.

"I don't think I should."

"It's not like you're a kid with a bedtime,"

she interrupted.

"No, but I do need to get some sleep."

"Tell you what. Have a snack with me, and then we'll call it quits." There was that persuasive attitude coming out. No wonder Ms. Goodwin had relented.

We ordered some pot stickers and potato skins to munch on, and Sandra had another vodka.

Eventually, the conversation meandered to the events of the past couple of weeks. Sandra put down her drink and said, "So, Daisy, who do you think murdered our friends?"

"I don't know." I shook my head. Didn't want to mention that she was highest on my suspect list. Not sure that would fly too well. "I keep hoping it's not someone in our group."

"Nonsense. Police said we were the main suspects."

"Main, but not only."

"I think we should have listened to you last week when you suggested we stop meeting for a while."

"Well, at least we have our buddy system. Just the same, tonight's arms exhibit was a bit over the top."

"A bit! Sweet Jesus. When Eleanor pulled that gun from her bag, I thought we were all goners."

Odd, I hadn't thought that. Eleanor's gun didn't look like the kind on television where the bad guys hold on with two hands before spraying crowds with bullets. Eleanor's gun looked like one of those old-fashioned revolvers the good guys point and say "Don't make me do it." They never seem to go off.

I gave an exaggerated shudder. "I think Toni's grandson was the scariest thing I saw tonight. Did you notice his icy glare at each of us?"

"Whew. Can you imagine that kid coming by for trick-or-treat?" Sandra put her hand over her excessively large cross.

It surprised me to be enjoying our conversation. The appetizers finished, Sandra ordered another vodka. We chatted about the group, about the murders, and about faith. She let me know that she'd plied poor Ms. Goodwin with a shot of booze to relax the librarian and encourage her to change her mind about our group.

"Where did you find alcohol in a library?"

Sandra gleamed. "Always keep a small 'emergency stash' in a flask in my purse."

"Clever." It seemed to me that such an emergency stash would have helped in my old job. Share with parents. Help kids take naps. Perhaps it was best that I retired. I shook my head.

Sandra ordered another round. I had progressed to lemon-lime soda by this time.

A knocking sound I couldn't place drew my attention. "Sandra. Do you hear that?"

"Hear what? I'm not hearing much of anything right now."

"A knocking sound. There. There it goes again."

Sandra chuckled. It was a delightful throaty sound and softened her overzealous features tremendously. She must have been quite popular in her youth.

She held up her cross. "It's been banging me all night," she said and burst out laughing.

This tipsy Sandra was a whole new woman. She was actually quite pleasant. "Why such a large cross?" I asked.

"Protection," was the reply. "Came from Lourdes, you see."

"So you really do have a lot of faith."

"Not enough. Never enough. Just want God to love me."

"I thought that was a given."

"Well, yeah, but He also has to decide who gets into heaven and who goes to hell and who's stuck in purgatory for ever and ever. Amen." Sandra was beginning to sound like

Kitty and Eleanor during our girls night in.

"Purgatory?" We didn't have purgatory in my old church. Or maybe we did and I'd forgotten. I remembered Art saying something about getting stuck in purgatory.

"Place God sends you if He's not sure what to do about you. Me? I think living on earth is purgatory."

"Interesting. Do you think Todd —"

"Hell. Todd went straight to hell. The end. Amen."

"Why?"

"Gay. Broken pot if ever there was one. Probably believed in abortion too. Hell for him. Poor soul. I should pray for Todd. Won't. I'll pray for Rico."

"So you believe Rico needs your prayers?"

"More than you know." Then she made a zipping motion across her lips and threw away her imaginary key.

I guessed Rico was off limits for our discussion.

The bill came.

"I got it," said Sandra. "Thanks for coming, Daisy. I don't like to drink alone."

"Really, Sandra. I can help with the bill."

"Teacher? Retired teacher? No money. No money at all. I got it. Here you go, Ted, you handsome man." Sandra beamed at the barkeep.

Ted smiled back. "Always a pleasure, Sandra." He swept away with her credit card. I wondered if I should look over the bill for my group leader but thought better of it. She was apparently among friends here.

As she signed the receipt, Sandra said, "I almost forgot. There's a reason I asked you out tonight."

"Oh?"

"Daisy, you were so kind to give me a lift on my errands a couple of weeks ago" — I didn't see it coming — "Won't you join my family and me for dinner on Thursday? It will be a belated thanks for your kindness."

Now whenever Sandra invites someone over, we know that their hatchet time is coming.

"Oh, Sandra, I don't think I can. Besides you paid my restaurant bill."

"Nonsense. Simply won't take no for an answer. Six-thirty. On the dot."

I nodded my head, and Sandra swept out of her seat. I guessed we were ready to go, so I stood too. As we made our way to the front of Pete's, I had the feeling I should be more conscious about looking around, but a quick glance only showed me a few guys at the bar and a dark-haired woman in a booth next to where Sandra and I had sat.

Well, Gabe had succeeded in giving me the jitters. Maybe I should have taken his stupid old pepper spray.

"Give us a hug, then," said Sandra. "Peace be with you." She walked out into the night. I was impressed by her ability to walk straight. If I'd had that many drinks, I sure wouldn't have been able to.

I sat on a bench near the front door and put my head in my hands. The enormity of Sandra's invitation hit. I was going to be kicked out of the writing group. My brief and uninspired writing career was apparently coming to an end. I felt like the Halloween pumpkin left back at the patch to rot. Tears welled up behind my eyes and my head started to throb.

"Boo!"

I jumped and squeaked. "Gabe! What are you doing here? You scared the pants off — er scared me half to death."

Gabe's eyes gleamed like sapphires in the evening light. "I told you I was going to make sure you got home all right."

"You have to stop. You're giving me the chills with all this cloak-and-dagger behavior."

"Daisy, I let you out of my life before. Don't know why. But —" He stopped and looked carefully at me. "You all right?"

"Fine." Then I shook my head slowly. "No. No, I'm not fine. I think I'm going to be kicked out of my writing group."

He looked relieved, then shrugged. "No big loss."

"And when you jumped out at me right now, I felt more than a little startled. I think I've been tense since this whole murder business started. And I keep having the feeling I'm being watched. How long have you been following me?"

Gabe frowned. "I only came out tonight."

"It's probably just nerves, but I could swear . . ."

"Daisy, can you be more specific? When did you get this feeling of being followed? Where precisely are you when this happens?"

"It's only a feeling, and lasts a mere second or two. Nothing I can pinpoint."

"I want you to be very cautious. Get in your car . . . Wait. Have you been drinking? Because if you have, I can —"

"No, I have not been drinking. You should have offered Sandra a ride."

"I don't like Sandra."

I laughed at that. "I saw a different side of her tonight."

"Daisy, you're a special friend. I let that friendship go a long time ago, but I'd like to get it back."

I tingled as Gabe leaned over and gave me a kiss on the cheek.

"When this is over," he whispered.

There was such promise in that phrase. I smiled up at him. "Good night, my friend." I got in my car and for once that feeling of being followed was comfortable.

CHAPTER 27

When crusted eyelids refused to open the next morning and joints hurt when I rolled over in bed, I knew I was in trouble. No one plans to have a bad day. They don't get up and say, "Gee, I'd like to feel miserable today." But sometimes you wake up and plain hope you have the aspirin handy.

I stood up against the wishes of my protesting muscles and shuffled to the bathroom. There I found a wretched imitation of myself in the mirror. Hair stuck out in electric-socket fashion, and dark rings made me look as if I'd lost my last boxing match. My skin glowed a sickly yellow. Sickly. That was it. I was catching a bug.

I returned to my welcoming, still-warm blankets, thinking that today would be a great day to stay in bed. Pounding on my back door banished the thought.

Chip stood in the doorframe, looking like a freshly groomed businessperson, except that he held on to Thunder, who was trying to charge ahead into my kitchen.

The news writer made a halfhearted attempt to restrain his monster. "Whoa, boy. We haven't been asked in yet."

I felt like saying they weren't going to be either, but Thunder pounded past me and started sniffing around.

"He's not going to think my house is his bathroom, is he?"

Chip laughed, a tad too heartily. " 'Course not, Ms. D. He's a bit curious, that's all."

Georgette didn't care for Thunder's curiosity and made a beeline back toward my bedroom. Thunder dashed after her.

I couldn't help it. "Gives new meaning to 'curiosity killed the cat,' doesn't it?"

Again Chip played into my weak early morning humor. "You're such a great sport, Ms. D. That's how I knew I liked you."

"What do you want?" I crossed my arms and tapped my toe.

"Why should I want anything?" Chip knew better than to play me for too long. I glared at him and he relented. "I have an assignment all the way out in Basalt this morning. I can't take Thunder with me, and on such short notice, I didn't know who else I could call." Puppy dog look.

I shook my head no. "What happened to

Ms. Flavor-of-the-Month?"

"Tina? She doesn't date guys who are too short for the height requirement rides at Elitch Gardens."

Ouch! Chip looked devastated. I felt horrid. How could someone be so cruel as to say that? "Oh, Chip, I'm sorry, but I don't think today would be a good day. I don't feel well, you see."

"You look fine to me. Tell you what. You just head to bed. Thunder won't be any trouble at all. Only have to hop up every now and then to let him outside."

"I don't know, Chip."

There was a loud meow, a bark, and a crash that came from the direction of my bedroom. I went running, and right as I left view of my kitchen, I heard Chip shout, "Should be back here by five. I'll bring you some chicken soup."

"Don't do this, Chip!" I shouted back, but the door had already slammed shut.

My bedroom looked like one of those ransacked apartments in the movies where someone has done a search for drugs or money. Although I hadn't made my bed yet, someone had rearranged my sheets and blankets all across the floor. The water in Errol Fin's fish tank was sloshing back and forth. My vanity stool was pushed over, socks from my tipped sock basket were dotting the floor, and all I could see of either Georgette or Thunder was the dog's tail sticking out from under the box mattress.

"Get. Out. Here!" I shouted. Damn that Chip. I didn't feel well, and I sure didn't need his obnoxious mutt on my hands for the day.

Thunder shuffled out from under the bed, took a look at my angry face, and slunk over. His ears, which had recently begun to stand up German-shepherd style, were pinned low, and his front shoulders hunched over as if he knew he was in trouble. He was brave enough, however, to come take his punishment.

I leaned over, putting my face as close as possible to the dog's. "You are not to make a mess of my house. Understand?"

He licked my nose. Ugh.

"And you are *not* to bully my cat."

He panted.

Good enough. I rubbed Thunder's neck behind his ears. I guess he took this as a sign that all was forgiven. He grabbed a sock from the floor and jumped up on my bed.

"Oh, no, you bad thing! Get off my bed. No dogs on beds." I dove toward him to drag him away.

Thunder interpreted this as an acceptance

of his invitation to play. He bounced a step out of my reach, sock still in mouth, a line of drool soaking into it. His tail waved a friendly salute over his back haunches, while the front of him sunk low. I could swear the brute was smiling under my now drool-soaked sock.

"Get off!" I yelled. I made another grab, then another.

In a couple of minutes, when he'd had enough, Thunder dropped my footwear, jumped off the bed, and trotted toward the kitchen. I heaved a sigh and lay on my unmade covers. Nobody plans to have a bad day, but that doesn't mean bad days don't happen.

A while later, I sat on my living room couch holding my temples. The aspirin bottle had contained only one pill of the lightest dose possible. While I'd managed to reassemble my bedroom into recognizable shape and put on some comfortable, albeit less than fashionable, jeans and a fleece top, I was still feeling under par.

Thunder and Georgette were sparring on and off. He seemed to like her well enough, but my poor kitty could not get the beast to stay away from her, and she was missing this morning's three-hour nap. Not good on cat nerves. Or mine.

The two frenemies chased each other around the main floor and upstairs into bedrooms I no longer used for anything but storage. That made the rooms all the more interesting, I guess, as first Thunder, then Georgette, came down adorned in Christmas tinsel and assorted feathers from pillows that had, no doubt, met an untimely end because of these two.

By eleven in the morning, my nerves were frazzled from trying to control my charges and cleaning up their messes.

"Thunder, you have to go," I said, putting on his leash.

This act only got him more excited, and he sat at the back door, tail wagging in anticipation.

"Oh, no. No walks. You're going to go play in your yard for a while."

I dragged the cur to his house next door, which took about fifteen minutes. We managed to unlatch the gate and put him inside with only a little more trouble than he was worth. I slammed the gate shut and looped Thunder's lead into one of the chain-link holes.

Huffing from the effort to put the dog in his proper place, I bade him goodbye. "Now, you be a good boy, and I'll be back for you in a while."

Thunder started whining.

"Hush, boy. I won't be too long."

Howl.

"Shut up, you stupid mutt!"

Amazingly, Thunder sat, then lay down and heaved a sigh. Well, who would have thought that Thunder could behave this way? I returned to my house, only to find Georgette at the back door, trying to get out.

"Oh, no, little miss. That big bad dog is out there. You don't want to go outside." She meowed somewhat louder as I took her back to my bedroom and put her on her cat bed, which sat next to my people bed. With one last admonishment to be good, I left and shut her in my room, crossing my fingers for Errol Fin.

CHAPTER 28

Enough for one morning. Fortification in the form of an indulgent, warm lunch was in order. I headed to my local Chinese food place and ordered egg drop soup and sweet and sour pork. Along with the check came my fortune cookie.

I love fortune cookies. That lemony sweet and crispy bite at the end of a meal is superb, and I believe that if I eat the whole cookie — like that's difficult — the fortune inside will come true. I also tape my favorite fortunes to my refrigerator:

Honesty will reward you well.

If you develop the habits of success, you will make success a habit.

How can you have a beautiful ending without making beautiful mistakes?

Quickly, I cracked open my cookie and read today's good thought: "Not all rules are meant to be broken." Well, duh. As fortunes go, this was unimpressively obvious. I wadded up the scrap of paper and almost left half the cookie. Then I remembered what a bad day this was and grabbed it back again. I popped the second half into my mouth and marched off to my pharmacy for some aspirin.

Shopping at smaller places, packed solid with good things to buy, was a delight. My pharmacy was no exception. I walked in and was greeted with a wall of Halloween candy, scary witch masks, and a few glow-in-the-dark skeletons. Charming.

Making my way to the medicine aisle, I grabbed what I needed, then stopped by the card and book aisle on the way out and picked up a new Bee Robb book. Some tingling romance this afternoon would surely put me back in good spirits.

As I drove toward home with my treasures, I saw police lights in my rearview mirror. Probably an accident up the road. I pulled over. To my surprise, an officer stopped behind me and got out of his car. I opened my door to greet him.

He put a hand on his gun. "Stay in the vehicle, ma'am."

I retreated quickly. What was this all about? The police officer knocked on my window, so I pushed the button to roll it down. "Anything amiss, Officer?" I was looking into the face of a boy who looked almost old enough to wear zit cream.

"License and registration, please."

"What is it?" I handed him the papers.

He stared at my stuff, then turned to me. "This your vehicle, ma'am?"

"Of course it is. You can see that with those papers."

"Yes, ma'am. Are you aware that your license tags have expired?"

"What? It can't be. I didn't receive any reminder card."

"I'm sorry, Ms. Arthur, but the cards are sent only as a courtesy. You are still responsible for renewing your plates, with or without a card. These plates expired in August."

"Oh, my stars! I am so sorry. I can take care of this right away."

"You do that. Meanwhile, this ticket" — he ripped a paper off his pad — "is due in thirty days. Please wait here. I'll return your documents in a moment."

My head started throbbing again. What a bad, bad day. How could I have missed something as important as my license plate renewal? I thought of my fortune as I stared down at the ticket.

Not all rules are meant to be broken. Well, duh. Expensive, duh.

"Here you go, Ms. Arthur. You may want to drive right over and get new stickers. Wouldn't want you stopped again."

"Thanks," I said. *For nothing,* I thought.

"Sorry to have upset you. By the way —" The officer caught my gaze.

"Yes?" I sighed into the boyish face that said he was not at all sorry to upset me.

"Sergeant Taylor sends her regards." The youngster had the audacity to wink at me. I didn't trust what might come out if I spoke, so I took my papers and rolled up my window. Good thing I'm a civilized adult. Otherwise I might have stuck my tongue out at him. Him and Sergeant Taylor, wherever she might be.

After waiting a good half-hour in line, I had a new, one-inch-by-one-and-one-half-inch sticker, worth two hundred dollars plus driving violation fees. To think the stickers I used to give away to students for good behavior were so much larger, and vastly prettier.

Grumpy and still dealing with a headache, I went home. I was going to eat a whole plate of cookies and read my new novel.

When I pulled into my drive, I remembered Thunder. I stomped over to check on him. The gate was unlatched. I tilted my head heavenward. Could this day get any worse? I tried the gate a few times and saw that the latch was, in fact, broken. Had Thunder and I done that when I put him in? But then the big question came to mind — where *was* Thunder?

Luckily, I only had to call once. He came bounding around the back of his house as if my voice was the best thing in his whole day. I couldn't help but smile. He dashed up to me and sat right in front of my shoes.

"Good boy!" I was so pleased he didn't jump on me that I forgot all about the messes he and Georgette had made of my house.

"Want to come over for afternoon nap time?" I rubbed his head and grabbed the leash off the fence. I snapped it on my charge and went home.

A few minutes later, the throw on my living room couch enveloped me, and I had a cookie and book in hand. Georgette selected my arm chair to curl up in, and Thunder lay right next to me on the floor. I took a deep breath. Peace. Life was good after all.

Then I opened my novel and began reading. Within a couple of minutes, everything in the book felt familiar. By the end of the first chapter I realized that I had bought this very same book during the summer and had read it one weekend up in the mountains. I couldn't believe it.

I got up and stomped off to Art's den, where I stored all my books. There, on a shelf near the desk, it sat. For heaven's sake!

I needed a friend and a good shoulder to cry on. Gabe? No. He'd be at work. Kitty? I could talk with her. I picked up my phone and dialed.

She answered on the third ring.

"Kitty? It's Daisy. Do you have a few minutes?"

"Sure, Daisy. What's up?"

"I'm having a bad day and need to vent. You okay with that?"

There was a slight hesitation on her end. "Well, I do have to get to work in a bit, but I suppose." She didn't actually say, "If you have to," so I ignored her reticence.

"Thanks, Kitty. You're the best." I told her about Thunder, the book, the expired tag. "And to top it off, I have been noodling all day about that dinner with Sandra tomorrow. Do you really think she's going to cut me from the group?"

Kitty waited a moment before answering. "Daisy, no offense, but will you grow up a bit?"

I was shocked. "What are you talking about?"

"Look. It doesn't matter what Sandra does tomorrow. You're going to be fine. You can write with or without the Tuesday group. And bad day? Think about Rico and Todd. Theirs were bad days. You're simply dealing with pet-sitting. If you can't handle it, you shouldn't accept when this Chip guy asks you for help."

"But he —"

"*He* nothing. Learn to say no when you need to, or don't whine about it." I hadn't ever heard Kitty sound so firm.

"I can't do that."

"Conflict, Daisy. Learn to deal with it, or Sandra pushing you out of the group will be the least of your worries."

This wasn't exactly the sympathetic ear I'd been hoping for.

"Kitty, you really sound upset. What's wrong?"

She sighed. "Maybe it's the weather. I have a headache too. Maybe those murders are starting to get to me. These were real people, real friends who were killed. And the police haven't caught who did it. I don't like being told I shouldn't leave town, or having my writing friends suspected of murder."

"I know what you mean. I've been trying to figure the murders out too. Maybe we

263

could get together and think it through."

"No offense, Daisy, but you ought to leave police work to the police. They might be slow, but they're professional."

I tensed. "Easy for you to say, Kitty. *You're* not the one steadily moving up their suspect list."

"Just drop the investigative thing," she replied. "This is serious. We're amateurs and likely to shoot ourselves in the foot."

Then it hit me. Kitty. Bright, passionate, martial arts expert. What had Gabe said?

". . . but your friends, as you call them, are legitimate suspects."

She didn't like Rico after he found her porno shots on the Internet. "Kitty, why are you so interested in seeing me drop the case?"

"Drop the case? Daisy, do you hear yourself? You're not the police. What do you know about solving murders?"

"I know that it doesn't take a rocket scientist to see who's upset, who would like to see Rico and Todd dead, who has the talent to kill them and the opportunity."

"Are you actually accusing *me* of killing them?" I heard the disbelief in her voice.

I was silent. I believed Kitty could surely have killed Rico, if she'd had a mind to. But Todd? Why Todd? And I liked Kitty. I couldn't like a murderer, could I?

Kitty broke into my thoughts. "I see. I thought we were friends."

"Oh, I'm sorry, Kitty."

But Kitty had hung up. I tried to call her back. No answer and no answering machine.

I gave up after trying for the third time to reach Kitty. She must've had caller ID on. I waddled back and lay down on my bed. The day tumbled in on me. Exhausted, I started to cry.

Visions of Rico and Todd and their bad days swam before my eyes. The fights with Gabe and Kitty replayed themselves and encouraged me to feel bad about who I was. I thought of tomorrow night's dinner and my end to the writing group. The tears came, and I wallowed comfortably in them. After all, no one was around to stop me, or care that I was upset.

My pillow was wet long before I was ready to stop crying. I rolled over and there was Thunder, chin resting on the bed, eyes staring at me with a sympathy I felt to my soul. "Oh, Thunder, I can be so stupid sometimes!" I hugged the dog, sniffling all the while. He stood there and let me hold on.

CHAPTER 29

I must have cried myself to sleep. I woke to the feel of a hot water bottle on my tummy. The hot water bottle morphed into Thunder lying there with his chin resting on me. Still achy and tired, I told him all of my woes. He made small whimpering noises. I told him about being jealous of Sergeant Taylor, and he made guttural sounds. Finally I told Thunder about how I really would like to be the special person in Gabe's life, but Gabe thought I was a criminally insane woman. Then I cried some more.

At last, Thunder heaved a sigh and crept closer to my face. He gave me a sweet lick under my chin, and I couldn't help but laugh. I loved that dog. "Are you telling me to grow up too, good boy? You're probably right."

Thunder yawned and stretched. He jumped off the bed, and Georgette jumped from a hiding place at the foot of the bed too. Thunder trotted to the hall, where he stopped and looked back at me as if to say, "Follow me. I'll show you what to do."

I followed him to my back door, slipped on his leash, and took him to my car. After listening to my moaning for so long, he deserved a good walk.

We walked around the park at Aspen Grove for nearly an hour. The fresh air and quiet helped my headache tremendously. Finally, Thunder dragged me toward the woods.

We neared a thicket of trees when a rustle in the grass stopped me. I do *not* like grass rustling. Could be any creepy thing, especially on a cold, gray day like this. A snake immediately came to mind, though my old student, Nick, told me snakes only come out in warm weather. I was glad I had Thunder with me all the same.

The creepy-crawly sound turned into a mass of yellow fur, followed by the old fisherman that Thunder and I had met in the park on our first visit. Today, the man still had on his fly-decorated hat and waders, but he also wore a heavy cardigan and flannel shirt.

His dog — Rocky, was it? — was wet from the river. When Rocky saw Thunder, he ran up to my dog, sniffed, and shook out enough water so Thunder could have a good shower too. I guess this made them best friends forever, as each was enthusiastically wagging away.

"Hello, Rocky," I said, smiling at the retriever. Then I lifted an unused bag out of my pocket and greeted the old man.

At first he didn't place me. He squinted at the brown plastic in my hand. Then recognition of sorts crossed his face. He harrumphed and walked on, calling his dog to him.

"One day, they'll be our friends," I said to Thunder. I patted my pal on the head, and we continued on our way.

At six-thirty there was a knock on my door. Thunder lifted his head, then lay back down. So much for watchdog skills. I went to the door. Chip walked in with brown bag in hand.

"Chicken soup," he said. "Thanks again for watching him. I hope you didn't have too much trouble."

I put a finger to my lips and led Chip back to my bedroom. There, on my bed, lay Thunder and Georgette, snuggled up like best friends. The television had on a program that both my little friends seemed to be enjoying: *My Good Dog Home Videos.*

CHAPTER 30

The view out the Martins' living room window was like an old master's painting. The western sun touched the Aspen trees that lined the property all the way down to Marston Reservoir, the largest of Bow Mar's three lakes. Early evening dots of light sparkled on the water's surface, and if I hadn't been so tense about my upcoming expulsion from our writing group, I would have enjoyed staying and staring at the peaceful scene for a good long while.

"Can I refresh your wine, Daisy?" Sandra smiled at me from the living room bar area. "I can't imagine what's kept Philip so long. I expected him home from work by now."

I turned to respond. "No, thanks. Still driving home yet tonight."

"Oh, I think we could arrange a ride for you, if need be." Sandra winked and gave me another smile, one that said something's up. Goodness! Was she tipsy already, or did she actually like telling people to leave her group?

"I also need to keep my wits about me," I said. "Adam here is crushing me badly in chess."

It was true. Adam, Sandra's ten-year-old son, had taken precisely four minutes to checkmate me in our first game, and seven minutes in our second. I was feeling pressured already at five minutes into our third. Apparently the boy played chess daily, while I last played about twenty years ago.

Adam shook his solemn head. "If you move that piece, Ms. Arthur, I will be able to take your bishop."

I glanced down. Doggone, he was right. Quickly I removed my hovering hand and selected a different move.

Adam giggled and took my other bishop. "Check."

"I think you cheat!"

Adam giggled again. "Would you care to concede now, or should I keep going to checkmate?"

The back door to the house slammed. We both jumped. Adam's smile slipped away.

"Dad's home," he said. He started putting captured pawns in a box. "We should probably put these away."

I cringed too. Dad's home. That meant

time's up. Here's the hatchet coming out for Daisy.

Sandra went to meet her husband.

"Darling, you're here." Her voice floated out to us from wherever the back entrance was. "I know traffic had to be miserable or you wouldn't have been so *late* for our company."

I couldn't make out the entire conversation, but Mr. Martin's side sounded defensive. Something about "he's coming in a bit" and "stupid plan" floated out to me. Who was "he"? What was the plan? The movie screen in my mind replayed through the several scenes of dismissal I'd been imagining since Tuesday. How I wished I could go home.

Suddenly, Sandra appeared in the doorway with a handsome man at her side. She smiled a wide, brittle mask of hostess calm. Her husband didn't bother with such detail.

The man was a giant. He could have been a professional football player in his younger years. He still had a solidness that I wouldn't want to challenge. No wonder Sandra had brought Loathsome Les here to expel him from our writing group. Kinda like the kid who holds his pit bull nearby before challenging the school bully to a fight.

I gulped.

"Daisy, I'd like you to meet Philip," said Sandra, walking into the room. "Philip, my writing colleague, Daisy Arthur."

"Phil," he corrected his wife. I found my hand enveloped in a bear paw. "Sandra says I have kept dinner and you waiting. My apologies."

"No, not to worry," I said. I felt like I needed to keep the peace. This massive man could do some real damage to a person. Any thought of arguing my case for staying in our writing group died on the spot. "You have a lovely home, Phil, and Adam has kept me on my toes."

I turned to smile at my young host, who was hunched over the chess board. Adam glared at me. What had I done wrong? The boy slouched further down in his chair. His eyes shifted from his father to his chess game and back. He looked as if he wanted to disappear.

"At that chess again?" Philip sneered. He turned to me. "I'm not so academic. Prefer football, myself. Keep telling Adam here, become a kicker. Can make millions and help me in my retirement." Phil laughed at his nonexistent joke about having an athletic son.

Adam blushed.

"How 'bout a drink, Daisy?" Phil headed

to the bar and began pouring into two glasses. Sandra had disappeared to the kitchen to work on dinner. I wondered if maybe she had her husband do the dirty work. This didn't bode well for me.

Phil came back over to Adam and me. He gazed down at the chess board a moment and pushed over Adam's king.

"Hey!" said Adam.

"You concede, son. Now, put this thing away and stop bothering Ms. Arthur."

Adam didn't say a word, but from the boy's look, Philip better hope his son never grew to match Phil's own size. Adam's green eyes flashed toward his father, and his small hands shook. I could tell puberty was right around the corner, and with it would probably come some impressive fireworks in the Martin household. Adam stomped off, presumably to his bedroom.

"Kids," said Phil. He shook his head, then turned to me. "But let's talk about you, Daisy."

In fight or flight situations I tend to be the flying type. I felt bladder pressure under the massive Philip's gaze.

"Mind if I use your restroom?" I managed to squeak out.

"Sure." Phil pointed the way.

When I returned a few minutes later,

beside Sandra and Phil, the living room held a new visitor.

"Daisy!" Sandra smiled at me as if I were some lost relative recently returned to the fold. What was with this smiling thing? "I'd like you to meet a friend of Philip's, Milo Grinnel. Milo, this is Daisy Arthur."

A man as tall as Philip but maybe a quarter of his weight stepped forward. He was about my age with gray hair receding past his ears and a smile no horse would own. Teeth splayed themselves in all sorts of directions, the only commonality between the chompers being their exceeding length and yellowness.

"Howdy, ma'am. Recently moved in from Dallas. Work with Phil here. Most folks call me Grins for short."

"Charmed," I answered, trying with all my might to keep my eyebrows from arching into my own hairline and not stare at those immense fangs.

"Sandy here tells me you're a writer," said Grins. "I write too."

"You do?" Sandra and I said it simultaneously.

Grins chuckled. "Well, not books precisely, but my writing requires creative thought processes too. I write customizations for Invesco's accounting software."

I had to look elsewhere. "And do you write software too, Phil?" I asked.

"No, no. I leave that for the brainiacs. I sell leases for the boxes at the field." At my blank stare, Phil elaborated. "You know, where all the bigwigs sit for games?"

"Ohhh." Sales. It fit. Besides Phil's posession of a genuine charisma, honestly, who would risk saying no to him?

Sandra's smile extended again. "Phil closed a deal today for a doublewide box for three years with —"

"Let's not talk shop," said Phil. "Sandra, that lamb is smelling good."

"Oh!" said Sandra. "I almost forgot. Philip, will you fetch Adam and we'll eat? Daisy, Mr. Grinnel, shall we?" She moved with movie star grace toward the dining room.

Grins and I followed. There were name tags at each place.

"Now who would have switched those?" said Sandra. "I had put Daisy next to Mr. Grinnel, not Adam."

Adam and Phil came in. Before Sandra could do anything about it, Adam grabbed my arm and pulled me down in the chair next to him. He "accidentally" dropped his fork on the floor between us. I reached down for it.

Adam dove over too. "That guy has bad breath!" he whispered to me. "You can thank me later."

It was all I could do to keep from laughing outright. I coughed and sat up.

Dinner was everything right out of a magazine. Perfect soup, lamb, vegetables, and rolls. Wine flowed freely. There was even a small taste glass of it for Adam. Sandra could put White House chefs to shame.

Philip played the perfect host and regaled us with sales stories of the rich and famous throughout the meal. Adam sat quietly for the most part.

"More tea, Daisy?" Sandra held a pot aloft.

"Thank you, no. This dinner is delicious, but I'm not sure I could squeeze in another bite." I looked across to Grins. "Mr. Grinnel?"

"Aw shucks, gal. Jus' Grins. I prefer it." He turned to Sandra. "And thank you, my charmin' hostess, but I too have had enough."

"Adam, eat up your okra," said Sandra. "We don't waste food, especially when there are so many unfortunate children in the world who would love to eat that up. Philip, will you offer Daisy some of that salt by your elbow?"

Adam shoved a piece of vegetable around his plate.

Phil pushed the salt my way. "Anything new or exciting happen at school, son?"

"No, sir," mumbled Adam.

I admired Phil's effort to bring Adam into the conversation, so I tried another tact. "Adam, thanks for playing chess with me earlier." I turned to his parents. "You must be very proud of your son. He is extremely clever."

Philip sniffed.

Grins' head snapped in Adam's direction. "Boy? You play chess? That's one of my favorite games. Perhaps we'll play together someday. This ol' dog has a few tricks up his sleeve yet. Maybe I could teach you a thing or two."

Adam shot a look at me before responding in a mimicked southern accent. "Why suh, I bet my pappy would be downright pleased for me to turn out jus' like you."

It was Philip's turn to cough into his napkin. Sandra gave me a measured look, then turned to Adam. "Well, Adam. Mr. Grinnel gave you a nice compliment. What do we say to such things?"

"Thank you, suh," said Adam. He stared down at his plate.

The silence after Adam's mimicry was

excruciating. Philip tried a new subject. "Hey, Adam. Mom says you haven't had an accident in over two weeks now. I'm proud of you, son." Philip smiled at his boy and Adam blushed.

Sandra spoke up. "Philip, I don't think Adam likes to discuss such things in front of guests." She smiled sweetly across to Phil, who scowled back.

"Bedwetter, eh?" said Grins. "Boy, you and I sure do have a lot in common."

I turned toward Grins. "You're a bedwetter?" Adding adult diapers to the conversation was something I didn't want to contemplate.

"Oh!" said Grins. "Not anymore, but when I was a boy, whoowee! 'Course, my Uncle Bob had a lot to do with that."

We all stared at Grins waiting for more.

"Uncle Bob was one of them — can I say it in front of the boy? — pedophiles. My daddy 'bout murdered him when he found out. The family packed Uncle Bob off to the Philippines and I've been grinnin' since."

He demonstrated, and I dared not even look toward Adam or Phil. There was a regular coughing fit going on.

A humming sound emanated from Philip's end of the table. He pulled his cell

278

phone from his pocket and checked caller ID. "That's Jeff from the office. Probably have to go back into work tonight." His look challenged Sandra to reply.

"I'm sorry to hear that, dear," she said. She glared at her husband and stood up. "Even if you don't care for any, Daisy, I think I'll freshen my tea." Sandra grabbed both the teapot and her cup in one smooth movement and walked toward the kitchen.

Phil looked as if he wanted to stop his wife.

"We'll discuss this later," she hissed to him as she passed his chair.

Phil scowled.

"Lovely wife," said Grins. "If I found me a woman like that, you might see this old dog settle down."

Did he actually look at me? Lord, no. I could handle anything — even being ousted from our writing group — anything but that.

Wait a minute. Was *that* what this evening was about? Matchmaking? I stood up.

"Think I'll go help Sandra with that tea."

I stomped into the kitchen. "Sandra, we need to talk."

She had her arm in a cupboard but turned when I came in. "Not too impressed with Mr. Grinnel?" She pulled her arm out of the cupboard, a bottle of whiskey in hand.

"Sure you won't share some 'tea' with me?"

"Look, you can expel me from Hug 'N' Kisses if you want, but I'm not going to have you matchmaking me with —"

"Expel you? From Hugs 'N' Kisses? Why would I do that?"

"Well, someone said that when you invite people to your house, they're told not to come back."

"That was only Les the pervert." Sandra laughed. She poured a finger of whiskey, then sipped it from her teacup. "The group probably thinks I'd do such a nasty thing because no one ever accepts my invitations."

Sandra cocked her head to one side and gave me an assessing gaze. "You can't write a prayer, Daisy, but you give good critiques and you make my writing look professional by comparison. Do stay with us."

"Do I have to date Grins?"

Sandra burst out laughing. "Gawd awful, isn't he? Phil wants to 'get him laid' because he thinks then the geek will stop showing up for dinner at our house. I'm so sorry, Daisy. I'll make it up to you." Sandra couldn't control herself any more. She laughed and laughed. Tears streamed down her cheeks. I held out a teacup and joined her.

Adam walked in with a pile of plates.

"Dad's on the porch, smoking. He told me to clear up."

Sandra pursed her lips. "I see. I'll deal with him later. Perhaps we three can eat dessert out here."

Putting down her tea, Sandra began bustling around the kitchen. She dropped a fork, then a knife, scooped them up, and got fresh from the drawer. She pulled a tray of elegant-looking tarts from the refrigerator and put them on doily-lined plates for each of us.

I cleared my throat. "What about Grins? How 'bout I take one out to him?"

Sandra put another tart on a plate. "Here's one 'just for Grins,' " she said and burst out laughing again.

"Sandra, stop," I said, but I felt equally silly. "This'll give him something to sink his teeth into."

The three of us burst into fits of laughter. With a few drinks in her, Sandra could sometimes be the life of a small party.

I grabbed tarts for both men and slipped out to the living room with them.

"Phil's on the back porch," said Grins. "Got another call."

Escape from the tooth fairy! The night was getting better and better. I smiled my thanks to Grins and slipped through the sliding

281

glass door to the back.

Philip's back was to me and in the fading light, I could hardly make out his silhouette. The red glow from his cigarette helped. Must be on the phone. "No, no, Jess. I have to be later tonight." He hunched into the night, cradling the phone with both hands.

"She has company — no, someone from her writing class — no, *not* attractive — Jess. I am too coming — yeah — okay — yes, I love you."

Oops. I didn't want to hear this conversation. I put the tart on a table and quietly stepped inside before Philip saw me.

When I made it back into the kitchen, Adam had gone to bed. Sandra leaned back against the ledge and stared at me. She took a deep breath, then turned to her cup for another sip of "tea."

"Daisy, you look like you've seen a ghost." She sighed. "Don't tell me. 'Jeff' on the phone has suddenly become 'Jess' or 'Jill' or 'Monica Lewinsky,' perhaps?"

"I'm sorry, Sandra. I don't know what to say."

"Say nothing, then." She put her cup down with enough force to make me jump. "Why do men have to be such shits? Always late. Always deserting you. Men. Why bother with them?"

282

"I'm sorry, Sandra," I repeated. No clever words came to fill this horrid void. I reached for her hand. She pulled away and stood at her starched best.

"Don't be. I have everything a woman could want." Sandra's arm made a sweeping gesture to encompass the entire room. "Handsome husband, plenty of spending money, impressive house. And once, I even thought I had a remedy for Phil's philandering."

Now I understood how difficult things were for her. How alone she must feel. Now I understood what she'd been hiding and why I had been suspicious of her. I put my own cup down and nudged it toward the sink.

"I think it's time for me to go."

Sandra nodded, eyes glistening. She escorted me to the living room to say goodbye to the men before we walked to the front door.

"See you Tuesday," I said, stepping onto the front porch. A manila envelope was tucked under the Martins' welcome mat. "Looks like someone dropped this by for you." I bent to pick up the envelope and handed it to her.

"Must be the homeowners' association." Sandra pulled the contents out of the envelope and began skimming down. "I'm head of the social committee." She froze. She stared at the paper, her hand shaking.

"Sandra? Are you okay?"

My hostess blinked. Then she realized I was standing there. "Daisy, did you? — No, of course you wouldn't — Would you?"

I was confused. "Excuse me?"

But Sandra made up her mind I wouldn't — whatever it was she thought I might — and replaced her blank stare with the brittle smile I'd seen when she introduced Philip to me.

"Thank you for visiting this evening. I'll see you Tuesday." She stepped back into her house and closed the door. No hugs or peace-be-with-yous.

How strange. As I crunched down the dark gravel drive, I stewed in thoughts of the odd evening, of not being fired from my writing group, of Sandra's marital problems. The cool autumn night enveloped me as I mused on. I heard a car start up and drive off from the nearby street. Peculiar. Houses weren't close enough in Bow Mar to be aware of a neighbor's car starting.

Suddenly, old movie clips popped into my head. Clips of people hearing a car drive off as they reached their own. Then *kaboom!* I pulled my hand from my door handle. Why did I feel like I was being watched?

Had to get over this being-followed feeling.

CHAPTER 31

What could Gwendolyn do to make things worse for herself? I rearranged the pencils and pens in my jar again. Readers stay with books because of conflict. I hated putting my heroine into uncomfortable places. It wasn't realistic. *I* sure didn't run into conflict that often.

Georgette Heyer wasn't much help either. She lay on my desktop and fanned her tail across my monitor, purring.

Thunder barked next door. Again. Luckily, I had finally picked up a book on German shepherds and saw that this breed likes to "talk" a lot. Understatement of the year, if you asked me. Thunder's woofing made it hard to focus.

Concentrate, Daisy. You can do this. Perhaps Gwendolyn could . . . could what?

The phone rang. My sister didn't bother with any usual niceties or to ask if this was a good time to chat.

"Oh, Daisy, you'll never guess what my *foundling* of a daughter has done now!" she said.

"Hello, Camellia. You sound upset." I rolled my eyes and found my comfy chair in the living room. Camellia lived in Florida. She only called when there was a problem she couldn't handle — about once every month or two. When she started a call in hysterics, it could only get worse. I looked at my watch. One forty-six. I calculated that I could stay on the phone for about a half hour and still get my chapter completed.

"She ran away! Fourteen, and she thinks San Francisco would be fun to slip off to for a while. *And* with some boy!"

I made appropriate noises to Camellia and grabbed a notepad. Could my niece possibly be a good Gwendolyn? This might be interesting.

Twenty boring minutes later and having an ear that was burning from the phone covering it so long, I'd had about all I could handle of Camellia's diatribe against her daughter. "Don't you think June's escapade sounds a bit familiar, Camellia?"

"What do you mean?"

"What about the time you and Timmy Dix ran off to South Dakota for the weekend? Scared Mom and Dad to bits."

"That? That was only a teenage lark. It was a great weekend, and I only ended up grounded for a month. Plus, I was sixteen at the time."

"And your point is?" I doodled a quacking duck on my notepad.

The phone was silent a few moments.

"Daisy, now you know why I always call you. You keep things in perspective for me. Patience with June, right? Grounding for a month, but patience?"

"Right." I chatted a couple of minutes more and let Camellia go. I had work to do.

No sooner had I sat down at my desk when my front doorbell rang. Dang it! I really needed to get to my writing.

"Leaf blower delivery," said a man in a brown suit with a clipboard-looking gizmo and a big box.

"I didn't order anything," I said and started to close my door. I wished I had ordered that. With the ashes, cottonwoods, and other large trees on the street shedding leaves faster even than my falling-out hair, a blower could come in handy.

"It's for the guy next door. Said we could leave it with you if he wasn't home."

"Me?" I eyed the box. It stood almost as tall as I did and was about two feet wide on both sides. I couldn't envision hauling it next door by myself. "It looks heavy."

"Yes, ma'am. 'Bout twenty-five pounds."

"Can you leave it at my neighbor's and I'll watch it?"

"No, ma'am. The package needs to be signed for at the place of delivery, but I'll put a note on your neighbor's door."

I reached for the delivery guy's pad and signed. I'd have to be sure to thank Chip for the lovely porch decoration.

Back to work. Now where was I? Ah, yes. Gwendolyn.

"Gwen made a desperate plan with Grant to ignore her mother's request to go to the Smiths' holiday party. That's where she'd *tell* her mother she was going. Then she and Grant would slip off to Aspen for a weekend of skiing and hopefully more . . ." Now *that* was a good potential conflict in the making. I smiled.

Another knock on my door. Sighing, I promised myself to put a do-not-disturb sign there one day. I marched off to the front.

"Hi, Ms. D." Chip leaned against the doorframe like some hooligan, but he had on a jaunty outfit of khaki pants, shirt, and tie. Must've come directly from work. "I see you got my leaf blower. Isn't she a beaut?"

"About that blower, Chip."

"Yeah, I know. I won't keep it to myself. It's a Stihl BR 500, after all. Awesome force. Once I power that baby up I'll blow both our yards to infinity. And back."

"I was going to say, you can't feel so free to have your packages dropped off at my house. I'm trying to work here." I crossed my arms for emphasis, but the offer of blowing my leaves did sound pretty good.

"Sorry, Ms. D. How's the book coming anyway?" Chip grinned at me.

I knew he wasn't at all interested. I shook my head. "Well, there's not exactly any writing on the wall for inspiration, or in my computer either."

Chip grinned. "Writing. Author. Ha! You can do it, Ms. D."

I sighed. "Why don't you come in for some oatmeal-raisin cookies, and I'll tell you about it." I didn't need to ask twice.

Chip sat at my table munching cookies and drinking milk. "Oh! I almost forgot." He leaned down into the backpack he kept constantly with him. It was a ratty old thing, but it seemed to be Chip's security blanket. Probably slept with it. Poor Thunder came in a distant second to the backpack. I wondered if Chip's many girlfriends were even lower on the priority list.

"Here it is." Chip sat back upright with a

290

folder in hand.

"What's that?"

"That, my dear Watson, is the lowdown on your cleric." Chip gave me a Cheshire-Cat smile. He seemed to be waiting for some reaction, so I obliged.

"Cleric?"

"Yeah. The guy who drowned a couple of weeks back. Catholic priest?"

"Oh! Father Rico."

"Yeah. That's it. Rico Sanchez. I did some digging, made some calls." Chip shrugged in an I'm-just-your-everyday-super-hero kind of way.

"And?"

Chip leaned in conspiratorially. "And let's say your priest was no saint. Whoever knocked him off probably had good reason."

"What do you mean?" I wasn't sure I was going to like what Chip had to share. "Rico was always friendly and nice during our writing group meetings. Surely he wasn't into any illegal activities, was he?"

"According to my sources, *friendly* isn't the right word, Ms. D. If you're going to be an author, you'll have to be more precise than that. I'd say his friendliness was really a cover for him being a sex fiend."

"Sex fiend?"

Chip nodded, eyes gleaming with a gossiper's pride. "He worked for at least three parishes in the States before landing here in Colorado. Didn't stay at any of 'em too long, which I naturally found suspicious."

"I think priests are moved all the time."

"Not like Sanchez —"

"Father Rico."

"Whatever. Anyway, I contacted some of the parishes. Told 'em I was doing an obit. With some digging and prying, they gave me the scoop big time."

"The scoop? Big time? You mean gossip?" I handed Chip another cookie.

"Okay, so they told me about Sanchez — er, Father Rico — from the little they knew, or suspected."

I took a bite of a cookie myself and leaned in.

"I pieced together a profile that is not really printable, if you know what I mean." Chip took another bite of cookie.

"No. What *do* you mean? Was Father Rico some sort of *criminal*?" I wasn't sure I should encourage Chip, but learning more about Rico might help pin down who'd killed him and possibly Todd too.

"Not precisely criminal, Ms. D., but I'd keep my kid sister away from him. Quite a bit too likable that guy, and sex, sex, sex everywhere in his past."

"I know he had a lover —"

"Correction. Lovers. Men, women, perhaps even" — Chip dropped his voice to a whisper — "boys."

"No. I don't believe that." I thought about Adam Martin, Sandra's son. "Couldn't be."

"Got to the Diocese of Galveston from some parish in Mexico. Left within a year. Rumored to have had an affair with the choir director of a tiny church in the area. She was married at the time."

"Oh dear!" I felt bad even listening to this about Rico.

"Then there was Tampa, Florida. The parish he was at there kicked him out with rumors of three or four incidents. Two of those were with young men."

"Chip, I don't think I want to hear more."

"And here, about two years ago, his name was linked to an accident with a little kid. You know what I think? I think Rico was slipping down the slippery slope."

"Chip! You have no real evidence of that. Don't spread such rumors!" Then I thought about Adam Martin again. He'd recently stopped wetting the bed — after Rico died. Couldn't be. I shook my head, but Chip started talking again.

"No evidence yet, Ms. D. Not *yet*." Chip wiggled his eyebrows, and a chill went up my spine.

"I think you'd better go, Chip. I liked Father Rico, and I refuse to think such bad things about him."

"Okay, I'll head out for now. If I get this story really hot, though, I'll want a quote from you. Just to make the thing balanced and fair, don't you know."

I smiled weakly and showed Chip the door.

Back at last to my desk. I flipped on my monitor. Immediately my email notification dinged. The sender was the Jefferson County library system. I didn't have any books on order or overdue that I knew of. I opened the mail.

Tag. You're it. We both know who killed Rico and Todd. Do not reply to this email. Meet me tonight at ten o'clock sharp at Independence High School, teachers' parking lot. Come alone. Tell no one. I will give you the evidence you need.

Of course the email was unsigned. Odd, meeting at my old high school. Also, *I* knew who killed Rico and Todd? Preposterous! I thought about who from our group was most upset when the two young men died. Could be a clue there, but nothing made sense. Someone outside of Hugs 'N' Kisses must have done this.

An explosion of noise hit my ears.

I jumped a mile out of my chair and dashed to the window.

I saw some sort of spaceman guy in a camouflage jumpsuit with big orange ears and black-rimmed goggles staring at me. He had a backpack contraption strapped to his scrawny shoulders with a long tube held in one of his hands. Leaves danced frenetically around him. The other hand waved to me, then pointed to the tube. Even through my window I could hear, "Hundred and eighty-one miles per hour air velocity!" My neighbor-spaceman smiled.

I could have killed Chip right then.

Hmm.

CHAPTER 32

Even in the dark, my car knew where I was supposed to stop and pulled into my old space at Independence High. Nine forty-one.

True, Independence was still my home turf in a way, nothing having changed much since I retired a year or so ago, but when meeting a mysterious someone because of their peculiar email message delivered from a public library, it was good to arrive early and avoid any creepy surprises.

Judging by the lack of lights or people around, I guessed there was no home football game or school dance. Hadn't counted on that. Must've been a teacher workshop day. The place seemed deserted, and the few pink fluorescent lot lights made my spine tingle. I switched off my car's engine and got out.

Even though Littleton is right next door to Denver, it can be ominously quiet at times. I looked around. The chain link surrounding our lot was still dented where Tom Coleman got carried away celebrating his eighteenth birthday and ran over the fence in his new Mustang. Or was it a Lexus?

I looked at the school. In daylight, its brick facade would glow a warm red, but at this time of night it hovered as a massive black hulk, cold and menacing.

Behind me, I heard a car pull in. I rabbit-scooted away from its headlight beams. The car swerved, then stopped next to mine and someone got out.

"Daisy Arthur!" Sandra Martin started striding toward me. There was a slight stagger to her steps. Had she been drinking again? "I knew it was you. How could you?"

"Sandra? What are you doing here? Are you my witness?" Why would Sandra go to such lengths to be secretive? Why hadn't she given me her evidence when I was at her house last night?

"Witness? What are you talking about? I came with the money you demanded. I knew teachers didn't make much, but you must really be desperate to engage in blackmail." She had reached my side and towered over me, hands on hips, as if I was a roach in a birthday cake.

"Blackmail! I don't understand. I got your

note about evidence relating to who killed Rico and Todd, so I came. Sandra, you could've shared with me last night."

"No, I got *your* note demanding five thousand dollars to be quiet about *my sins!*"

Another car entered the lot. I didn't want to pay attention to it. Something was very wrong with Sandra.

I continued asking her questions. "What do you mean, your sins?"

The car rolled to a stop in some shadows, but there was no engine cut.

Sandra wagged a finger at me. "In the packet you handed me last night. You were very certain I had something to hide. And all this time I thought you were an easy-go-lucky hack."

The intruder's high beams flickered on. Its engine revved.

Sandra spun toward the lights and put her arm up to block the glare. "Good grief, who is that?" We both stood there staring at the vehicle that seemed to consist of nothing more than headlights shining on us.

The car squealed into motion. Must be that high school twit, Tom Coleman, coming back to finish his demolition job on the fence. I saw something protruding from the driver's side window. An arm with a stick or . . . I couldn't make out what.

The vehicle seemed to be coming straight in our direction. It was gaining speed instead of slowing down. For a moment my body froze in the glare of the lights and the disbelief that someone would play such a dangerous game of chicken with Sandra and me. Then I realized the car wouldn't be able to stop in time.

"Look out!" I grabbed Sandra's elbow and pulled her away right as the car swerved past us. Too late. I heard a sickening pop, then Sandra screamed out in pain.

Realization hit me full force. "Sandra! Somebody wants to kill us! Run!" I took off in the opposite direction from my group leader. Turning back, I saw Sandra holding her left arm, running for the parking lot's open entrance.

But the fiend on four wheels had doubled back and was chasing after her again. She stumbled along in the headlights' glow. The car's engine revved up. I couldn't believe what I was seeing. Sandra staggered forward, trying to keep her footing.

Again the driver pulled to Sandra's side. Again I saw the stick. Then whack! Sandra crumpled to the ground. Wheels squealed in a victor's taunt.

I ran to my colleague, forgetting my own relative safety out of the line of attention.

"Sandra! Sandra! Are you okay?"

That car swung around again. I grabbed Sandra under her arms and began dragging her. Which way to go? I spotted our own two cars. They were only a few feet away. If I could only get us between them . . .

In the distance, sirens howled. I didn't know who might have called the police but was grateful for the sound and hoped the law was headed our way.

Sandra had been deathly silent since she fell. She made no effort to help me get her to the precarious safety of our cars. I pulled her with all my might.

That demon vehicle lurched forward for another attack on Sandra and me. Oh, help!

One more jerk and I had most of both of us between the cars. I fell on my butt, Sandra's upper body cradled in my lap. Only her right leg stuck out. Her forehead pumped blood over the two of us. I put a hand to her wound, but the blood relentlessly seeped through my fingers.

There was a crunch of metal as the evil vehicle sideswiped Sandra's rear bumper. The thing moved too fast for me to make out color or model, much less see who drove the car. It rolled over her ankle and I heard more bones cracking. I pulled Sandra farther back between the cars. She made no sound. Her silence frightened me more than if she had been moaning. I screamed for her. I screamed and screamed.

It didn't help.

CHAPTER 33

I looked down into Sandra's face. She wasn't moving. Her right leg was twisted at an odd angle, and her left shoulder seemed to be in a tent shape rather than flat. Blood continued to gush from the gash in her forehead, a forehead now cold as a dead body here in the dark. I shivered and held my writing group leader closer against me. Her blood unrelentingly pumped from her wounds. It soaked through my blouse and I shivered in fear.

The roar of the devil car receded, so I took a risk and scooted out from under Sandra's body. I grabbed my car's door handle and pulled up. All I could see were the taillights of the monster that had pursued us. I couldn't read the license plate. The car was swallowed up in darkness.

Sirens got closer. Would they be attached to the one car I wanted to see now? Would Gabe come to our rescue?

Sandra let out an unconscious sigh. Oh, my God! Was she . . . I couldn't give in to bad thoughts. I tried to remember the CPR we had to take as teachers. Not much came to mind. I grabbed Sandra's right wrist and checked for a pulse. Couldn't find it. I reached a hand toward her neck.

The sirens were on us. Then silence. I heard a car door open and crunch closed. The parking lot seemed to flutter in red and blue light. Police. At last.

I stood up.

"Help!" I yelled. "Please help!"

A police officer flashed his light into my eyes. "What seems to be the problem, ma'am?"

"Someone just tried to *murder* us! Will you please put that light down and come help me?"

"Get your hands on the car, ma'am." The officer gestured with his light and put his other hand on his holster.

I complied.

He walked over toward Sandra and me scrunched between our two cars. He gave a low whistle and spoke quickly into the radio on his shoulder.

The officer started to squeeze into the space. "Are you hurt?" His attention fixed on the lump that was Sandra.

"No, but my friend —"

"What happened?" He was inspecting her.

"Please! She needs CPR right away."

"Step back. I've ordered an ambulance. Now tell me what happened."

"I couldn't find a pulse. Please, please do something!"

"She'll be all right. She's breathing on her own. You two have a fight?" He looked directly at me for the first time. A hint of a frown took over his features. "I said to step back."

"No! I told you, we were chased by someone in a car. They hit her with a pole or something. She fell. Then I tried to pull her to safety. Oh, please, let her be all right!"

Another police car arrived. Then a fire truck. Dear God, where was the ambulance?

"Help is on the way, Mack," said a female officer. She turned to me. Sergeant Taylor!

"Oh, Sergeant Taylor. It's my friend, Sandra. She's hurt badly." I tried to go to Sandra. Sergeant Taylor held me back.

"Daisy Arthur! What are you doing here?" she said. Her gaze swept over me from head, through blood all over my clothes, to toe.

I sighed. How apt. The ticket-with-her-compliments Sergeant Taylor. No matter. She was a police officer, and I was a citizen in need of help.

I sagged against the back of my car. "I'm not sure. I received an email this afternoon telling me to meet a witness here at ten. The witness would have evidence about the murders of Rico and Todd."

"Why would anyone write you about those murders? Ms. Arthur, that doesn't sound plausible," said the oh-so-efficient sergeant.

"I know. But that's the honest-to-goodness truth." I shrugged in the moonlight.

Sergeant Taylor inspected me with her flashlight. The up-glow showed her grimace. Even with that look on her face, she was quite attractive. All she said was "Daisy Arthur." Slowly she shook her head back and forth, perhaps not sure what to do with me. I knew the woman hated me.

"Sergeant Taylor," I said, telegraphing my own feelings that she was a wanton creature and desperate rival for Gabe's affections.

She smiled. It was a cold, calculating grimace. I could almost read her thoughts. Should she interpret this situation as she found it, or indulge in coloring everything with her knowledge of my recent challenges with the law? I think she was somehow listening to her bad angels.

"Step over this way," said the sergeant. "Under the light post." She grabbed my arm and started leading me away.

"Ow!" I said and shook her off.

We walked toward another part of the parking lot. I glanced back. The other police officer and firefighters had Sandra stretched on the ground behind the cars. From what I could tell, they were bandaging her.

Sergeant Taylor commanded my attention with a tap on my shoulder. "Now, let me guess. You had another misunderstanding. Perhaps your friend guessed you're a murderess?" She air-quoted the misunderstanding word. "Your little *faux pas,* Ms. Arthur, tend to leave quite a trail of disaster."

"Oh? What has Gabe told you?" He must have been her source of information.

"Gabe? You mean *Lieutenant* Caerphilly? He hasn't told me much, but the police file on you is growing by the moment."

"And how would you know that?"

She at least had the decency to glance away. "We're going to need you to come in for questioning." Sergeant Taylor straightened up, all business now. "Please turn around and put your hands behind your back."

"What! You're going to arrest me on top of all this?" I swept my arm around to encompass the police cars and the ambulance that had finally arrived and the attendants loading Sandra into the vehicle.

"On top of? *Because* of. The witness who called this in only mentioned two persons and a loud fight over money."

"How would they know what we talked about? And who are 'they'?" This air-quote thing was contagious.

"It was an anonymous call, but judging by the lights coming on in nearby houses, I'd have to guess the noise from your altercation with the woman in the ambulance garnered a lot of attention around here."

"Sandra. Sandra Martin, my writing group leader. Not just some woman in an ambulance."

Sergeant Taylor rolled her eyes. "This keeps getting better and better."

"Oh, stuff it! We were *not* arguing about money. At least I wasn't."

"That attitude won't help, you know." The sergeant sounded remarkably like a teacher at Independence I once knew and hated to the nth degree; a prissy, self-righteous thing.

"Attitude, my eye." I was getting more upset by the minute. "I was nearly killed!"

"It looks like your friend — Ms. Martin, is it? — is the one who was nearly killed. You appear to be perfectly fine, for an innocent victim, *if* that's what you are."

"That's what I are — am." I hated this sergeant.

"So, if you're innocent, why are you here? Why this precise place and time? You're retired from this school, aren't you?"

"Yes."

"You have no business in this parking lot, unless you lured your friend here for a purpose better explained at the station."

"This is outrageous! I didn't lure Sandra here. I was hoodwinked —"

"Oh, yes. Hoodwinked by email. You receive this email, somehow *anonymously,* telling you to come to your old school to meet your writing group leader, who would be unfamiliar with this location. You are to meet at a time when no one is around. You claim a third party arrives. Then, for no reason, this unknown assailant starts to chase you both. You, however, are unscathed in the encounter. Only your writing group leader is hurt, and she has significant, multiple injuries."

It sure sounded bad, the way the hatefully competent Sergeant Taylor put it. I hung my head.

"Like I said, Daisy Arthur, you are under arrest for assault on one Sandra Martin. Turn around and put your hands behind your back."

"Wait!" I cried. "What about the damage to Sandra's car?"

"Damage? I don't see any damage."

"It's right there! When the car hit Sandra, it also dinged her car."

"Well, I'll have to check into that" — she smiled at me and paused — "sometime."

Was this officer arresting me because she honestly thought I did something wrong, or because she was having fun on an otherwise quiet night? I crossed my arms and glared at her. "I won't allow this! And I won't put my hands behind my back like some common criminal."

"Have it your way," said the sergeant. She looked as if she was going to walk away, but then suddenly she turned and slammed me into the light post. "We'll go ahead and add resisting arrest to the charges. Now, you have the right to remain silent . . ." She rattled through my rights.

Something about a lawyer slid through my consciousness, but I didn't have a lawyer. Who'd have thought that as a retired teacher, romance writer, and dog-friendly neighbor, Daisy Arthur would ever need one of those?

Sergeant Taylor put me in the back of a squad car that was mercifully driven by a different police officer. He was much kinder in his manner toward me. Asked if I was comfortable and everything. His kindness pierced where Sergeant Taylor's coldness could not. The whole evening and past few weeks swooped in on me all at once.

My body took over from my brain and large tears rolled silently down my cheeks. I slumped against the seat and let my head loll back. How did all this happen?

CHAPTER 34

Sergeant Taylor. What did Gabe see in this cold woman? Her presence made the interrogation room as frigid as a ski resort without tourists. She'd peppered me with questions all night. Like a machine, the sergeant worked to make me spill more guts than I had. What was she after? How could I confess to something I knew less about than she did? Who was the mysterious caller that claimed there were two women fighting over money? How should I know why Sandra had a bundle of cash with her? I was consumed with fatigue. And anger. The orange jumpsuit Littleton's finest had lent me (to get out of my bloodied outfit) added nothing positive to my mood.

Finally, Sergeant Taylor stepped out, perhaps as tired as I. For the past fifteen minutes, I'd sat alone. I looked around. The "interview" room was nothing more than a tiny beige cubical inside a secured set of glassed-in rooms. Todd's description of this place came to mind.

Probably a breeding ground for every imaginable pollen spore.

Poor Todd. I could see why his allergies had kicked up. The overcrowded police station had people practically working on top of each other, files tucked in every corner, and, while there was a neatness to it all, the conditions were ripe for germ generation. I felt some allergies coming on myself, and I didn't usually suffer from them. I sniffed and reached for a tissue. At least they had unhandcuffed me. I felt embarrassed and petrified by this whole incident.

The police had taken my fingerprints again and my photograph without even giving me a chance to brush my hair or put on makeup. The photo happened in my street clothes, blood and all, so I must have looked like some monstrous criminal.

I loathed Sergeant Taylor!

The she-devil came back in the room. At least some of her crispness had worn off her stride, and she looked as tired as I felt. Even so, Sergeant Taylor's appearance was ten times better than my best-looking me. Jealously, I wished she would go grow a wart. Right on the end of her classically straight nose.

"Okay, Daisy, we're going to go over this again." Sergeant Taylor sat down across from me, her ever-present clipboard ready to scribble on.

I didn't feel like putting up with her rubbish anymore. "Number one. I am 'Ms. Arthur' to you, especially as you remain 'Sergeant Taylor' to me." I used Gabe's finger-counting strategy.

"And number two" — *you poop* — "I have recited the incidents of last evening and beyond several times. I've worked with special needs children for most of my adult life. Even they catch on faster than you. What's your problem?"

Sergeant Taylor glared at me with dark eyes ringed in lack-of-sleep circles. She'd taken the opportunity to freshen up, so her makeup was neat and bright, her dusky hair tied in a classic chignon, and, I suspected, she'd put on a fresh shirt during the time she deserted me.

Then she smiled. Goodness! Even in the comfort of my jealousy, I had to acknowledge how Gabe might have fallen for her. The smile transformed Taylor's face into one of authentic Renaissance beauty.

She spoke. "All you have to do, Daisy, is admit that you're involved with our two murders and last night's assault."

I seethed inwardly. *Daisy?* Hadn't I said I wanted to be called Ms. Arthur?

She threw her hands up. "Then we can be done." Sergeant Taylor made it seem so simple.

But, hadn't I heard that line on *The Closer* or something? The suspect admits all, in an effort to get the cops to shut up. Then *bam!* They throw the poor fool in the slammer. Personally, I was beginning to have a lot more sympathy for bad guys. Maybe I'd think about that in my next book. For now, a nice quiet jail cell might be better than this metal chair I'd sat in for too many hours.

"Well, Laverne —" I stretched and yawned. Two could play at these annoying legal mind games.

"Who's Laverne?"

"You."

"I'm not Laverne."

"You wouldn't tell me your first name and you keep using mine, so I made one up for you."

I'm usually a reasonably well-behaved person, but the little and uncomfortable sleep I'd had in this room since last night left me feeling uninhibitedly obnoxious. Conflict is good. Conflict is good.

"The name's Linda. Linda Taylor. *Ser-*

geant Taylor to you."

"Whatever."

"You think you're so cute, Daisy Arthur. You probably think Gabe is going to come to your rescue again." She spat the words at me like a rattlesnake.

"Well, I do feel like I need rescuing from you." I glared right back at her.

"You gave me good cause for arresting you."

I snorted. Yep. That contemptuous sound came from my nostrils. Oh, yeah, conflict is good.

"What? What's that sneer supposed to mean?"

Her question opened the door for my thoughts. "Tell me you haven't had it in for me since this whole thing started. Tell me you haven't wanted this precise situation since Gabe took me to the bar that first night."

"Shut up!" Sergeant Taylor made a slicing motion across her throat into the mirror. My expertise from watching television said she didn't want what I had to say recorded.

Turning back to me, Sergeant Taylor said, "Are you nuts? You want to get Gabe in trouble? You are one stupid bimbo." She continued a string of insults and charges at me. I sat calmly reciting my alphabet in my head until she was done.

Then I said, "Bet you're glad that wasn't recorded. Police harassment, you know."

Sergeant Taylor, now a bit more spent, gave me a cool sneer. "It might have been somewhat uncomfortable until I explained to the captain what a desperate criminal mind I was dealing with. After all, what I've said is the truth. You are a dumb, irresponsible problem just waiting to happen."

"What's that supposed to mean?" I didn't like her calmness. There was something calculating about it.

The sergeant smirked. "Did you think I wouldn't do a background check on you? Did you think Gabe's trust pulled you off the suspect list, even for a second?" She leaned over the table between us to get right in my face.

I leaned back in my chair. "What are you on about? I don't have anything of concern in my background."

She glared at me and pounced. "Cole. Bee. Stan. Ton." Each syllable was punctuated with her palm hitting the table top.

I gulped.

"You want to tell me about that?"

I glared back at her. "No." I didn't tell many people about Colby.

"Like I said, I did a background on you.

Only natural to ask why you 'retired' so early." There went those quotation fingers again.

"That's none of your business."

"Guess again. Maybe Colby was a murder case too. Maybe I should spend some time checking into that."

I jumped up. "How dare you? How dare you! I loved Colby. I loved all those kids. I wouldn't do anything to hurt any of them!"

"So you say."

"So I know." Tears welled up in my eyes. "Okay, you sick creature. You want to know what happened? I failed. I failed my charge and I feel guilty as hell. Damn you! But I did not kill Colby Stanton, or anyone else, for that matter." I flopped back down in my chair and buried my head in my hands.

I needed to talk this history out. Who cared if I ended up in jail? Maybe I deserved it.

Sergeant Taylor sat and leaned back in her seat.

I told the clipboard toter my story. "Colby smiled all the time. His eyes shone like the stars in a bright blue sky. At sixteen, he was a cheerful boy who never let the fact that he lived in a wheelchair, couldn't speak, and had no control over eating or defecating slow him down. I loved him. Everybody loved Colby. He was like a happy-go-lucky rag doll, and one of the most popular kids at school.

"One afternoon, while in the gym, Colby was playing basketball. The other kids would put the ball in Colby's lap, race him down the floor, then make the basket for him. He was thrilled. He whooped and giggled and smiled as everyone had a turn pushing him.

"Colby got too excited and started wriggling in his seat. I don't know how, but his feet came off the footrests and dropped to the floor. The boy pushing didn't see anything, but Colby's feet got caught in the chair, and the two young men fell over before I could stop them and right things. The other boy didn't have a scratch, but Colby hit his head and immediately slipped into a seizure. Have you ever had to deal with an epileptic fit, Sergeant?" I glared at her, tears in my eyes.

Colby. How could it all have happened? What might I have done differently?

Taylor had calmed down. She shook her head no.

"A seizure is an electrical malfunction of the brain. In Colby's situation, he had a grand mal. He lost consciousness and slipped into the most violent seizure I had ever seen. I ran to him and held his head. I sent my teacher's aid to dial nine-one-one. Colby jerked even more, and he soaked through his diaper. Seizures are scary stuff, Ms. Taylor. Thank your lucky stars you don't have to deal with them."

"Okay." The sergeant coughed. "We don't have to go into this any more."

"Oh, but we do. You think I killed Colby? Maybe I did. All I know is that most seizures end within two minutes. Colby was still shaking and unconscious at four. We were dealing with something called status epilepticus. That's where the body is unable to recover by itself. It's an emergency situation.

"My aid tried using her cell phone to make that emergency call, but couldn't get good reception. The school had been fiddling with interference to keep kids from using their cells on school property. Five minutes passed. She finally found a place outside the school building to make the call. Seven minutes. Colby's chest was pounding. The other kids were standing around in shock, crying, hugging each other, staring at their friend. I knew that staying calm was the most important thing I could do, but it wasn't helping. Ten minutes passed. The ambulance finally came."

Sergeant Taylor's eyes were glistening.

"I prayed, Sergeant. I prayed while that boy jerked in my lap. I prayed when the EMTs arrived. I prayed when they loaded him into the ambulance. He was still unconscious and seizing. I hoped. I prayed. Then, when I went to the hospital, Colby's parents told me that the doctors were able to stop the seizure." My tears flowed freely now.

Sergeant Taylor leaned in. "But I thought —"

"You thought right. I went home to a good night's sleep. No dreams. No worries. Just exhaustion. The next morning, Colby's mother came to the classroom. It was obvious she hadn't slept all night. Sometime after I had gone home and before school the next day, Colby went into another seizure. His body betrayed him again. He had a heart attack and died."

"So that doesn't make you . . ."

"A murderer? You're right, Sergeant. The Stantons, though, were in such grief. They wanted — no, they *needed* to blame someone. I was awash in guilt. It was easy to point at me."

The policewoman looked shaken for the first time since bringing me in. "Daisy, I don't think we need discuss this any more."

Gabe strode into the room. "Sergeant Tay-

320

lor, what are you doing?" He looked upset, but I was never so glad to see his familiar face. Sergeant Taylor, aka Nasty Laverne, transformed immediately into her cool, competent persona. I rubbed the tears from my cheeks with the back of my hand.

The sergeant straightened her shoulders. "I have Ms. Arthur in custody for suspicion of assault on Sandra Martin. Ms. Arthur and I have been discussing the details of last night's events."

At least she called me Ms. Arthur.

Gabe didn't look at me. He stared at his partner, then slowly pulled a plastic bag from his briefcase. In the bag was a ratty-looking piece of grayish paper. "Linda, you and I both know Ms. Arthur isn't our perp." He pushed the bag toward her. "Please go recheck this into evidence."

Sergeant Taylor looked as if she wanted to say something, but a glance in my direction turned any words into a sigh. "Yes, sir." She took the bag and left.

Gabe turned to me at last. "Can I give you a lift, Daisy?"

"I'm so sorry, Gabe. I guess I goofed up again." It took superhuman effort to bring my trembling lower lip under control.

Then Gabe grinned at me and shook his

head. "Life is sure never dull with you, my friend."

I basked in that grin and felt that the universe had at last righted itself.

I stood and winced at the stiffness in my legs and back. "Thanks." Middle age sucks big time. "A ride would be nice."

CHAPTER 35

"What was in the bag?" I glanced at Gabe. He always drove with his eyes on the road. Nice profile.

"The note from your windshield."

"You kept that? It didn't have anything legible on it."

"It's still evidence, and Sergeant Taylor knew that. I told her about the incident." Gabe's brow pinched and he whispered something to himself that sounded like, "Don't know why she didn't remember it."

Let me see. Gabe talking outside of work time to Linda about Daisy. Linda doesn't seem to remember the evidence that would've let Daisy out of that cesspool of a room. Go figure.

The question was, why would Sergeant Taylor be jealous of me? She was gorgeous. I was frumpy. She was professional sounding. I was a little frazzled most of the time. Anyway, things were straight enough that I could stop suspecting myself of having multiple personalities, one of which could kill my friends.

"Speaking of evidence, Gabe, how are things shaping up with all this? Have you heard anything about Sandra? I sure hope she's okay. We seem to be running out of suspects. Do you have any new ones? I can't imagine the stress you must be under."

"Used to have someone in mind for the doer, but after last night, I don't any more." He tapped his thumb on his steering wheel.

"When I worked with the special needs kids, there were several mix-ups and mis-communications. I used to figure out what they were trying to say by retelling their stories to Georgette Heyer."

"Who's that?"

"My cat — not the author. Somehow, things fell into place with the repetition of bits and pieces the kids said. Do you think talking things out might help you?"

Gabe looked as if he was fully absorbed in driving. Maybe he didn't hear me. I opened my mouth to re-offer my advice, but thought better of it.

After a few minutes, Gabe spoke. "Okay. We have two murders and one assault. All related. Common thread is the writing group."

"How exactly did Father Rico and Todd die?" I tried to speak quietly so Gabe could stay in his train of thought.

"Sanchez was knocked over the head a couple of times. Stone probably. Not big enough to crush the skull, but enough to give the vic a hefty lump, had he survived. Then he was either held underwater or he simply fell in the Platte face down to finish the job."

"And Todd?"

"Stevens had a lump too, but this one was at the front of his head. Probably hit it when he fell. He landed right near his desk, so might've caught his head on its edge. But Stevens was also stabbed with his pallet knife."

"Eeww." I couldn't help the reaction. Poor Todd. He was nicer than that sort of end justified. "And Sandra?"

"We haven't had the report from the hospital yet."

"Want to go over there and visit? I know I look horrid, but I've been very worried about her. Gabe, she looked like she might die, when I was — that is — when I last saw her."

Gabe broke from his train of thoughts. "You sure?"

I nodded.

His grin fortified me again. That and the knowledge my purse had a brush and makeup in it. Gabe swung onto Broadway Boulevard, and we headed toward the hospital.

"I'm still missing something," he said, back in puzzle mode. "It's usually a relative or lover who commits murder. In this case, there are no close-by relatives, and the two vics were the lovers."

"What about the notes?"

"Yeah, notes. The note near Sanchez simply said 'Snake' and had a Bible passage about trusting a snake highlighted. The other was printed off Stevens' own computer and said 'Rabbit.' There were corpses of each animal near the victims too."

"My stars! Not much to go on." I remembered the rabbit in the bag at Todd's apartment. Whoever was killing my friends had nasty anger issues. I hoped to never run into him on my own.

"Not much to go on at all." Gabe shook his head.

"Could there have been a cheating situation?"

"Cheating — oh, you mean an affair — no. Todd was the one with most opportunity for other lovers within his and Rico's relationship, but he seemed to be pretty monogamous."

"And Rico?"

"Hmm. Rico was an interesting one. We did some background work on the guy and found a string of broken hearts from numerous parishes where he'd worked. Tended to be in one place for only two to three years at a time."

"Wow. I knew he was charismatic, but lovers everywhere?"

"The disturbing thing was that he had both male and female lovers."

"Bisexual? I had heard that. But it's too hard to believe." Rico's intense gaze surfaced in my brain. Hadn't I been interested in it? Hadn't I thought about possibilities with this priest who shouldn't have been in my interest scope? I wondered who else might have succumbed to his charms. Now that both sexes could be Rico's targets, they both could be Rico's assailants. The question became, why go after Todd too?

"What if Todd wasn't the number-one lover in Rico's life?" I asked, trying to see things from a different perspective. "What if Todd was Rico's on-the-side relationship?"

"Good thought, Daisy. That begs the question, though. Who in your group was most involved with Rico?"

We hesitated in thought for only a second,

327

then Gabe and I said it simultaneously. "Sandra!"

CHAPTER 36

For the first time, Gabe took his eyes off the road to glance at me. "Seat belt on?" he asked. At my nod, he flicked a switch. The car rumbled into action, and I felt what it's like to be in a speeding police car with sirens on.

Gabe's hands grasped the wheel with practiced calm. My breath seemed to speed up to match the velocity of our movement. The standard police computer equipment mounted on the dash rattled and bumped with stoic nonchalance as houses, businesses, and slower cars on Broadway disappeared in a jet stream behind us. I stopped talking and let my hero focus on the business of driving. What a ride!

We turned off the siren as we entered hospital parking. We left the police car and walked into the building. Gabe strode with a purpose that left me jogging to keep up. We wove our way through the emergency room to the nurses' station. Gabe knew some of the staff on duty and soon had permission to visit Sandra in Intensive Care.

Sandra managed to struggle out from under her sedative-induced sleepy state. "Thanks for coming," she said. Her foot was elevated and her arm rested in a sling. A large bandage adorned her forehead, and angry welts and bruises seemed to be playing hopscotch all over her face and limbs. How could I have ever criticized her for being obsessively neat? Poor thing looked fragile, even smallish under the sheets. At least the staff were keeping her bedding in order. Even in a hospital, Sandra could maintain fanatical control.

"Sandra, I'm so sorry! I was terrified for you." I took her free hand in mine. "You are so brave."

Gabe remained quiet, standing next to me.

"Thanks, Daisy. 'Lo, Lieutenant. Can you catch who did this?" Sandra's eyes moistened, and tears rolled down the side of her face.

I felt my own eyes begin to water.

"We're doing our best, Ms. Martin. Do you think you can answer a few questions? It would help." Gabe reached in his pocket, but I laid a hand on his arm.

"Let's simply chat for a while," I said.

Okay, so my interrogation night with Sergeant Taylor was still wreaking havoc in my brain. I pulled a chair close to Sandra's bed, and Gabe retreated to hold up the room's wall.

"Thank you, Daisy," said Sandra. She looked worn and weary. "You . . . saved . . . me."

"From Gabe's questions? Oh. You mean last night. Gosh, I didn't do anything much."

"Ambulance staff brought me to. Said you pulled me between some cars. Saved me from more." Sandra's gaze floated toward the ceiling. "How could someone . . . why me?"

"That's what we're trying to find out, dear." I stroked her arm. "Last night you said something about money and blackmail. You thought I had something to do with it?"

"Yes. You put — envelope under mat. At least I thought you did."

"Under — oh! You mean Thursday? When I came for dinner?"

"Yes. Got your note . . . whoever's note. Threatened me and said to be at school. Come alone. Bring five thousand dollars."

"So you were being blackmailed? Oh Sandra, that sounds horrible!"

331

Gabe left his wall-propping post to come closer. "Hang on. Five thousand dollars? That's *all*? Five K's not what blackmailers are demanding these days."

"What?" I was incredulous. "There's a going blackmail rate sheet? What do you do, look it up on line? 'You did this, so I'll blackmail you such-n-such an amount'?"

Gabe glared at me.

Sandra sighed. "They probably knew . . . don't have much money of my own. My stupid fault. Shouldn't have . . . well, I was lonely. Still, that's no excuse."

I spoke as gently as possible. "Excuse? For an affair, perhaps? With Rico?" The last thing Sandra needed was judgment about her life right now.

She blushed, closed her eyes, and sighed again. "He was wonderful. Made me feel truly important, at least to him. Said I was the love he had looked for all his life. Then he died. Someone wanted . . . make our love public and tawdry."

Gabe leaned into the conversation. "What about Todd?" Sandra and I both turned to stare at him. Men could be so insensitive sometimes.

"We don't have to talk about Todd right now," I said after glaring at Gabe. Like Sandra would be up for talking about a rival.

Sandra stared at Gabe, then waved a small gesture of resignation. "It's all right. Rico brought Todd to writing group. About six months ago. Wrote reasonably well. Seemed like a sidekick. Didn't think much of it, but they always came to the library together. Rico hadn't a car of his own. Lovers? Todd seemed attracted to Rico, but not the reverse. Never considered it, until Rico died."

"So, you weren't jealous?" I tilted my head forward.

"Jealous? Of some dwarfy-wart who was a so-so writer? No. But then Rico was murdered. Thought for sure Todd did it." Tears rolled down her cheeks. "We both saw Rico was attracted to you. Jealous. Thought Todd must have been as well."

"Me?" I couldn't believe what I heard. Then I remembered Rico touching my arm. I thought I had imagined the connection between us.

Gabe stepped closer to me.

Sandra blew out her breath before continuing. "You, Daisy. There's something about you. You simply make people like you." She tilted her head. "Not sure what. Guess you're plain likable."

Compliments don't come often and I wanted to savor this, but it wouldn't help solve the case. "Thanks, Sandra. You can trust me, there was nothing going on between Rico and me. Now, where you and Rico were concerned, did you happen to tell anyone about your . . . er . . . liaison?"

"No. No one knew." Her forehead puckered slightly.

"But . . ." I supplied.

"Adam might have guessed something. Such a bright boy. Whenever Philip" — she glanced at Gabe and took a deep breath — "Whenever Philip had to go meet his mistress, I'd invite Rico over. Adam was home. Mostly in his room. Home."

Gabe couldn't resist his duties and fetched his notebook from his pocket. "How long were you and Rico involved?"

Sandra looked at me to answer. I patted her arm in encouragement.

"Not sure. Started so innocently. Rico came for prayer and Bible study. To help Adam grieve over a friend's death. Rico began that about a year and a half ago."

"Adam's friend?" I couldn't imagine losing a playmate so young. Poor Adam. What a rough childhood to live through.

Sandra shook her head. "Toby Brown. Carla's son. Toby died during a camping trip the boys were on. Adam said he saw what happened." Sandra shifted uncomfortably. "I asked at church if someone could come visit with Adam a few times. The church sent Rico."

I wanted to stay and talk more. Sandra seemed open to conversation, but the doctor came in and said it was time for Gabe and me to leave.

Gabe was silent all the way down the elevator and into the parking lot. But when he opened the passenger door of his car for me, he said, "Good job, Daisy. Not good to flirt with a priest, but otherwise, good job."

Gabe grinned, and I felt warm and cozy all over.

CHAPTER 37

Deeply engrossed in reading a book, I wasn't up for the tapping at my back door. Didn't people understand the concept that Sunday is the day of rest? This used to be Art's favorite day of the week. He'd watch whatever sport was playing on TV, and do right what the Bible asks: rest. I would putter in the garden, make a tasty roast for dinner, and prepare crafts for school the next day.

The tapping came again. I sighed, put my book down, and plodded to my door. Chip stood there with a big grin on his face and Thunder at his side.

"Hi, Ms. D.," said Chip. "Thunder and I are heading to Chatfield to take a nice long walk. Wanna join us?"

Chatfield was the closest of the state parks to where Chip and I lived. It was still a twenty-minute ride. I envisioned Thunder drooling down my neck the whole way there and back.

"That's kind of you, Chip, but no thanks. I'm engrossed in a novel today."

Although the grin slipped a bit, Chip produced a raw chicken. "Just thought I'd ask. Anyway, dinner last week with you was really good, and I was hoping I could talk you into . . . ?" He shoved the raw bird at me. I couldn't help but smile.

"You are incorrigible, Chip, but as I was only going to have a can of soup — hang on."

"What?"

"Let's raise the stakes here. You can leave the chicken with me and I'll roast it. Even make some mashed potatoes to go with the bird, but I get a rematch on that Scrabble game from last week."

Chip's grin widened to let in a sky full of sun. "You're on. We'll be back, say around five? I want to watch the game this afternoon. Denver's playing Washington this week."

"See you after the game."

Chip leaned over and gave my cheek a quick kiss. "You're the best," he said. I smiled, wondering if this is what it would feel like to have a son.

My buddies went on their way.

I'd no sooner put the chicken in my

kitchen sink for a quick rinse than my front doorbell rang. Chip must've forgotten something.

I swung open the entrance and Kitty charged in.

She stomped past me and whirled around to glare in my direction. "Where have you been?" Today she shimmered in a teal lamé shirt and black pants. I caught a light whiff of flowered scent as I stared in surprise. Were we talking again then?

"Hi, Kitty. Won't you come in?" I hoped my sarcasm wasn't too obvious.

"I have been so worried about you. Damn it, Daisy, you can't simply go under the radar and expect people not to get upset. You're my buddy, remember? Why haven't you answered your phone?" She burst into tears and rushed toward me. I had only time to brace for the impact before she was in my arms. "I tried calling you Thursday, Friday, and yesterday, with no answer. I thought you might have gone the way of Rico and Todd. You absolutely must call me every single day from now on. You hear me?"

"Hold it," I said, pulling my friend into the living room and onto my couch. "You hung up on *me* last time we spoke. How was I supposed to know to call?"

"I was only upset because you thought I

could murder people."

"I didn't really think that for more than a blink, and I rang to apologize several times."

"Yeah. My bad. It takes me a while to cool off. Daisy! I'm so glad you're okay. I thought I was going to walk in on a dead body today."

I laughed and hugged her again. "And I'm glad you didn't. Want some hot apple cider?"

"Ooh. Perfect!"

We headed into the kitchen. "I'm putting together a roast chicken for tonight for my neighbor, Chip. Would you like to stay? I'm sure he would share."

"Thanks anyway, Daisy. I have to be at work by six."

Sunday. Day of rest. Apparently, not for everybody. "Perhaps another time."

"We'll always have our girls' night in, right?" said Kitty. We both laughed.

I reached for mugs. "That was the best party."

"Wasn't it, though? You were such a sport to ask for help. Really put Eleanor at ease. I hope one day I'll be half the hostess you must be."

"Thanks, Kitty." By this time, I'd managed to heat the oven, make fresh cider for Kitty and me, and had dinner under control.

We headed back to the living room.

I talked as we walked. "It was so sweet of you to check up on me. I'm feeling guilty I didn't do the same for you."

"No worries. I'm only aspiring to be as controlling as Sandra." She laughed.

"Sandra! Did you hear? The poor woman is in the hospital."

"What!" Kitty looked as shocked as I felt as I remembered the last couple of days. I filled her in on what had happened.

"That's terrible. O-M-G! For some reason, I hoped the killing would stop with Rico and Todd. I'm having a hard time suspecting anyone else from our group. This is awful."

"All I can say is, I'll be glad when Gabe — when the police catch the perp."

"You still doing the pretend-detective thing? Perp, huh?"

I smiled. "Won't be long until I have the complete set of lingo down. I've been watching all sorts of detective television lately."

"Careful what you wish for, Daisy. Isn't it you who told me that?"

"Perhaps I did. I'm not wishing to get involved with murder every day. Personally, I think that's a real dead end for me."

"Will you stop, stop, stop with those puns

of yours?" Kitty giggled and rolled on my couch. "So, miss deadeye detective, who from our group did it? *Besides* me."

"I know it's weird, Kitty, but I keep thinking I should know. This steel-trap mind of mine, though. Don't ever bother with menopause. Killer on the brain cells. I know I'm missing something."

"You could try a free write on the subject. That might wrangle loose a thought or two."

"You want to sit and watch me free write?"

Kitty shook her head. "Oh, that's exciting. Not. How about we make a list of people, then fill in why they would or wouldn't be the murderer."

"There's a good idea. Let me fetch some paper." I ran to the den and reemerged with a couple of pads. An hour later, we had notes on each person in the group and several others besides. I looked over the list, fresh apple cider in hand.

"Kitty, I hate to say this —"

She perked up. "Say what?"

"Say . . ." I shook my head. Something wasn't adding up. "No. Something about our notes from Toni is really hitting me."

"Do you think Toni did the murders?" Kitty's sharp features focused on me.

"No. Not Toni, but the hypocrisy about

her son's molestation. There's something there."

"Daisy, we're at a standstill." Kitty gnawed on her lower lip. "What about Toni's grandson?"

I frowned in concentration. "Jamie?"

"Yep. He creeped me out, talking about permanent vacations and all."

"I think he was only acting tough for his grandma. He came home from school to be with her, remember? He wasn't even around when Rico and Todd were killed."

Kitty sighed. "I guess you're right. Boy, I want this to be over. I'm tired of looking at my friends like they might knife me at any minute."

Something in my heart said we weren't focusing on the correct concern. "I don't think it's someone from our group."

"But the police narrowed their focus on us."

I nodded. "That's what they said, but Gabe also told me they might widen their search."

"That lieutenant? What did he say?"

"He said he always tries to keep the options open until there is no doubt about who has committed the crime."

Kitty sighed. "Just in our case, he's in no doubt about our group."

"Then he's wrong. I know it."

"I hope you're right." Kitty sounded doubtful. "If someone I knew were planning to bonk me on the head —"

I couldn't resist. "It wouldn't be Eleanor."

"Not Eleanor?"

"Nope. She'd shoot you."

Kitty laughed, then pulled her cell phone from a pocket. "Oh, shit! Sorry, shoot. It's past five and I have to change before heading to work. I'm in trouble!"

We scrambled up from my living room floor, where we'd strewn the afternoon's work.

Kitty gave me another hug. "You know, Daisy, you may have found a real talent here." She gazed over my living room floor, tiled now with notes.

"What do you mean? We didn't figure this out."

"Perhaps not yet, but I suspect you will do it. Just make it soon, won't you? Please?"

Helplessness crept like ice into my brain. Who was I to think I could really solve one murder, much less two? And what about the assault on Sandra? Was it the same bad guy who did that?

There was a knock at my back door. I waved bye to Kitty out front and ran to open the door for Chip at the back.

CHAPTER 38

Creativity is the spirit behind every story, but determination and perseverance are the cousins who make a writer successful. I'd woken to a cold front, Monday gray skies, and a good, hot cup of tea. Perfect conditions for inviting my muse to visit. I huddled up in my grungy old bathrobe and fuzzy pink slippers. Damn the looks, I was going to write.

Georgette, my companion in creative endeavors, only took three practice moves before successfully leaping to my couch. She settled in her spot and stared at me with encouragement in her lightly gilded eyes.

I had, as usual, a clear schedule, so was resolute about writing today. I would remember to add conflict and . . .

And the doorbell rang. I waited a minute or two. Maybe whoever it was would go away.

The doorbell rang again. Dang. Seven-thirty in the morning and the solicitation parade was already beginning. I tramped to my front door ready to tell whoever it was that I was not interested.

I flung the portal wide, only to confront Sergeant Linda Taylor. She, of course, looked flawless in a camel pea coat and black pants suit. Suddenly, my comfy writer's outfit seemed a tad understated.

I heaved a sigh. "Oh, it's you. More questions?"

Feeling resigned, I turned away from her and walked back toward my living room. "Well, come in." Tossed the last comment carelessly over my shoulder. I know. Not too hospitable, but doggone it: did the woman always have to be so immaculate?

Taylor stopped at the threshold. "Really no questions. Apologies." I turned and saw for the first time a hint of nervousness about her. Oh yes, the hair was neat and tidy as always, the doe-shaped eyes done up with precisely the right amount of liner and mascara, the coat a trim, conservative covering. If I could get past my jealousy, I'd have to say that Taylor was — er — well-tailored.

But there was something else. There was a whiteness to the knuckles that held her ever-present clipboard. In fact, if she held the board any closer to her chest, I'd have to

guess the thing might run the risk of suf-
focating.

"Sergeant Taylor, please do come in." I
tried sounding if not friendly, at least civilized.

"Thank you." She stepped across the
threshold and carefully closed my front
door.

We crossed into my living room and sat. I
took my reading chair and Sergeant Taylor
sat in Art's old lounger. Taylor's seat
groaned and protested under even her slight
weight. I'd have to get that fixed one day.
Meanwhile, I appreciated what I took to be
Art's commentary on my visitor. Couldn't
agree more. Sergeant Taylor was a pain.

The police officer cleared her throat.
"Maybe I shouldn't have come." She half
rose.

"Do sit, Sergeant," I said. We were both
too old to play childish games over shyness.
"Might as well have your say, then we'll take
it from there."

The sergeant nodded her assent, cleared
her throat again, and re-sat. "Daisy —
excuse me — Ms. Arthur. It was wrong of
me to ignore evidence of your lack of guilt
in the murders of Father Sanchez and Mr.
Stevens. I apologize."

While not impressive or very sincere

sounding, it was a start.

I shrugged. "Why? Why did you ignore the evidence of my innocence?"

"Correction — lack of guilt."

"Whatever. Why?" To be visited at this very early hour for such a skimpy apology was almost as insulting as — no, nothing could be as bad as that interrogation. I shuddered at the thought.

"Because I thought you were guilty and . . . playing Gabe."

"Guilty? *Playing* Gabe? Preposterous!"

Taylor looked at me curiously.

I shook my head. "I guess people don't really say *preposterous* too much any more."

She shook her head. "Maybe that's why you're the creative writer and I'm — I'm only a cop." Sergeant Taylor dipped her head in self-blame mode.

Was she kidding me? I stopped her right there. "My goodness, young woman, I hope your mother never hears you talk like that. You are an impressive and scary police officer, you project a capable air in everything you do, and" — I guiltily perused my super-casual apparel — "you're one of the tidiest people I've ever seen. Here it is, the crack of dawn, and you appear looking like you freshly stepped off the pages of *Cosmo.*"

"Thanks." Taylor smiled but sobered immediately. "Anyway, I suspected you almost from the start."

"Me? I don't know whether to be horrified or flattered. How could I have stood out enough to be your personal choice for key suspect?"

"You're new to your writer's group. That makes you both an outsider and suspicious. By the way, why did you join that particular group?"

"I called the membership chair of the Rocky Mountain Fiction Writers and asked which critique groups met nearest my house."

"So you didn't even ask about romance writing?"

"Nope. I could have been in a sci-fi group or a suspense writer's group, anything. I merely wanted to belong to something and to try my hand at writing."

"Oh." Taylor looked disappointed. "But why did you attempt to seduce Sanchez the night before he died? We think maybe he disappointed you? Maybe you thought you'd get even for him not taking you up on any offers?"

"First of all" — I put my tea cup down — "I did not try to seduce San — Father Sanchez. It was Rico who was coming on to me."

"That's not what another witness said."

I let my mouth gape. "No! Who told you that?"

"It's evidence I'm not at liberty to discuss."

"Hogwash."

Taylor smiled again. "Well, would you really want to know who in your group thinks you're a flirt?"

I scowled. "I guess not. So far, though, the case you're building against me isn't very strong."

"Yes, but then your fingerprints were all over the second victim's apartment."

"Yours would have been too, if you'd visited him right after his police interrogation." Oh. The interrogation was probably a sore spot for both of us. Change subject, Daisy, you flirt. "Would you like a cup of tea?"

"That would be delicious." Sergeant Taylor graciously followed my lead into safer conversational waters. "Wish I'd stopped by that new muffin shop on Main. Sorry. It would have been nice to wake you with something more than an apology."

"The apology works. I'll pop some toast." I'd made my way to the kitchen by now and shouted out to her. "Might as well take off your coat while I get things going." Flirt. I kind of liked that. Went well with being a romance writer who was learning to like conflict.

I stepped back into the living room to see Taylor's coat neatly placed on the back of Art's chair, but no sign of the police officer.

"Taylor? Sergeant? Where are you?" I wandered through the living room into the den, my writing office, and caught Sergeant Taylor shuffling through my drawers. How dare she? I stomped my foot and the officer jumped.

"Apology, my eye. Get out and don't come back without a warrant."

Taylor had the courtesy to blush. "Ms. Arthur, I am so very sorry."

"Don't bother saying more. It would only be a lie."

Taylor winced. She even looked good doing that, damn her. "No. No it wouldn't," she said. "I'm only trying to protect Gabe — Lieutenant Caerphilly."

"Protect him from what?"

"You."

"Oh, that's rich. What, do you think I'm going to knock him off too? Pre— ridiculous."

Taylor sighed and threw up her hands in surrender. "You win. If you'll hear me out, I'll tell you why I'm really here."

Against my better judgment I did precisely that. We went back into the living room and over tea and toast, the young woman told me about how she had wanted me to be the main suspect because she could see that Gabe was interested in me, but didn't sense any true feelings in return. She said she'd seen how hurt he was when some of his first dates went awry after his divorce, and how he'd struggled to bring up Ginny on his own. The sergeant admitted she'd warned Gabe not to trust a witness or a suspect and had even gone so far as to dig up my retirement story.

"So, Ms. Arthur, while you may not have committed the murders, I felt you still might be dangerous for Gabe. But, after Friday evening at the police station, he made it clear that he'll take care of himself and that I better apologize if I wanted to keep my job in his department."

"But you're not really sorry." I didn't pose it as a question.

Sergeant Taylor looked at me carefully for a moment. "I'd do it again in a heartbeat. I watch his back. He's my partner."

"So what you're saying is that you're in love with him."

She looked at me long and hard. "Let's just say he's a special man."

I crossed my arms. "Agreed. So?"

"So, you treat him well." She patted the gun holstered at her side. "Remember. I've still got his back. And I've got my eye on you. Always."

The threat was undeniable. Question was, what exactly was the relationship between Gabe and his capable, fully armed assistant? "Understood," I said. I led her to the front door. "And Sergeant Taylor?"

"Yes?"

"Thanks for being honest with me. You can call me Daisy."

"Good. Daisy. It suits you. Bye."

"Bye, Linda."

She turned back, professional to the core. "You may call me Sergeant Taylor."

Then she was gone, this police woman I might one day learn to respect, but couldn't like. Ever.

CHAPTER 39

The clackity sound of my keyboard had been silent for more than a half hour. Gwen sat on my latest pages, a blob of inertia and adolescent impotence regarding her lover, Grant. I wanted to barf. My muse, so full of promise in the morning, apparently had other appointments for the afternoon. I gazed out my window toward Colorado's granite sky and made a decision. If my muse would desert me so unceremoniously, I could do the same right back.

So I bought a leash at PetSmart and "kidnapped" Thunder. I left a note for Chip not to worry; I was headed to the river behind Aspen Grove. It was the most creative writing I'd done all day.

Thunder and I drove down Santa Fe, past the community college and the Catholic seminary toward Aspen Grove. How things had changed in the past fifteen years. The old country lane had become a business mecca, and my destination was one more assault on what used to be the rural feeling of my part of town.

I heard a merry ding and checked my dashboard. The low gas light had come on. Dang!

Thunder and I pulled into a gas station. Although I tried to think about writing, foremost on my mind were the murders and Sandra, so I autopiloted my gas routine. I jumped out of my car and began pumping.

Then a big tan-and-black head accompanied by batwing ears popped out my open door. Before I could stop him, Thunder leapt from my vehicle and sniffed the gas pumps.

"Thunder, come here!" I tried to sound firm but calm, as the dog books instructed. Thunder had obviously read other dog texts, because his reaction was not to come, but to wag his massive tail and run off. He turned to see if I was following.

"This is serious, Thunder. Danger!" I tried to keep the panic from my voice. Santa Fe is six lanes of cars all going over the forty-five-mile-an-hour speed limit. I ran toward my charge.

Thunder took my approach as acceptance that I wanted to play tag and edged closer to the street.

I grabbed my head and squeezed my eyes shut. "No! Thunder!"

A high-pitched whistle came from somewhere behind me. I opened my eyes to see Thunder trotting past me toward the sound. A tall, jean-clad man stood outside the doorway of the gas station's snack shop with something in his hand. His cowboy boots had the look of authenticity about them and, as Thunder went to investigate, he was rewarded with a treat from the handsome stranger. The cowboy grabbed Thunder's collar and led him back to me.

"Burger," he said by way of explanation. "Good dog you have, ma'am."

"Thank you. He's my neighbor's. I just walk him from time to time." I enjoyed looking up into the man's rugged face. I reached out to shake his hand and realized I still held the dog's leash in mine. "Oops. Sorry." I pulled back and switched the leash to the other hand. "I'm Daisy."

"Ms. Daisy, I'm Clint." He shook my hand, then nodded toward the leash in my other. "May I?"

Deftly, Clint clipped on Thunder's tether without incident. I noticed my cowboy was wearing a wedding band. Oh, well. I remembered happier days at Independence, when the other teachers would say window shop-

ping could be as much fun as buying sometimes. Now I knew what they meant.

"Thanks so much, Clint," I said. "I guess
I have a lot left to learn about dog-sitting."

He smiled. "These guys can be a handful.
Had several as a kid. People think shepherds
are vicious because they don't generally
wander around with tongues hanging out,
but I think they have the goofiest personalities of all the breeds. Add that to their
general intelligence, and you're always running after 'em."

I laughed. "You're absolutely right. I know
Thunder knows the commands I give him,
but whether he complies or not is another
story."

"How old is he?"

"Nine, no — he recently turned ten
months."

"Give him another six to eight, and you'll
never want to let him go. Loyal as all get
out, these guys."

"Clint, it's been a pleasure to meet you." I
would definitely write about this encounter
in my journal. A true angel moment. It's so
comforting to know the world can be uplifting sometimes.

Clint smiled at me again. "Pleasure was
all mine, Ms. Daisy." He turned to Thunder.
"You be a good boy, now, hear?" He growled

at the dog, who wagged effusively in reply.

Thunder barked and let me lead him back to my car. We finished filling the tank, keys firmly in my hand, and Thunder shut in behind closed doors. We drove to the park behind Aspen Grove without any more Thunder adventures.

"Now, big boy, I need you to let me think." We left the car. "You've had your fun, so now it's my turn. I want to go back to the scene of the first crime without any extra escapades, hear me?"

Thunder wagged his tail. I could have sworn the dog grinned. Losing it, Daisy. Dogs like Thunder don't smile. I couldn't help myself. I beamed back at him and rubbed his head.

We wandered into the tall grasses that had turned from soft green to gold in merely the week since our last visit. Autumn in Colorado seems to creep in quicker than night turns to day.

As we neared the wooded area, I saw the old man of the park again. And Rocky. Today's waders were accompanied by a windbreaker jacket over his cardigan. His hat was no longer full of flies or lures or whatever you call them, but was a sturdy, warm knit cap. Wish I'd remembered to wear one of them.

The old man nodded. "You seem to pet-sit a lot."

"Actually, I borrowed Thunder for the afternoon. I'm not too fond of walking in the woods, and Thunder here helps me overcome my jitters."

"Dogs are good for that." He made a move to walk on, then stopped. "You're a good woman to help with the dog. With some training you'd be a good pet-sitter. The dog — Thunder? He seems to have taken a real liking to you."

I glanced down at my side. Thunder was sitting, looking up at me with loving eyes. I smiled and gave him a pat. "I've taken a real liking to him too."

"Hmm. Can he have a treat?"

"Of course. You don't have to ask."

"Oh yes, you do. Dogs get allergies all the time. That, and not all dogs have soft mouths. Best to ask permission."

"Soft mouths?" I looked at Thunder. His jaw seemed nice and firm to me.

"Soft mouth means that when a dog takes a treat, he doesn't take half your hand with it."

"Oh. I'm not sure . . . yes. I think Thunder has a soft mouth."

The man smiled and gave Thunder a dog cookie. As my pooch munched away, the old geezer stroked his sides and looked into Thunder's eyes, even grabbed his ears.

I backed up a bit. "What are you doing?"

"Sorry. Old habits. I was a vet."

A vet? General Geezer? "Oh! A veterinarian. In that case, pet away."

"Your dog, or your friend's dog, has great lines, clear eyes, healthy-looking ears. This is a superb specimen of shepherd."

"Superb or not, I think he's perfect." I reached down and scratched Thunder. Rocky, the old geezer's dog, seemed to feel left out, as he came over and nudged my hand for a bit of attention for himself. I buried my hand in his fur and scratched at his shoulder blades. Perhaps I could learn to like dogs after all.

The old man looked up at me from his examination of Thunder. "You know, the American Kennel Club has a certificate of recognition for well-trained dogs. I think they call it the Canine Good Citizen award. Bet, with a little work from you, this fellow could earn one of them."

"Does Rocky have one?"

"Yep. It was a high priority with me. Got it about five years ago. Training was fun."

General Geezer went on to explain a few of the requirements, like sit, stay, act politely with strangers. I thought that if they had that certificate for people, the world would be a much happier, safer place.

I felt a warmth toward the old guy that opposed the cold front sweeping off the foothills. When I really looked at this man, his face wasn't etched so much by years as by a life well-lived. He had a kind smile and a capable way with both dogs and me. A bit gruff, but he was the kind of person I'd like to have as a friend.

I stuffed out my hand. "I'm Daisy. Daisy Arthur."

"Sam Waters."

I looked over Sam once and couldn't help it. I giggled.

"What's so funny?" His furry eyebrows drew together, ready for a fight. Then he nodded his head to see what I was looking at, and a slow grin spread over his face. His tummy rumbled out a joyful blast of laughter. "Waters. Waders. I get it. Ha!" Then he reached down and plucked a wild aster and with great show said, "Not quite a Chrysanthemum leucanthemum, but for Daisy, a flower."

I chirped my giggle again. Suddenly, we were like two little kids laughing and walking along, our dogs trotting companionably behind.

"Try this one," said Sam. He dropped

Rocky's lead and told his dog to heel. Rocky did as he was bidden.

"That's amazing. I don't think Thunder could do that."

"He won't if you don't ever try to trust him. Start small. I know he's only a pup, but take a few steps. If he wanders, step on the end of the leash. He'll catch on."

We practiced this "off leash" lesson for a few minutes, each time with more success.

"Thanks, Sam. You're a gem."

"Daisy. Have to go now, but I'm sure we'll see you again." His face shone. I wondered how I could ever have thought of Sam as an old geezer. As they left, I turned to Thunder. "See, boy? Told you they'd be friends one day."

Thunder barked, but miraculously stayed with me as we walked in the opposite direction. I needed to return to Rico's murder site, and I was glad for Thunder's company.

CHAPTER 40

Crime scene. Yuck. In the afternoon light, with the cottonwoods now bereft of half their leaves, the place felt colder, fiercer than before. Much of the yellow police tape had fallen away by the time I reached the spot, but it still gave me chills. Did I really need to be here? Couldn't I have figured this out from Kitty's and my notes? I stepped gently forward. A twig snapped under my foot and I jumped.

"Thunder, help me out, will you? Last time we were here, you proved Todd didn't kill Rico. Now I need you to show me who did."

Thunder wagged that tail again and sniffed among the bushes. Nope. No help at all.

Why would Rico have come here? Was he an outdoorsman like the old geezer — like Sam? Why was he killed here? I tried to picture him. Would he have come alone? I know I wouldn't. Still, it was more than that. Rico was social — too social — to go for long walks by himself in the woods.

And Todd wouldn't have agreed to walk with him. Todd knew better than to come to this dirty, albeit majestic place. Would Sandra have come to meet Rico here?

Sandra of the perfect hair, starched everything, and coping mechanism of pretend tea? It didn't feel right. Another muffled crackling sound and I jumped. It was only the wind, but my jumping stirred up Thunder, who started to wander off. I let him lead me further up the river path.

"Rico, what were you doing here?" I said aloud as I rounded a bend in the path. I almost bumped right into someone coming from the other direction.

"Oh! Sorry!" I said.

The woman hiker smiled at me. "No problem. The paths can be quite narrow."

"Can I ask how you happen to be walking by yourself out here?" I had to ask. This was not something I'd do on my own.

"Sure." The woman shrugged. "I love walking, and my husband doesn't. Each week, usually Mondays, when he's at work, I steal an hour for myself and explore this park. It's really beautiful, isn't it?" She lifted her gaze and looked across the river toward the mountains. This woman looked very much at home here in her khaki cargo pants and thick-soled boots. Her red and black flannel jacket was right off the cover of some hiker's magazine, no doubt.

I looked down at my own jeans and loafers, feeling somewhat vulnerable. "Yes, but still, I think you're very brave. I have this beast of a dog with me so it's okay. I don't think I could walk in the woods by myself, though."

Sorry, Thunder. You are a beast sometimes.

"That's why I carry my stick." The woman proudly held it out for me to see. The staff's woodgrain wove a mesmerizing pattern up to a baseball-sized knot on top. "This gives me a chance to push away things in my path without risking bites." Her smile dimmed. "Unless . . . you mean the murder that happened here?"

I hadn't, but now that she mentioned it, I shrugged. "It was close by, wasn't it?"

"Yes. Unsettling, but I'm not going to let one incident stop me. I make sure to keep a good grip on my walking stick here. And of course I wouldn't go around after dark." She nodded back to her silent companion.

I gave myself an internal shake. "Good idea. Incidentally, do you know if the path we're on loops back to the main parking lot?" I pointed back in the direction I'd come from.

"No, it doesn't. I usually get on at Hudson Gardens and walk south till I hit the open ground and paved walkways. Then I turn around and head back, past the seminary."

"Goodness. I didn't know you could go so far."

"These greenbelts are the best part of Denver. If you wanted, you could walk all the way to downtown, or get off wherever's convenient."

I thanked my unofficial guide, and she disappeared around the corner again.

As we traveled farther on the path, I imagined all the places it was possible to go. My students would have really enjoyed field trips here. They'd have learned so much from the adventure. Of course, Carl couldn't come with his wheelchair, and Tammy would be hard to keep out of the river. They'd all be muddy from head to toe. I would've had to bring Sally, my head aide, to scout out the place for ideas on how we could make it work.

Hang on.

If I came here with the idea of planning an outing for my group, wouldn't Rico have done the same? Didn't someone say he helped with the youth group?

In my mind's eye a partner appeared with Rico. Someone different from Sandra or Todd. They might have even walked to this area with the intention of planning a youth outing in these woods — and yes, it all fit.

Oh my stars! I knew, without a doubt, who killed the not-so-saintly priest. But Todd too? I could be wrong, but instinct said I wasn't. I'd have to check it out.

Thunder and I trekked back toward my car and cell phone. Exhilaration ran through me as things, at last, made sense.

I dialed for Chip. No answer. I left a message. "Hello, Chip? It's Daisy. I'm keeping Thunder a little while longer than expected. Think I may have stumbled on a solution about who killed Rico and Todd. Going to check it out. Thanks. Bye."

I turned to Thunder, who was busy lapping at the bowl of water I had poured for him. "C'mon, good boy. We're going to go get religion!"

CHAPTER 41

Thunder and I drove the short distance to the Denver Seminary's compound. Why hadn't I noticed how close to the park it was before? I pulled my Nissan into the complex and parked. The multiple housing and business buildings except for the church looked almost identical in a blood red and ochre sort of way. Very dormitory feeling. Where to begin? How do you find the proverbial needle in a haystack? Was I even looking for the right needle?

I turned to my furry friend as I pulled my keys from the ignition. "Thunder, I'm going to have to trust you in my car for a while. Will you be good?"

Thunder panted, then made a licking gesture with his tongue.

Good enough for me. I cracked my windows, and took off his leash. Gabe's reprimands still rung in my head. Make sure my dog has plenty of cool air and nothing to

367

choke on.

"This shouldn't take long, buddy." I locked my door, then took off to the closest building.

When I entered, there was no receptionist. I was greeted by a bank of unmarked mailboxes. Hadn't figured on that. Two or three more residential buildings produced the same result.

I walked across to one more place. If nothing worked out here, we'd have to go home. After all, I couldn't be sure of my conclusion, not being a detective or anything.

The new building was set up for family counseling. A woman near my age sat behind the desk wearing a busy-doing-nothing kind of attitude. Signs everywhere admonished visitors to be on time for appointments.

"Excuse me." I smiled at the woman. She didn't bother to return the gesture. "I'm looking for someone who might be living here?"

"This is the family counseling center," she said. "We don't have people living here."

"But all these buildings —"

"Are someone else's concern." She shuffled papers, trying, it seemed, to ignore me.

Sheesh, long week already, and it was only

Monday. I tried again. "But surely you know or perhaps could find out if someone lives at the seminary?"

The woman heaved a sigh, removed her glasses, and spoke directly to me at last. "Do I look like a Google search directory to you? I'm very busy here and don't have time to locate your misplaced friends."

I scanned the reception area. Some toys sat in a nearby corner, but otherwise it was empty. A Janet Evanovich novel was splayed near the woman's elbow. Patience, Daisy.

"I'm sorry to impose. It's that I really need to find out if — that is — where a person lives. She's very danger— impor— tant."

The woman was all primness as she said, "All of God's children are important."

"Look, lady, I don't want to study theol- ogy with you. I only need some informa- tion." Couldn't anyone go the extra mile these days?

"You needn't get snooty about it. I said I don't know how to find whomever you may be looking for." The woman pursed her lips starchily and busied herself straightening papers. My fingers itched to go over and push her pile onto the floor.

The door leading to a hallway of offices opened. Father John from Sandra's Most

Holy Saints church stepped out.

He didn't notice me, but spoke to the receptionist. "Mary, I need to find Sean O'Neal. I think he lives in student housing here."

"Certainly, Father," said Mary. She tucked a loose strand of graying hair behind her ear and flipped open a binder. "Here he is. Apartment thirty-two seventy-nine. That's in building four, right down near the greenbelt path."

"Father John," I called. He turned and stared at me. No recognition.

"I'm Daisy," I said. "Daisy Arthur. I was at your parish a few weeks ago, the day after Father Sanchez was found."

"Ah, yes!" said Father John, recollection at last registering on his face. "You came with Sandra Martin. How is she? I didn't see her at Mass yesterday."

"She's still in the hospital, but I think she'll be all right."

"Hospital! I didn't know. What happened?"

"She'll be all right, Father. She's at Littleton General, and I understand will be heading home in the next day or two. But Father, I'm looking for help."

"Yes, my dear?"

I glanced at Mary, tempted to smirk.

Father John would surely help me. "I came to find your youth director, Carla."

"Carla Brown? But of course. Only why would you need to see Carla?"

Gosh, what a good question. Could I tell this man, standing in the middle of a family counseling clinic, that I was looking for his youth minister because I suspected she was a murderer? Not precisely tactful. And there was Mary Contrary, showing more than enough interest in my private conversation. Maybe I could make something up.

"I . . . er . . . have some old school supplies. Thought she could use them. I was in the neighborhood and guessed she lives here." Not bad, ol' girl. That sounded at least plausible.

Father John's smile was hot cocoa on this cold day. "Ah. How kind of you." I felt a pang of guilt for my fabrication, and hung my head.

Father John placed his hand on my shoulder. "I can't give out people's addresses; I'm sure you realize that. However, I'd be happy to give her whatever you have."

It felt like his gentle gaze saw right through my lie. Now what? Lie again, or spill the beans?

"It's a rather large box of items, Father," I said, crossing my fingers behind my back. I sure hoped God was all-forgiving. "I'll drop it off over at your church next time I'm headed in that direction. Thanks, anyway."

"All right, dear child. Peace be with you." He made the sign of the cross in front of me and disappeared into the hallway guarded by Monster Mary.

"See?" said Mary. "No one gives out private information around here." She looked at me as if she were ready to stick out her tongue. Why is it I cannot abide such self-righteous people in my life?

"You do have the information I need," I snapped. "So you lied. That's a sin. Now you won't give me that information, and it's really important. Do I look like some sort of axe murderer to you? You could have helped, but you just plain *wouldn't.* You could've opened your stupid binder and —"

"Please control your voice." Mary Superior tilted her chin up.

"Control my — that's it! Do you know who I am? Do you? I am a romance writer. I am going to put you into my next book, and, by golly, you will never get the guy! You will be a doomed spinster forever!"

Mary's jaw dropped. I couldn't tell if she was frightened or amused. I didn't care. In one smooth movement I swished her papers to the floor and took off at a run.

She was jibbering incoherently at my beastly behavior as the door closed behind me.

Whew! That was strategic and tactful. Daisy, you'll have to apologize sometime.

I'd already spent about a half hour running around the seminary, and was out of ideas for finding my haystack-hidden needle. I stepped into the complex bookstore. Just being amongst books would help me calm down, and think.

Carla was close by; I could feel it, but I wasn't so sure that she was the murderer I sought. My own behavior toward that Mary woman was worse than I'd ever seen in Carla. How could I have done such a rude thing to someone I didn't even know?

Think about the murder, Daisy.

In the woods it had been it so clear. Now I realized Carla could've had the opportunity for killing Father Rico, but what about her motive? And what about Todd? As far as I was aware, she didn't know him. Then, running down Sandra?

I must be mistaken. Maybe the woods had merely left their fingerprints on my sensitivities.

I bought a book on meditation and headed toward my car and my dog.

CHAPTER 42

As I walked across the parking lot pulling my lightweight jacket tighter around me, I envisioned a nice cup of tea with navy bean soup for dinner. When a cold front sweeps down from the mountains, soup is the best protection against a chilled, creaking, and lonely house. My tummy grumbled. Maybe Daisy Arthur, super sleuth, could go home and make sure her conclusions were drawn from the right set of facts.

When I reached my Versa, it surprised me to see the door open. I wouldn't have done that, especially as I had just had that runaway incident with — Thunder! Oh my stars! Where was Thunder? I dove into my car, hoping in vain that the beast would still be there. I couldn't believe he might open a door and run off. The back seat was empty, the floor well unoccupied. No Thunder. No leash.

Wait a minute.

This was too much. A dog who could open a car door and bolt, but before doing so, had the forethought to grab his leash? Someone stole him. From a seminary? Chip would never believe this. Or forgive me. I wouldn't forgive me either. Poor Thunder!

Who would have done something like this? Who would steal a dog from a car at a religious place like the Catholic seminary? Who would be brave enough to put their arm in the window of a door guarded by a big German shepherd?

I jumped out of my car to look around. Thunder. Where was he? I didn't want to call Chip. I absolutely *had* to find Thunder.

Perhaps I should call the police. But the last thing I needed was another "incident report" by Littleton's finest. I shuddered at the thought.

Santa Fe loomed a short distance east of me, and Thunder had tried to run into that traffic only a little while ago. I hoped that wasn't his direction. At least the cars weren't rushing forward. Traffic backed up by this time of day, so if Thunder wandered there, he might still be okay. I trotted quickly toward the street, calling as I went. No sign of him.

The best chance of recovering my charge was within the seminary. I walked back toward the buildings. People were stepping about, pulling their coats around them. I wished I had worn more than my old sweatshirt and windbreaker. It was getting cold.

"Excuse me," I called to a passerby. "Have you seen a German shepherd around here?" The man shook his head and walked on. A second person said yes, but pointed out a German shorthaired pointer. I repeated the question a few more times with no luck.

My watch showed nearly five-thirty. I had just about a half hour of sunlight left to find Thunder. Perhaps I should call Chip and face the consequences.

Oh, why had I lied to a priest? God was probably in a bad mood today. I bit my lip in thought.

"Excuse me," said a young woman. She had a pink nose and charming face under her wool cap. "Were you asking about a dog?"

"Yes!" My heart jumped. The girl was an angel — had to be. I was forgiven. Yippee!

"What kind of dog?" she said.

"German shepherd."

"I can't say for sure, but I saw someone walking with a big black-and-tan dog about ten minutes ago. They seemed to be struggling about which way to go."

"That's gotta be Thunder! Thank you so

much! Can you tell me where they went?"

The young woman pointed. "Into the woods, by that path over there."

I thanked the woman, who wished me luck and walked off.

The woods. Dark, scary, without-my-dog woods. The hair on the back of my neck stood on end. Sun's going down — woods. The I-don't-want-to-go-into woods. Perhaps I should call Chip now. He would understand. I started dialing —

A yelp cut through the crisp air. It had to be Thunder. What was happening to him? The yelp slapped my ears again. Goodness, how bad was my guy hurt? I dropped my phone into my bag and took off at a run.

"Thunder!" I yelled. "I'm coming. Thunder!"

CHAPTER 43

I ran until out of breath. In other words, I made it about fifty feet.

But Thunder was in trouble. My short sprint landed me on the path I most dreaded. I had to push on. My lungs felt ready to burst. Cold mountain air will do that to you. So will a lack of exercise. And old age. But I forced my legs to keep moving. Worry will overcome many obstacles. And I was worried.

"Thunder! Here boy," I called. No answer. No more yelping, but no response either. For some reason, *The Wizard of Oz*'s *"Lions and tigers and bears, oh my!"* kept running through my head. My only hope was to keep calling out on the off-chance Thunder would recognize my voice and decide to come to me.

Meanwhile, the cloudy afternoon was fading fast. Shadows lengthened, wind sang in ghostly chants among the treetops, and bits of dried-up leaves tumbled about in the undergrowth. At least I hoped they were leaves. With the fading light, I couldn't see well. To stay calm, I decided to talk to myself between calls for Thunder.

"He's a big dog. He'll be okay. Yes, he's only a puppy, but he's a big puppy. Who in their right mind would steal a mutt — correction, German shepherd — with all the trouble that would bring?"

I muttered and stumbled along, anxious about both the dog's and my safety more with each step.

Then I heard it. A high-pitched yelp again. The painful sound was torture to my heart! Oh my Thunder! Please, please, God. Let him be okay. I ran in the direction of the cry.

A bulging root tripped me and I stumbled forward, landing on my knees. As I struggled up, I saw a pair of work boots and jean-clad legs in front of me. Relief surged.

"Thank goodness! Someone else is in these god-awful woods!"

"You!" Carla and I said it as one, as we came face to face.

I hoped to sound tough. "What the hell are you doing here?"

"I would ask you the same question," she shot back.

"I'm looking for my dog." Did Carla steal dogs as well as direct youth? With the direction of my thoughts, it was easy to suspect the young woman of every crime imaginable since Eve bit into the apple. It all seemed to fit. Would it be smart of me to say so? "He was around here a few minutes ago. Perhaps you've seen him? Big, black-and-tan thing?"

"I think not. I have been walking in these woods for a while, and *your* dog has not crossed my path."

Why did Carla emphasize the "your"? And now what? Would it be smart to accuse her of being a liar? I tried a different tack. "So, you've been walking in the woods. Alone? At this time of day?"

"I often walk in the woods. It helps me think. And I am not alone." She glanced to her side.

I expected some thugs to emerge, like in the movies, but Carla stared lovingly at a large walking stick in her hand. "I always carry my friend with me," she said.

This gives me a chance to push away things in my path without risking bites.

Would Carla try to push me away with the stick? "It really is a big cane." I shook my head. The stick was even larger than that carried by the hiker I'd met earlier. "Isn't it heavy?"

"Sure, but I am strong." She suddenly grabbed the cane over her head with two hands and brought it down inches from my right side.

I gasped and jumped away.

Carla bent down where her stick had landed. She emerged again with a dead snake in hand.

"Protection is important when traveling the woods alone," she said. "This one was nonpoisonous." She looked a tad disappointed at that fact, and flung the limp rope-like creature deeper into the woods, away from our path.

Shock left me bereft of words or air.

"You should not have come out here without your dog, Ms. Daisy," said Carla. "But perhaps I could help you search for it."

Gee, what a proposition. Search a dark woods alone, where there were definitely snakes and other unpleasant critters — so much for Nick's theory of snake hibernation — or walk with someone I suspected of murdering two people with an attempt on a third. And what had she done with Thunder?

Carla must've seen my brow pucker. "You

do not want help, perhaps?"

"I thought I'd go home and come back tomorrow, in the daylight."

Her laugh sent a chill right through me that had nothing to do with the weather. "Ah. A little rabbit, are we? Well, come. I will show you a shortcut back."

That sounded reasonable. Carla strode with a confidence I could only assume came from her familiarity of these woods. I followed her for about five minutes, but nothing civilized came into view. I touched a blood-red leaf as we walked. One of the few remaining. It was sticky wet, and I pulled away. Goodness gracious, it really *was* blood!

"Carla, are you sure this is the right path?" I asked, trying to keep the panic from my voice.

"Oh, yes, Ms. Daisy. This is the way for you." She glanced back over her shoulder and smiled at me. I followed on, all the while noticing more blood on leaves. These were definitely not friendly woods.

Suddenly, Carla stopped. We looked down a gully into the Platte River. The water ran black in the evening shadows. I realized we were at the spot Father Rico had died. And I gulped.

CHAPTER 44

The black water gnashed over the rocks in its bed. Flickers of sunset's last light reflected off the movement like teeth gleaming in a National Geographic lion feast, and the powerful, hungry sounds of rushing water added to my desire to run. Carla stopped me with her words.

"You shouldn't have come, Ms. Daisy. I tried to warn you. You should not have come."

I turned to look at the youth director. She wore a face as sad as the executioner's at an innocent man's hanging. "Warn me?"

"Yes. Twice. I put the spider note for you — 'Keep out of God's work or else.' You are a widow, no? The Western black widow is a beautiful spider. I thought you would like it. It suits you."

"Ahh. I wondered. The writing washed away, you see."

"Then the email. I told you I was aware

you knew about me. Frankly I was surprised to see you that night, at the parking lot." She turned back to the river. "But having you there to — how do you say it? — to take the fall for Sandra's accident. Well, that made my work easier." She smiled at her memory.

Then Carla's face drooped into somberness. "He deserved it, you know," she said. "He was a horrid man. The snake from the garden of Eden."

"Father Rico?" I emphasized the *father* word, hoping to plant more positive thoughts. I was finding the woods very claustrophobic at that moment.

"Just Rico. He didn't deserve to wear any religious garments. A blasphemy on the Catholic Church and in the eyes of God."

"He hurt you."

She shrugged. "Yes."

I sat down. The earth was cold and moist, but this would allow me to grab onto something before Carla could drag me over the side of the embankment. Perhaps I could survive.

In my classes, I had calmed students by showing interest in what upset them most. "Can you tell me how you came to see Rico as such an evil man?"

"Wasn't his — how do you call it —

philandering enough? Couldn't you see the evil in him?"

I thought of the man who had been a part of my writing group a few short weeks ago. Had I seen his philandering side? He'd been courteous to everyone, except to Todd that one evening. And Todd was his lover. But lover-like?

Then I remembered all the hints about him lately. I remembered him holding my arm — stroking it. Was he really interested in me? I had assumed he was not, because of our age difference, but I remembered the magnetism I'd felt at his touch. I remembered the intensity of his gaze into my own eyes, the softness of his hand on my arm, and even at this later time, I felt a small thrill.

"You *do* see," said Carla.

"Yes, I do, but should a person be killed for having an abnormally active sex drive?" Could I say *sex* to a youth director? What was I talking about? This youth director was no innocent. She might be a murderer. "Carla, did Father Rico — Rico — did he perhaps, seduce you?"

Her laugh was bitter and long. "He told me we were meant to be together throughout eternity. Said I was the love he had looked for all his life. Our love was sanctioned by God, though Rico's work kept him from acknowledging that."

"I'm so sorry, Carla. But didn't you see he had so many lovers —"

"No! He had none! Not when he — when he — raped me!"

"He *raped* you?"

"What would you call it when a man of twenty-seven has sex with a girl of sixteen?"

"I don't understand. Rico only came to Colorado a couple of years ago. Neither of you is anywhere near that age."

"Yes, but he came from Mexico, like me."

"Oh, my stars! He had sex with you when you lived there?"

"When I was young and susceptible to such 'charms.'" She threw out the last word as if it were poison. In an instant I understood her hurt.

"So you followed Rico to this parish?"

"That is what he said, but this is not true. I came here when the youth minister job opened up, more than three years ago. Rico didn't arrive until almost a year later."

"And when he was placed here?"

"He didn't even *remember* me!" She spat on the ground.

I edged away an inch or two. Carla was angry enough that I remained in danger. How could I get her to keep talking but calm down?

A breeze blew over us, and I looked into the treetops. Their branches silhouetted against the darkening sky offered no comfort. How could Rico have been so cruel as to not even remember Carla?

"Carla, dear, some people are not as sensitive as we'd like."

"What *sensitive*? You take away a girl's virginity and you don't even remember her? You cause her to be disowned from her family. She has to survive in Mexico City with the crime and the horrors and the oh-so-friendly *turistas*? An' ju don' *remember* her?"

Uh-oh! Carla was talking to Rico and not to me. I was in trouble now. "Carla, Carla, he's gone. Rico's gone. Someone killed him, remember?"

"I remember," she said. Carla dug into the ground with her stick. "I remember that pig telling me my son and I were not important in his greater plans. He was going to be a bishop, and he would not allow us to get in his way. He accused me of following him to Denver, mainly to ruin his career, and he would not have it."

I saw Rico from a new light. Sex addict who had a cold, ambitious streak. He had truly hurt this woman deeply. The pain showed on her face even now.

"I'm so sorry, Carla." I stood and tried to hug her.

"Sorry. Bah!" She ripped away from me and pulled a weed from the ground. She threw it into the river below.

I inched backward. Calm, Daisy. Stay calm. Sweat broke out on my brow. Why hadn't I simply called the police with my suspicions? I could be home with my nice soup dinner by now, instead of trying to figure out how to stay out of the reach of Carla's nasty stick. Why hadn't I taken Gabe's pepper spray? Stupid me. Now I might never be home again. Carla had a crazy look about her I didn't trust.

"Carla, let's go home. I could make you some nice soup and tea."

"Home? Home? Home is in a small village in Mexico. It is a place where my *Mama* and *Papá* have no little Maria Carlotta any more. How can we go home?"

"Things change, Carla. Parents forgive. People forgive."

"Forgive? Did Rico forgive me for ruining his career? No, he did not!"

"But you didn't ruin his career."

"Yes, I did. I came to a parish that he was at too. I reminded him of our love, and he said I ruined his chances for being a bishop."

Personally, I hadn't thought about it much, but I couldn't see Rico as a bishop. Rico couldn't truly be the pastor at a Catholic church, much less someone higher up. He was too worldly by far. Not at all like that gentle Father John of Most Holy Saints.

"Rico hurt you with those words, Carla, but —"

"Hurt me? Hurt *me*? *He — killed — our — son!*"

Carla's cry filled the woods with anguish. It was the long tormented howl of a parent in grief. The sound rent the evening air with a deep, undeniable pain I understood from my own loss. Even so many years later, my heart cracked again for my Rose.

All around tree branches drooped with our sorrow. The wind stopped its ghostly stalking of dried leaves. Even the river's churning seemed to quiet in Carla's song of sorrow. I knew I could have run away then. I probably should have, but I reached out to Carla instead, and pulled her into a hug.

"Tell me about him," I said. "Tell me about your son."

"*Mi Tobias. Mi bebé.*" Carla's shoulders shook. There were no words, but tears streamed down her face. I held her as any mother might hold a child in pain. After a few minutes her sobs slowed. We sat on the ground, the menacing stick forgotten for a moment.

"Rico got me pregnant at my small village in Mexico," she said. "I had to leave the only life I knew. My papa said it was only until the baby was born. I would give the child up for adoption. There were places in Mexico City that would take care of such things. Then I could come home again." Carla sniffed.

I dug in my purse and pulled out a tissue. My cell phone was there, but I couldn't think how to use it without risking Carla's ire. She took the tissue, wiped her face, and went on.

"Only . . . when Tobias was born, I could not give him up. He was so beautiful, and I loved him in a heartbeat. I decided to stay in the big city and raise him myself."

"But . . . ?" I supplied the nudge she needed.

"But life in Mexico City was rough. When he was five and six years old, Toby often came home with bruises and bloody noses. It was not a good place for him or me. One time I helped a *turista* escape from some robbers, and in return he helped me get to America."

"And you came here?"

She nodded. "We were in Houston first,

but I saw the job here and applied. My priest in Houston, a very good and kind man, recommended me and I got the job."

"Then Rico came?"

Carla's face clouded over. "Yes." She curled her lip. "At first, he didn't remember me, but when I mentioned our village, he knew. I told him he was Toby's father, but Rico would never admit that truth to me or anyone else. He told me to be quiet about such nonsense or he would have me fired."

I cowered under the weight of her pain. How could Rico have been so unfeeling? So despicably cold? I shivered.

CHAPTER 45

Carla's story shocked me to the core. I was unprepared to face this different side of Rico. This new and shameful side. And yet . . .

Even though Rico used words like trite, long-winded, *and* grandiloquent . . .

Something in my brain had sent off warning signals. I knew Rico was dangerous, even back then, in my first encounters with him. His looks, his beautiful accent, threw me off track, but in that quiet part of my heart, I knew.

Rico was cold and calculating. He slithered the knife into my critique so sweetly, that only upon later reflection would I know I'd been stabbed. The past few weeks I'd been so busy trying to play at detective that I forgot to spend real, honest time reflecting on the victim. Now things clicked. Somehow I knew Carla was telling the truth.

But my emotionally wounded companion

had gently pulled away from me and stood once more. She stared into the grayness that wove into the fabric of the woods, searching for memories that both hurt and healed her in their telling.

"Then they went on that camping trip." Carla's voice dropped to a whisper. "The sheriff came with Rico to tell me my son . . . my son was dead. I screamed at Rico. I knew he did it, but he told the sheriff people make 'wild accusations' in their grief. They said it was an accident, but I knew. I could see it in his eyes. When the sheriff's back was turned, Rico smirked at me. Oh yes, that *híbrido* killed my son."

"There was no investigation?" I, too, stood.

"Why? Who would be foolish enough not to believe a priest?"

"I see." I hung my head. She was right.

Angry energy drove Carla to walk in circles as she talked. Dry twigs snapped under her force.

"Adam Martin knew. Toby and he were best friends. After the accident, and when his mother was visiting the church, Adam would sneak off to help me prepare youth projects. We would talk a bit and always about Toby. Then one day . . ."

I let Carla think for a moment before

prodding for more. "One day?"

"Rico came into the youth center. He saw Adam with me, and a look of pure evil rage crossed that man's face. It was gone so quickly I could have imagined the look, but then Rico called Adam away, and I never saw the boy after that. I knew that Adam was my proof. I asked Sandra to talk to her son about the accident, but she only had Rico come visit Adam for prayer counseling."

"So you took matters into your own hands."

Carla splayed her open palms and shrugged. "The sheriff wouldn't do anything. No one believed me."

"What happened?"

"I started watching Rico. I'm not sure what I was looking for. Then opportunity came. Things were not going well for Rico and his gay lover, Todd."

"You knew Todd?"

"Only from afar. I recognized him. And I knew he was Rico's lover." She spat on the ground again. "A rabbit, Ms. Daisy. A rabbit."

I thought of gentle-spirited Todd. His blue eyes had sparkled with the fun spirit he'd injected into our critique meetings. How could he have hooked up with the likes of

394

Rico . . . Hang on. Rabbit? Isn't that what Carla had called me? Wasn't that what was left at Todd's murder scene?

I had to keep Carla talking. My life depended on it. "So, opportunity?"

"Rico was planning a catechism class and wanted a small retreat place away from the parish. He was going to start in the church here, at the seminary, and lead the youngsters on a walk. I know the woods well and told him I would help him with planning their path."

"You brought him here?"

"Yes." She laughed at her memory. "He was so arrogant! He acted as if only a man could be adept in the woods. Kept trying to touch me and 'help' me . . . *me*! . . . over roots and rocks. Perhaps he forgot that he'd already had me as a lover."

"That must've been annoying."

"Yes, but suddenly I knew. We sat down and reviewed his lesson. We opened the Bible, and a perfect passage from Genesis caught my eye . . . 'The serpent beguiled me, and I did eat.' I highlighted it. Rico laughed at my silly reminder of his sins. Then a snake slithered nearby and Rico was afraid, so I smashed it with my stick." She looked lovingly at the rod only a few feet away.

"What I had to do became clear. It was a message from God. Rico, the snake, would be no more. He took his mind off me, denied my son as his own, and continued the devil's work he'd always done. So I bashed him on the head with my beautiful stick."

"And you dragged him to the river."

"No, Ms. Daisy. The fool got up and staggered to the riverbank. I guess he was — what is the word — *dizzy*? Suddenly, it came to me. A small shove would do. A small shove and Rico fell. I could have left him, and he probably would have drowned, but he might not have. He was a tricky devil. I just helped make sure of what was supposed to happen anyway. Then I washed my stick in the river. Far away from here."

Carla shrugged again and smiled.

I looked from her to her stick and a chill ran over me. Was I looking at the instrument of my own demise?

CHAPTER 46

The stick seemed to gleam in the last rays of daylight, especially the knotted end that was solid enough to kill a man. If that stick could talk, who's voice would it use? Carla's or Rico's? Both were trouble where I was concerned. Carla was finished with her story about Rico. Now what?

New subject, Daisy, quick. "And Todd? The rabbit?"

Carla's gaze dragged itself from the instrument of revenge to my face once more. It took her a moment to understand what I was asking about.

"Todd? Oh. I called him that day saying I had some of Rico's things he might want. I even brought a big box with me. When I pulled in the parking lot to his apartment, you and I almost collided our cars. Remember?"

Ah, yes. The parking lot fender bender I barely avoided. I nodded my response. I

397

hadn't seen the other driver clearly. Didn't know it was Carla.

"He said Rico never mentioned a Toby, but men will say anything. He had to know about Rico's son. They were lovers, after all. Then Todd showed me his disgusting painting of Rico."

Carla's face distorted with revulsion. Then she relaxed and shrugged. "It was almost too easy. I had brought along my walking stick and bashed him on the head too. Odd, I always thought heads were hard, but Rico's and Todd's smashed right in."

"You're the one who took Todd's painting."

"I burned it. A priest, even one such as Rico, should not be seen so."

So even Todd's artwork was gone. I shook and put a hand to my head. What a shame.

Carla laughed. "You act like a rabbit, Ms. Daisy, but I believe you think like a hawk. You showed up at Todd's when the police were there, so I knew you suspected me. I've been watching you since then, you know."

The walking-over-my-grave feelings. They hadn't been my imagination. This woman's anger had passed all boundaries, and still it clung to her every fiber.

"So you decided to 'bash' Sandra as well,

and pin it on me?"

"She had to know what Rico did to my Toby. Adam *must* have told her."

If only Carla knew how dysfunctional the Martins were, she would never have made such an assumption. But she didn't know, and telling her didn't matter any more.

Carla continued. "Then you were early and Sandra was late. I didn't allow for that."

"And how were you going to go on after these — er — events?" I tried to remain calm. Had to keep her talking. Had to think. I looked around for a path smooth enough for a quick get away. I had to get away. Gabe needed to hear this story. Pay attention, Daisy. What was that crazy woman saying now?

"I was going to go back to Mexico. I *am* going back to Mexico. Only you have figured everything out, so now, Ms. Daisy, my rabbit friend, I must bash you too." She actually pouted at that, as if she were sad over what she was about to do.

CHAPTER 47

I had to think quickly, act fast. Carla leaned down to get her stick. Lucky break. I swung my purse as hard as I could. She whirled at the energy in the air. My purse hit her in the ribs. The blow wasn't enough to do damage, but Carla fell off balance. A crazed look of fury enveloped her features.

I didn't stay to see more. Rabbit she had called me, so rabbit I became. I ran and ran through the woods, stumbling and crashing into trees and bushes. Snakes were forgotten. Coyotes or even mountain lions were no threat. Only Carla, yelling now with fury, was real.

I dove behind a cottonwood and grabbed in my purse for my phone. I dialed nine-one-one, then crouched down.

A few feet away in the underbrush lay something furry. I almost screamed, but then recognized my Thunder. Oh, heavens above. He was dead! I leaned over to pet him but was rewarded only with sticky blood on my hand.

"Thunder! Oh, please, Thunder, don't be . . ." I shook his warm body, willing him to be okay.

The emergency dispatcher came on line. I was crying so hard I could hardly hear her.

"Help," I cried. "I can't talk more. Help, please, help!"

A noise in the trees behind me forced me to freeze where I kneeled.

"Come out, little rabbit," called Carla from somewhere nearby. I dropped the phone and took off at a run again. Leaves crackled under my feet. Branches from bushes whipped my arms and face. I didn't care. Had to run. Run for my life.

Rustling sounded to my left, so I scooted in the opposite direction. The rustling followed me. Carla was inching closer with each step.

I found a dirt path and was grateful for the relative quiet of my steps. Now if only my heart would stop pounding so loudly. The Independence High drum corps was hardly louder. Thunder, Thunder, how could I have been so bad for you? How would I ever escape Carla and her stick?

The rustling continued, and I ran on. Blackness enveloped me. I perked my ears in an effort to hear the water of the Platte. Somewhere far, far away, the traffic from Santa Fe droned on. Would this be the last sound I ever heard?

The rustling of Carla's footsteps was closing in on me fast.

I ran with all my might and crashed into something softer than a tree. We both fell down.

"You!" Again, Carla and I yelled out simultaneously. How had she gotten in front of me? I knew I had heard the steps behind . . .

My adversary was truly athletically gifted. I struggled to my feet. Carla was faster.

I couldn't see her walking stick by now. Night was full on, but I knew the wicked stick was there. The dim light allowed me to barely make out Carla's form.

"You put up a good chase, little rabbit," she said. While she, too, panted, her voice held a calm determination.

I knew she'd made up her mind, and I was going to be her next victim.

"Please, Carla. It doesn't have to be this way."

My answer was a whooshing sound near my right ear. Then a thud as Carla's stick hit the ground. I jumped to my left. Whoosh-thump. I jumped to my right. Whoosh-thump. I wasn't going to be lucky much longer.

Suddenly I heard a ferocious growl, like the deep dark voice of a bear. Heavens above, what was that? Something leapt from the underbrush.

Carla screamed. The growl continued. The sound of breaking bone, which I knew from Sandra's accident, reached my ears.

"*Mi brazo! Mi brazo!* My arm!" Carla's cries were pure agony. I peered through the darkness.

"Thunder!" I cried. The dog held Carla pinned to the ground; her right arm lay at a sickening angle.

I unsnapped Thunder's leash and used it to tie up Carla, broken arm and all.

"Good boy, Thunder. Good, good boy. How badly are you hurt?"

Carla cried out. "I am hurting too much!"

"Not you," I snapped. I reached for Thunder, but he jumped away from me and repositioned himself on top of Carla. He stared at the deranged woman and kept growling.

Suddenly the woods were filled with beams of light, and someone called out with a megaphone.

"Daisy! Daisy Arthur! Can you hear us? Can you answer?"

Could I answer? What a question.

I screamed and screamed. I emptied my lungs, refilled them, and screamed some more.

In an instant, Gabe found me. With a few well-chosen commands he had everything under control and me in his arms. My body shook. I couldn't stop yelling. Then I heard a soft hush in my ear. Gabe's hand cradled my head into his neck. He took a blanket from one of the other officers and wrapped me in it, then whispered "Shh" to me quietly until I could stop bellowing.

I was safe at last. Then my world went black.

CHAPTER 48

We — Toni, Eleanor, and I — sat in a booth at Pete's Pub. Our sad, small writers' group had dwindled, at least for tonight, to three. Kitty had called to say she was working. Sandra was still in the hospital, stuck for one more night.

The doctor in the ER room said I had suffered shock from my encounter with Carla, and to expect nightmares, but that returning to a safe routine would be very good for me. Even if the routine called for a move away from the library for an evening.

I looked around our group again. Rico and Todd were gone forever. It was still so hard to believe. I pictured Todd's smiling face when he had first welcomed me to the Hugs 'N' Kisses group and felt a bittersweet satisfaction with the memory.

Toni finished reading her submission for the night, and while Eleanor and I made our editing marks, she stood and offered to order drinks for us at the bar.

"No Yellow Tail for me," said Eleanor with a wink in my direction. "I'll play it safe with a Manhattan."

"I'll stick with pop tonight," I said. "Lemon-lime, please."

Toni acknowledged our wishes and walked away.

"So Daisy," said Eleanor, "are you okay? I mean, that was a lot for anyone to handle, that business with the Catholic youth minister."

"I feel for Carla," I said, "but I'm very grateful that Chip had called the police when he got my phone message. It would have taken them longer to find me if they only had the nine-one-one call to go by."

"I think you're incredibly brave. You know, there's more to you than I ever thought at first." Eleanor gave me an encouraging nudge and winked again.

Toni returned with our beverages, and we dug into our reviews. I looked across at her and smiled. "I really, really like this. Your descriptions are so strong. 'A sky painted with the sorrows of the years.' Love it."

Toni nodded her thanks.

Eleanor went next. "I agree, Toni. Your writing gets more precise and eloquent all the time. How many books have you written at this point?"

Toni searched the ceiling for her answer, then turned to us. "This is my fourth."

"Are you planning to start submitting to publishers this time?"

"Not yet. I really enjoy the writing process, but I'm not quite ready for any big-time pressures."

Eleanor nodded her head in agreement. "Unfortunately, I think you're right, but by the time you complete your next project, let me know. I think my editor may be interested in your style."

"That's very generous of you." Toni smiled and sat taller in her seat.

I didn't bother to check in on the ready-for-publishing of my work. The harsh critique two weeks ago at Kitty's had made it plain how I stood with regard to writing. I sat quietly, hoping not to draw attention to myself, but Eleanor looked across the table to me.

"Don't worry, Daisy. You've made some impressive improvements over the last couple of weeks. Keep trying. One day, you'll get better." There was a friendliness to Eleanor's tone that took away any sting to her words.

"I think I do have an idea for another story," I said. "Gwendolyn really wasn't strong enough to carry *Love Finds a Way* to completion, but now Florence . . ."

Eleanor rolled her eyes and shook her head.

Toni took a sip of her drink, then spoke. "I think, as we don't have other pages to read tonight, we should talk about rebuilding our group."

I gave a thumbs-up sign. "Great idea. Do you have anyone in mind?"

She thought for a moment. "Well, when I was being interviewed by that Sergeant Taylor a few weeks back, she mentioned she's always been interested in writing."

Eleanor brightened at Toni's comment. "Oh, that nice police woman? She could add a lot to a group like ours."

Sergeant Taylor. Oh. My. God. What had she said the last time we spoke? *I've got my eye on you. Always.* I pictured her angry face in the interview room at the police station. It would be hell working with her.

But Kitty was repeatedly telling me I needed to embrace conflict. I felt the blood rise in my cheeks just thinking of Sergeant Taylor. Conflict was too clean a word for Sergeant Taylor and me. "Sounds terrific," I said, trying to hide the lie in my voice.

"Then it's settled," said Eleanor. "Daisy, you seem to have a better acquaintance with the police than any of the rest of us, so you can ask Sergeant Taylor to join us. But while we're revamping our membership, maybe we can consider a new name. It was quite embarrassing when that police lieutenant called us the 'hugs and kisses,' like we were a strip joint or something."

Toni laughed. "That was quite awful."

I took a sip of my soda. "Kitty wants to add a murder to her next novel. Kind of makes hugging and kissing a misnomer, doesn't it?"

At that moment, the door to Pete's opened and a couple walked in. Sergeant Taylor and Gabe Caerphilly. Joy of joys. It didn't take them long to do the surveillance once-over and spot us. I turned my back to them, hoping in vain that they would retreat out the door. They walked over.

Gabe spoke. "Good evening, ladies. Mind if we join you?" His handsome face was relaxed and cool, as if last night he hadn't found me in a deep dark woods with only a dog for protection — as if I hadn't been screaming like a banshee into his, now probably deaf, ear.

"Not at all," said Toni. "Daisy, scrunch over and let the police sit down."

I did as I was told, using superhuman effort to keep from glaring at Toni and the sergeant. Gabe slid in beside me, and I immediately felt the warmth of his body next to mine. Luckily, the group began to chatter as Gabe waved over a waiter.

After ordering, Toni took charge again. "Linda, we were just talking about you."

"Me? Why?"

I shrank back into the booth's leather so she couldn't move around Gabe to scowl at me.

Toni smiled. "I mentioned that you might be interested in writing, and we need new group members."

"Oh, thanks, Toni. But I don't write romance. Suspense is more my thing."

"That's great!" said Eleanor. "We were also talking about changing the name of our group. We could expand our focus to general fiction. Interested?"

"I'm not sure. Daisy, what do you think?" Sergeant Taylor leaned forward so she could see me around Gabe.

"She already heartily endorsed you," said Toni. "Said 'terrific.' We meet Tuesdays, normally at the library. Oh, but you know that. Any chance you can come?"

"Sounds like a plan." Sergeant Taylor looked over at me with that Queen Cleopatra smile. I sighed inwardly and voiced a quick approval.

Beneath the table, I felt Gabe's leg rub against mine. I stilled, hoping the connection wasn't merely an accident. He rested his leg next to my own, and I felt the heat pass between us. I stared at his profile. There was nothing to suggest he noticed what he was doing, but I sensed his focus was exactly where he wanted.

Soon Sergeant Taylor, Toni, and Eleanor were in deep discussion over new names and new focuses for our group. Gabe and I sat quietly, sipping our drinks.

Eleanor spoke up louder than the others. "How about something dashing, like 'Rocky Roads'?"

Toni shook her head. "No, it needs to be more positive."

"It needs to sound professional," said the sergeant.

Everyone turned to me. "You're being rather quiet, Daisy," said Eleanor. "Do you have any thoughts?"

"Well, I was remembering Todd and Rico." Everyone fell silent.

"They were like angels. No, don't look at me that way, Eleanor. The other priest at Rico's church told me about people having special messages for us, and that makes them at least temporary angels. What was Todd's and Rico's message to us? I think if we used their initials as some sort of acronym, then they'd never fade away but be a part of our group forever."

"Sounds good," said Toni, "but what do you make of R-S-T-S?"

"Well, I would combine the last names to one S and put Todd first. TRS: The Right Stuff."

"If we add the silent W for write, then I agree that Daisy has something there," said Eleanor. "I like the use of the homophone. Sure beats being a strip joint."

Everyone smiled.

Gabe raised his glass. "A toast to The Write Stuff. May your words never fail you."

We all lifted our glasses and said, "Cheers."

It wasn't long before the sergeant and Gabe announced they had to go.

"Stepping to the women's room," said Sergeant Taylor.

"Good idea," said Eleanor.

"I need to get ready for the drive home too," said Toni.

Suddenly Gabe and I were alone. He made no move to give me more booth room and looked down at me with his boyish grin.

"What, no bathroom, Daisy?"

"I'm less than ten minutes from home. I'll wait."

"You're amazing." Gabe suddenly looked serious. "Quite a scare you gave me — us, last night. You all right?"

"Umm," I said.

Jeez, Daisy, and you want to be a writer? I didn't trust myself to say more.

Gabe tried again. "I wanted to stop by sooner, but all the paperwork stole my time."

"Gabe, you're not my guardian. You were there for me last night when I needed a friend. Thank you."

He smiled. "I'll always be there for you, my friend. My Daisy."

Sergeant Taylor cleared her throat near our table. "Ready to go, Caerphilly?"

In one swift movement, he was in the aisle next to her. "No problem, Taylor." He laid down money for the bill. "Tonight's on the Littleton police, Ms. Arthur. With our thanks for helping us solve the case of Faith on the Rocks. Please say goodbye to your other group members for us."

I nodded and they were gone.

413

CHAPTER 49

"How does it feel to be a hero, Daisy?"

Kitty sat on my sofa, her petite body framed between Father John and Sandra. Today's outfit was a vision in orange. How did she do it? Everything should have looked gaudy, but on Kitty the bolder the color, the better she looked.

Gabe sat in Art's old armchair across from me. I smiled.

I turned my gaze to a photo Chip had given me. In it Thunder sat, bandage on head and tongue hanging out, happy-dog style. I shook my head. "Thunder's the real hero. Me? I'm just glad it's all over. But I think at least I learned something as well."

"What's that?" said Gabe. His purply-blue eyes glowed softly, and I felt a tremendous spirit of friendship in the warmth of my living room.

"That sometimes I project myself as a rabbit, but it's always my choice whether or not to be a victim."

Father John spoke up. "That's quite profound. Do you mind if I use that in a homily I'm working on?"

"Not at all, Father." I smiled. Father John was someone I would like to know better. His voice resonated with kindness, fairness, and a general well-being toward the world. In short, he was what I always pictured when I thought of priests.

Sandra cleared her throat. "It surprised me that I could honestly feel sorry for someone who became a villain." She sat with her leg propped up on my coffee table. We'd rigged a pillow under her broken ankle, and her sling-clad left arm had plenty of space between her and Kitty.

"Villain? You mean Rico?" Kitty asked.

"No," said Sandra. "Unfortuately, I think Rico got what he deserved. Adam told me how Rico threatened to hurt him if he ever told that he saw Rico shove Toby over that cliff. I never connected Adam's bedwetting to fear. My poor son. How I fell for that man's fake charm . . . Well, it's neither here nor there. No, I feel sorry for Carla."

I shifted in my chair to look at Gabe more directly. "What do you think will happen to her?"

He sat quietly for a few moments. I liked

415

how he always seemed to think carefully before speaking.

"It's hard to say. If she had killed only Rico, I would've said that a light sentence was possible. But she also killed Todd, and she tried to kill Sandra, then you."

San_a grimaced as she shifted in her seat. "Well_'ve forgiven her. Won't that count for so_ething?"

"I c_'t predict what will happen in a courtr_m, but I can get you contact info for C_a's lawyer if you'd like." Gabe reache_nto his pocket for his notepad. Did this ma_ever take a day off?

My k_hen door banged at that moment. We all_mped.

Chip_lled from the back of my house. "Ms. D_Ms. D., it's me." I rolled my eyes. When h_Chip and I become such close friends_t he'd feel free to walk in on me? "The ya_s are looking leafy again. What say I cra_up ol' Stihl Baby and blow 'em away? Yo_e not writing are you?" Chip cut himself _as he entered the living room. "Oh! So_Ms. D. I didn't know you had company.

As if he_uldn't see the extra cars parked in my driv_ay? Some reporter.

"It's ok_Chip. Come and meet my friends."

Chip mumbled the usual courtesies to Sandra and Father John. To Gabe, he said, "We've met. I'm the investigative reporter-neighbor. Mind if I call you for quotes sometimes?"

"As long as you get the quotes right." Gabe smiled and pulled out a business card.

When I introduced Kitty, Chip lost all words. He stared at the rare woman he could really tower over. She smiled shyly up at him, and he placed a hand on his heart. They stared a good five seconds, entranced. Then Kitty looked around at the rest of us and blushed.

She turned back to Chip. "You say you have a Stihl leaf blower? My brother has one of those. Family hates all leaf blowers because so many tend to be noisy, but I think the Stihl isn't bad for noise, and its power rocks!" Her tiny nose crinkled above her smile, and I thought Chip was going to fall over dead on the spot.

"You do? Awesome! Wanna go check mine out? We'd have to find you a pair of ear protectors, but they're orange and would be fantastic with that outfit."

Kitty nodded, and they headed toward the back door. "Great to see you're okay, Daisy," Kitty called over her shoulder. "Gabe, thanks for the lift, but I think I can find my own ride home."

The door closed behind them. I'd have to write this first meeting down. There seemed to be a romance novel budding right before my eyes. Gabe and I looked at each other, and all four of us burst out laughing.

"Aw, smitten," said Father John. "Think they're Catholic? My wedding calendar books up fairly quickly."

Sandra sighed. "Young love. If only life could remain like that." She straightened in her seat as much as possible. "But it doesn't."

I turned to my friend. "What do you mean, Sandra?"

"I've been doing a lot of thinking since our dinner and this . . . this mishap. And" — she glanced at Father John — "I've been talking a lot with Father John." Sandra cleared her throat again. "I think we both know, Daisy, I have a drinking problem. It isn't easy to admit, but I'm an alcoholic. I've been so unhappy for years that I took to self-medication as a way to get through my days."

"Have you talked with Philip about this?" I leaned closer to Sandra.

"Some. Mostly I told Philip that we're through. I am divorcing him and getting an annulment from the Church."

My heart dropped. "I'm so sorry, Sandra."

She smiled at me. "Don't be."

She then turned to Father John. "When we get healthy within ourselves and turn to the Church from our strengths instead of our weaknesses, our faith life becomes richer, and we're less susceptible to those who would use us . . . inappropriately."

Father John nodded approval and patted Sandra's free hand. "Sandra will be joining Most Holy Saints' Alcoholics Anonymous program next week. She'll accompany Agnes, from the church office. It's time we put our house in order."

"No one better than Sandra for that," I said. Okay, it slipped out. I cringed, but Sandra smiled at me.

"This means, Daisy, I won't be at our writing group for a long time. You'll need a new leader."

I ran through the fast-dwindling roll. "Perhaps Toni?"

"Actually, I was thinking of you."

"Me? I couldn't do that! I don't have the skills for such a big job."

"The writing group leader doesn't need actual writing skills. You only have to be good with people, and, Daisy, that you are. Now don't be a rabbit! Take charge. Won't you?" Sandra gave me one of her best smiles, and I wanted to say yes to her proposal on the spot.

"I don't know, Sandra. This is rather sudden."

"Tell you what. Think about it for a day or two. I'll call you next week, and we can discuss it." She was back to her general-in-charge mode, and I felt helpless to do anything more than nod.

"Good," said Sandra with a nod of her own. "Right now, I hate to rush, but it's Saturday afternoon and Father John has five o'clock Mass. Father? A little help, please?"

The good priest stood and gathered his flock member to her crutch. He supported her toward the door. "Thank you for the lovely cookies and tea."

I smiled at the priest and handed him one for the road. "They're my favorites, oatmeal raisin."

"Everything in moderation, my dear," he said and winked.

"Especially moderation." I replied. Then it hit me that this was not what Sandra needed to hear. But Sandra laughed as well.

"You'll make a great group leader," she said.

"Shame you're not a Catholic," said Father John.

"Shame." I closed the door on the parting

pair. Sandra would be all right. Curious that I'd never imagined her tough life before all this. I wondered how many other people I had formed the wrong opinion about.

I turned back to my living room, where Gabe stood with the remnants of the afternoon visit.

"You're a good person, Daisy Arthur," he said.

I smiled my thanks and started picking up dishes and cups. Gabe put out a hand to stop me.

"Won't you sit with me for a few more minutes?"

I put the dishes down on the coffee table and sat in the spot Father John had recently vacated. "What is it?"

Gabe sat back down in Art's old chair. The chair groaned. "Daisy, I misjudged you," he said. "It doesn't happen often. I'm usually good at reading people, but you . . . you always say or do the unexpected to me."

"What? I'm perfectly logical. Can't live with an engineer for so long as I have without picking up very good reasoning skills." I tilted my head in a birdlike fashion in his direction.

"There you go, coming at me from left field again. What engineer do you live with? Georgette? That fish, Errol?"

421

I laughed. It felt good to laugh again. "No, silly. My Arthur. I know he died ages ago, but you don't live with someone for more than twenty-five years without picking up some of his personality traits."

"Oh, I'm sorry. I forgot." Gabe looked around the room. A picture of Art sat on my mantel. "Maybe I should go."

"Don't." I reached toward Gabe. "I mean, yes, I loved Art, but he is in heaven now with our daughter. I have to live here on earth, and Art wouldn't have wanted me to hide myself away behind my front door, not to live out my own life."

Gabe smiled at me, then his brow puckered. "Art? His name was Arthur Arthur?"

"Art's mom was a bit like me, I guess. She always wanted Art to be a writer. Only she wanted him to write stage plays."

"Arthur. Author," said Gabe.

We laughed. Gabe slapped his knee.

A loud crack filled the air and suddenly the chair he sat in, Art's chair, collapsed. Gabe fell into a pile of tapestry and old bits of wood.

I scrambled off the sofa and grabbed his arm. "Are you all right? Oh, gosh, I'm so sorry! I didn't know that thing would break."

"It's okay." Gabe scrambled out of the

mess and onto his feet.

Suddenly we were standing face-to-face only inches apart. I still held his hand. His lovely, strong, warm hand. My heart started beating fast. Damn these hot flashes! I hadn't felt so breathless since Humphrey Bogart kissed Ingrid Bergman goodbye in *Casablanca*.

"It's okay," Gabe said again, this time whispering the words.

I had half-closed my eyes, ready for Gabe's kiss when an explosion of noise hit our ears. Gabe's head snapped to the side, and my lips ended up brushing his shoulder.

"What the flippin' . . ." said Gabe. He strode toward the window.

"I believe that's a Stihl 500. Blows leaves to kingdom come and beyond." Thanks Chip. And Kitty.

Gabe turned and came back to me. "Look. Let's get out of here, Daisy. Just the two of us. There's a great steak place south of C-470 and Santa Fe. We could have a date. A real date. No murder talk, no Ginny, just us."

"No Sergeant Taylor?"

Gabe grimaced. "Sergeant Taylor? Why her? Work and personal relationships don't mix."

"Does she know this?"

423

"What makes you ask?"

"From the little I know of her, Sergeant Taylor seems to have missed that memo." I shuddered at the various memories I had of Linda Taylor and me.

"You flatter me. While Linda is beautiful and great to work with, she's too young for me. And it would be too complicated to get involved."

"I'll trust you on that, Gabe. For now, though, you have to trust me with the other man in my life. How 'bout I meet you at the steak house?"

Gabe looked surprised.

"There's a place I recently heard about up at Windermere and Belleview. It's sponsored by a group called Englewood Unleashed, and I'm taking my hero there for an hour of free running with the pack." I scooted Gabe out to his car, smiled, and headed toward my neighbor's.

"Thunder!" I called. "Thunder. Wanna go for a ride?"

ABOUT THE AUTHOR

Liesa Malik grew up in the suburbs of Detroit and has several family members still living there. She acquired an associate's degree in Commercial Art and a bachelor's degree in Mass Communications — Journalism only to turn around and spend the next several years in business and raising two children.

Her older daughter is a dentist and her younger was a special needs child. Currently, Liesa lives with her husband; her obnoxious, yet lovable German shepherd, Prophet; and their big fat cat named Nalla, in Littleton, Colorado.

The employees of Thorndike Press hope you have enjoyed this Large Print book. All our Thorndike, Wheeler, and Kennebec Large Print titles are designed for easy reading, and all our books are made to last. Other Thorndike Press Large Print books are available at your library, through selected bookstores, or directly from us.

For information about titles, please call:
(800) 223-1244

or visit our Web site at:
http://gale.cengage.com/thorndike

To share your comments, please write:
Publisher
Thorndike Press
10 Water St., Suite 310
Waterville, ME 04901